## PRA
## SURGARL

"Davis's latest in her Su -tered around another to d Robyn have a blend of good chemistry and sweet romance. A suspenseful plot coupled with smooth pacing makes the reader want to keep turning the pages." —*RT Book Reviews*

"Really moving . . . amazing story and I loved every bit of it. Four and a half stars!" —Night Owl Reviews (top pick)

"With *In His Sights*, Jo Davis has hooked me yet again. [From] steamy, passionate scenes to [scenes] dripping with suspense, nothing is missing from this book! Highly recommended for those readers who are looking for a book to draw you in and keep you mesmerized until the end!"
—Joyfully Reviewed (joyfully recommended read)

"*In His Sights* is another wonderful story that was romance suspense at its best. In the middle of this suspenseful intense mystery, the romance was great, as I loved both Chris and Robyn. Jo Davis does it again with a fantastic addition to this fabulous series." —The Reading Cafe

***Hot Pursuit***

"With her descriptive storytelling and sharp banter, Davis's way with words will keep the reader hooked. . . . Once again, Davis hits it out of the park." —*RT Book Reviews*

"Scorching hot." —*Publishers Weekly*

"A wonderful series that has it all: exciting stories, [a] superhot couple, romance, danger, suspense, friendship from a great group of secondary characters, and hot hot hot sex."
—The Reading Cafe

"This exciting contemporary romantic-suspense story continues the saga of the delicious detectives in the Sugarland Police Department . . . a thrilling story." —The Reading Addict

*continued . . .*

"An adult romance tale which piles on the tension from the start and doesn't let up." —Fresh Fiction

"A roller coaster of emotion and action that will keep you gripped until the last page . . . with just the right combination of both romance and suspense." —Cocktails and Books

***Sworn to Protect***

"[A] strong series launch . . . a satisfying, fast-paced read." —*Publishers Weekly*

"What's not to love about sexy men in blue with fast hands, true hearts, and the courage of their convictions? Davis certainly knows how to draw the perfect balance of vulnerability and strength. . . . She wraps it all up in an action novel that falls just shy of a police procedural, but with plenty of pure, steamy romance and family drama." —*RT Book Reviews*

"If you like romance, action, and mysteries, then you will love this book." —Once Upon a Twilight

"Jo writes stories that keep you hooked until the very last page and clamoring for the next book to release." —Book Monster Reviews

"A smart, sexy, and fast-paced read." —Fresh Fiction

## PRAISE FOR THE FIREFIGHTERS OF STATION FIVE NOVELS

"The perfect blend of romance and suspense. . . . Jo Davis creates a great combination of romance, steamy love scenes with mystery and suspense mixed in." —Fiction Vixen Book Reviews

"Once again, Jo Davis has rocked it in this series!" —Night Owl Reviews

"A great blend of hot romance with suspenseful, well-plotted action." —Fresh Fiction

"Grab a fan and settle in for one heck of a smoking-hot read. . . . Fiery-hot love scenes and a look inside the twisted mind of a killer make *Line of Fire* stand out." —Joyfully Reviewed

"Surprisingly sweet and superhot. . . . If you want a hot firefighter in your room for the night, grab a copy and tuck right in with no regrets." —The Romance Reader

"A fast-paced romantic suspense thriller."—The Best Reviews

"Four stars! A totally entertaining experience."
—*RT Book Reviews*

"Exhilarating [with] a two-hundred-proof heat duet . . . a strong entry [and] a terrific, action-packed thriller."
—*Midwest Book Review*

"Jo Davis turns up the heat full-blast. Romantic suspense that has it all: a sizzling firefighter hero, a heroine you'll love, and a story that crackles and pops with sensuality and action. Keep the fire extinguisher handy or risk spontaneous combustion!"
—Linda Castillo, national bestselling author of
*The Dead Will Tell*

"One of the most exciting 'band of brothers' series since J. R. Ward's Black Dagger Brotherhood. It's sweet and sexy, tense and suspenseful." —myLifetime.com

"A poignant and steamy romance with a great dose of suspense." —Wild on Books

"Hot, sizzling sex and edge-of-your-seat terror will have you glued to this fantastic romantic suspense story from the first page to the final word." —Romance Novel TV

## ALSO BY JO DAVIS

Sugarland Blue Novels

*In His Sights*

*Hot Pursuit*

*Sworn to Protect*

*Armed and Dangerous* (novella)

Firefighters of Station Five Novels

*Ride the Fire*

*Hidden Fire*

*Line of Fire*

*Under Fire*

*Trial by Fire*

# On the Run

A Sugarland Blue Novel

Jo Davis

A Signet Eclipse Book

SIGNET ECLIPSE
Published by the Penguin Group
Penguin Group (USA) LLC, 375 Hudson Street,
New York, New York 10014

USA | Canada | UK | Ireland | Australia | New Zealand | India | South Africa | China
penguin.com
A Penguin Random House Company

First published by Signet Eclipse, an imprint of New American Library,
a division of Penguin Group (USA) LLC

First Printing, April 2015



ISBN 978-0-451-46793-5

Printed in the United States of America
10 9 8 7 6 5 4 3 2 1

*In loving memory of Nancy Lynn Boyd.*
*Best friend, confidante, sister by choice.*
*If only I had known that our last hug would have to sustain me for a lifetime . . .*
*I would've held on a lot longer.*
*I would've tried harder.*
*I would've forgiven sooner.*
*I wouldn't have taken one single laugh for granted.*
*I would never have stopped searching for you.*
*If only.*
*I love you, old friend.*
*Missing you is an ache that will never ease.*
*Wait for me.*
*Until we meet again.*
*Tonio's story is for you.*

# Prologue

The stench reached his consciousness first.

Then the pain. All-over, racking agony that proved he wasn't dead yet, though he didn't have a clue how that could be.

Awareness of being trapped came next. Buried. But not in the dirt. As he tried to move, various items surrounding him shifted and rolled away. With his fingertips he felt . . . cans. Paper. Slime. Old food? Cold knowledge gripped him, turned his blood to ice.

*After the bastards finished with me, they threw me in the garbage. Literally.*

*Move, Salvatore. Move or you're dead.*

Using his hand, he sought the air. Pushed and clawed, twisting his body in the stinking refuse. The weight on top of him was heavy but not crushing. They'd meant to hide his body, completely confident he wouldn't wake, or make it out even if he did. He tried not to think they might be right.

At last, fresh air. But as he broke through the pile, the heap sloped downward sharply and he was tumbling sideways. For several feet he fell, jabbed and poked by sharp edges until he landed in the dirt at the bottom, the wind knocked out of him. Breathing was almost impossible, his lungs burning. He was hurt inside, and out.

His eyes opened to slits, and he tried to peer into the darkness. All he could make out was a sea of garbage. No moon or stars. Worse, little hope.

They'd thrown him into the dump miles outside the city, where nobody in their right mind would venture.

*Don't give up.*

Drawing his legs under him, he pushed upward. His legs were like rubber, his strength almost nonexistent. He made it halfway to a standing position before crashing back to the ground with a hoarse cry. God, the pain. His entire body felt hot and cold by turns, and swollen like a balloon. Any second, he would split and spill onto the ground like the plastic bags all around him vomiting their guts. His skin and clothing were wet, too, from head to toe.

He knew it wasn't all from the slime of the trash.

Shaking, Tonio crawled forward on his belly, inch by inch. Time lost meaning. An hour or three might have passed, though he didn't think it had been so long—he would already be dead.

Wetness ran down his forehead, down the bridge of his nose. Gradually he grew cold. So cold he knew he'd never get warm again. What was he doing? Too much blood loss. Confusion. He tried to remember, couldn't.

Knew that was the beginning of the end.

*Anthony. I'm Anthony Salvatore, and I'm a cop. Have to get out of here, get help. Let them know—what?*

Her name whispered through his mind like a promise. Or a nightmare. He didn't know which, and now he might never.

*Angel.*

*Have to let Chris, somebody, know about Angel. Because if I fail . . .*

Brother or not, Rab would kill her. He would show her no mercy, and she would end up here, in a grave next to Tonio. He couldn't let that happen.

"Angel."

Her name was on his lips, her beautiful face in his mind and the memory of her warm, supple body close to his heart when his strength finally deserted him.

He'd wanted years to learn her secrets, her joys, and had been granted only weeks. It would have to be enough.

"Be smart, baby," he rasped. "Stay safe."

Against his will, his eyes drifted shut.

And Tonio surrendered to the darkness.

# *1*

*Five weeks earlier*

Detective Tonio Salvatore leaned against the bar in one of his favorite dives where the regulars only knew him by his first name, and sipped his whiskey, neat.

They didn't know what he did for a living, either, and nobody ever asked. He figured that, if anything, they had him pegged for a dangerous thug of some sort, maybe into drugs or fencing stolen goods like three-quarters of the guys there. Dressed as he always was when he came here, in leathers, a tight black Metallica T-shirt, heavy boots, a five o'clock shadow on his jaw and a bandanna around his short raven hair, it was a reasonable assumption.

It didn't hurt that he was six-four and muscular, and looked mean even though he wasn't unless he had to be.

Stroker's was a rough place with an even rougher clientele, but it suited him despite his job—or maybe because of it. It was the perfect place to keep his finger on the pulse of Cheatham County's criminal activity without risking being seen and recognized in his nearby city of Sugarland, Tennessee. He wasn't here in any official capacity, though. He just wanted to relax, incognito.

And maybe see some action that involved the weapon in the front of his leathers and not the one strapped to his ankle.

Taking another sip of his Dewar's, he savored the smooth flavor and recalled the sweet little piece of work from last weekend. The blonde, what was her name? Trish? Tess? Didn't matter. She'd been all over him from the minute she spied him at the bar, and it hadn't taken her long to maneuver her way between his legs as he sat on the stool, then proceed to check his tonsils with her tongue.

His cock stirred as he remembered giving her a ride on his Harley to the motel down the road, his go-to for the one-night stands that provided him and his chosen partners with relief. No way was he taking any of them home. He wasn't stupid.

The blonde had hugged him tightly from behind, pressed her breasts against his back, her hot crotch against his ass, and he'd nearly wrecked trying to get them to the motel. Inside, they'd been naked in seconds and he'd been eating her out, enjoying the moaning and breathy little whimpers coming from her throat. She'd dug her fingers into his short hair and held on for the ride as he'd thrown her onto the bed, slid his cock deep, and fucked her so hard the headboard had cracked the plaster on the wall.

Looking around, he hoped she'd be back tonight.

"Another round?" the bartender asked. The guy's name was Rick, and he was as tough as anyone here.

Had to be to work in a place like this. Tonio knew for a fact that the man kept a baseball bat behind the counter, and wouldn't hesitate to use it.

"Sure," he answered. Fuck it, he was off duty tonight. Always made sure he never drank when he was on call, either, and he wasn't tonight.

"Comin' up."

His night improved when the little blonde with the perky bust and tight jeans strolled through the front door. He turned back to his drink, making sure not to clue her in that he'd noticed her arrival. As he thought it might, pretty soon a warm body sidled close to him, and a woman's voice whispered in his ear, "Fancy meeting you here, Tonio." Small teeth nibbled at his ear lobe. "Buy a girl a drink?"

"You bet." Damn, what *was* her name?

"Hey, Tess," Rick said in greeting. "What's your poison tonight, baby girl?"

Settling on the stood beside Tonio, she brought a long, manicured nail to her lips in thought. Then she grinned. "How about a Screaming Orgasm?"

Rick snorted, then smirked at Tonio. "Don't think you need me for that one, but whatever the lady wants."

While Rick mixed her drink, she swiveled to face Tonio. Leaning over enticingly, she showed every bit of the rosy nipples on display under her plunging blouse and eyed him like a cat ready to pounce on a mouse. They both knew she wouldn't have to work real hard to catch him.

"Watcha been up to, sexy?" she asked.

He shrugged. "Not much. Messing with my bike, doing a little business to keep a roof over my head. The usual." All true, even if he'd just strengthened her perception of him as a criminal. Why he was playing this game, he wasn't sure.

But they were both enjoying it, so what was the harm? He might learn something interesting.

"What do you do to keep that roof over your head, hmm?" She grabbed the drink Rick slid over, and took a healthy swallow.

He'd stepped into this willingly. But there was no question he had to develop a cover now. Besides Tess, Rick and a couple of other men were very interested in his answer and trying to pretend they weren't. Who knew, he might luck onto a case that would lead somewhere, eventually to arrests for drugs or something else. Sure, his captain would have his balls for going out on his own, but if it led to something big, he'd forgive Tonio just as fast.

"I acquire things," he heard himself say. "For those who want them."

She arched an eyebrow. "What kinds of things?"

"Whatever you want, for a fee."

"Anything?"

"Pretty much."

Tess wasn't fazed. "Good to know. I might be persuaded to pass that along."

"Up to you." Pulse kicking up a notch, he tossed back the rest of his drink, letting his demeanor say he didn't give a shit whether she did or not. But he'd gotten a nibble that might lead to something bigger, and the game was on. The high was better than any drug.

Almost better than sex. But not quite.

After taking another drink, she slid a hand up the thigh of his leathers and brushed her fingers across his tightened crotch. "I can provide something *you* want, too."

His dick was throbbing in his pants. Hot. "Yeah?"

"Oh yeah." Leaning into his chest, she took his mouth and tangled her tongue with his. Her nipples grazed his chest and peaked to tiny eraser points, rubbing. Driving him crazy.

"Want to get out of here?" he asked between heated kisses.

"Sounds like a great idea," a woman's voice said. And it wasn't Tess's.

Tonio and his hookup turned toward the woman who'd stalked up to them without either of them noticing—and Tonio's breath caught. The woman was several inches below Tonio's height, perhaps five-nine, long-limbed, with a killer body that looked like she'd just stepped from the pages of a skin magazine. Long dark hair fell past her shoulders, almost all the way to her waist. Her eyes were large and green and her nose was a sharp blade above a lush mouth made for sucking cock. Full, ripe breasts pushed at the snug cotton shirt that had been cut with scissors or a knife to make the low V-neck, and made sleeveless as well. She wore tight jeans and black ankle boots with silver conchos studded around them. Encircling her right upper arm was a surprisingly feminine Celtic tattoo. His mouth watered. The look that would have come across as tacky on anyone else was stunning on her.

Definitely centerfold material.

"What the fuck do you want, Angel?" Tess was clearly less than pleased with the other woman's presence.

"Are you really that stupid?" Angel stared at her, then shook her head. "You know this is Rab's territory. He's not going to be happy to find you here again, and he's not taking you back."

What? Stuck in the middle of Tess trying to make another man jealous? *Fuck.*

"You think I give a shit what that asshole brother of yours thinks or what makes him happy? Maybe it's *you* who doesn't want me here," Tess said smugly. "He hasn't said a thing to me."

"I happen to know that's because he hasn't seen you." Angel sighed. "Look, I'm telling you this for your own good. He—crap, too late. Here he comes now."

Angel really did look worried, Tonio had to admit. When Tess glanced toward the door, she did, too. Who was this Rab guy who had the women so nervous? Tonio followed their gazes and cursed inwardly.

The man who held their attention was a frigging tank, maybe even an inch or so taller than Tonio himself. He was about thirty, bald, and wore his tats proudly as sleeves down both thick arms. Several pendants bounced against his broad chest, and he wore jeans that emphasized his muscular thighs. There wasn't an ounce of fat on his frame.

Rab headed straight for their group, a steely expression on his face. Tonio slid from his stool and planted himself slightly in front of the women on pure instinct; this wasn't even his fight, for God's sake, and he wanted no part of their argument.

"Bitch," the man growled, throwing his sister the barest glance before focusing on Tess. "What the hell are you doing here?"

Tonio's back went up. He absolutely *hated* any man who addressed a woman as *bitch*. Only bottom feeders resorted to that kind of talk to make themselves seem like bigger men.

"What do you think?" she purred slyly. Curling into Tonio's side, she wrapped an arm around his waist. "I'm here for a drink, same as you. A little company, too. No harm in that."

"There is when you know goddamn well I don't want to see your face." His eyes were dark and cold, like black marbles. He hadn't acknowledged Tonio at all.

"Fine," she said airily. "I guess I won't introduce you to my friend Tonio here, who has a special talent."

That icy gaze settled on Tonio for the first time, and inwardly he actually shuddered. That didn't happen often. There weren't many people who scared him, but there was something about this man he perceived as dangerous. Even deadly. Maybe it was because he was too still, too calm. As though watching and calculating.

"What talent might that be?" Rab drawled, checking him out from head to toe, his disdain clear.

"Acquisitions," Tess said pointedly.

*And here we go.*

That caught the other man's interest. "What's your specialty?"

"Don't have one. Someone wants something, I get it." That was taking a risk, not specializing. It might sound too close to fishing on Tonio's part. Too suspect.

Rab studied him for a long moment. Tonio held his gaze, not backing down. *Never, ever volunteer more than you're asked. That's the first rule of being undercover.* Eventually the other man spoke again.

"You got a last name?"

"Reyes," he lied.

"You got a number?"

*Shit.* He couldn't give out his real cell phone number—he'd have to get a burner, fast. And have an unpleasant conversation with Rainey first thing tomorrow. He was onto something here, he could feel it. The room had hushed, every single person there tense. Belatedly, Tonio noted the men, all dressed in similar fashion, who'd risen to their feet and moved subtly behind Rab. None of them appeared to be the stereotypical bumbling backwoods yokels. They looked tough, and serious. He'd bet most of them had done hard time.

This man was no small-time player.

"I'm around," was his only reply.

Several men flexed their fists. Looked to Rab, who held them off with a slight flick of a hand. *Jesus*. He'd escaped getting the mother-fuck beat out of him by the skin of his teeth, and all he'd wanted was a cold drink and a hot woman. In that order.

"I expect you will be," Rab said, his warning unmistakable. "Same time tomorrow night. Here. We'll talk."

Dismissing Tonio, the man strode away, taking up residence at a table in a corner of the bar. The only vacant table in the place, which must be reserved for him. Angel stepped closer to Tonio and tilted her head toward the corner.

"You've got his attention," she said, sounding less than pleased. And still concerned. "I hope you know what the hell you let in when you opened that door."

"Interesting way to talk about your own brother."

A second of unease flickered in her jade eyes. She glanced around, and apparently decided Rab's men were no longer listening. "My advice? Don't come back. Ignore it at your own risk, and my conscience is clear."

"Noted." Angel, warning him off. He was even more intrigued than before—and he knew he'd be back.

Angel turned her attention to Tess. "And you? Don't let the door hit ya where the good Lord split ya."

"Fuck off, Angel."

Angel glanced between them, a smile curving her lips. Without another word, she turned and walked away, joining a couple of women at a different table. Girlfriends of two of Rab's men, maybe. She didn't look Tonio's way again.

"Come on," Tess urged, voice irritated. "Let's go."

Taking her hand, Tonio led her outside to his motorcycle. His mind kept going back to the mysterious woman, Angel. Sister of the man he might be working undercover against, in order to expose any number of crimes. Certainly off-limits.

And yet—

No. There was no use going there.

Against his back, the little blonde was warm and willing. His libido resurfaced with a vengeance and his cock woke once more. By the time he parked outside the motel, he was so damn hard he could hardly walk. He needed relief, and Tess was pretty. Great in bed, too.

After obtaining his key, he dragged her inside and stripped off her top. Her breasts weren't that full, but they were creamy, the tight peaks pink and lickable. She was a bit skinny, but that hardly mattered as he watched her slip off her jeans and get naked.

He stripped off his shirt and she attacked his belt with fervor, unzipping it to expose his aching erection. His shaft throbbed, almost deep purple with want. Then she sucked him into her mouth and began to work him over, and he went up in flames.

"*Dios*, yes," he hissed. "Like that. Suck me."

She did, as enthusiastic about it as she was last week. He watched his dick slide between her lips, wet and shiny, and couldn't help imagining a different woman doing him. One with long dark hair and plump lips. Groaning, he picked up the pace.

When he was near the edge, he gently disengaged, chuckling at his lover's whimper of displeasure. Quickly he removed his boots, finished stripping his pants, retrieved a condom from his wallet, and gloved up.

"How do you want it, honey?" he asked, moving in close. He took her mouth in a heated kiss.

"Eat me, then fuck the shit out of me," she demanded breathlessly.

"Not a problem." He winked, liking her giggle. Tess was rough around the edges, and knew some dangerous people. She was dangerous to *him* because of the company she kept. But she was cute, and in some ways, maybe more naive than one might guess.

"Kneel by the bed and lean over the mattress," he ordered.

She hurried to do as he said, and spread her legs wide. Crouching behind her on the carpet, he bent and spread her with his fingers. Then he gave her slit a slow lick, laughing when she squirmed, pushing back, wanting more.

He wasn't a selfish lover. It was important to him that a woman enjoy herself to the fullest, and he set about making sure Tess was satisfied as well as himself. He lapped at her, tasting her essence and loving every second.

"Delicious," he murmured.

She gasped. "Shit. Tonio . . ."

"Need my cock, honey?"

"Yes!"

"Say it. Tell me what you want." He loved to hear the words.

"Fuck me," she breathed. "Please."

Needing no further encouragement, he lined up with her entrance and pushed inside. Her sheath was so hot and tight around him, he almost came like a sixteen-year-old on the first stroke. Holding deep, he calmed the fires a bit, and then began to pump.

*"Dios, bonita,"* he muttered. "Such a sweet pussy."

Her reply was incoherent, just the way he liked. He fucked her slow and deep, at first. Gradually he picked up speed and soon he was shafting her hard. Her trills of pleasure echoed throughout the small room, driving him over the edge. His orgasm exploded and he emptied his release into the condom, filling it.

She came down with him, channel spasming pleasantly around his cock. He fucked her a few more times to wring out every last bit of ecstasy for them both, then pulled out gently. After helping her up and onto the bed, he went to the bathroom and tossed the condom, then cleaned up. Then he took her a warm cloth, waiting as she used it, and tossed it into the bathroom.

He reached for his shirt, fully intending to leave.

"Can't we have another round?"

He studied her, lying on the bed, naked. Inviting. Straight blond hair fell attractively around her face, and she pouted.

"Sure, what the hell?"

Abandoning his shirt, he climbed into bed and under the covers. And he wondered if this was the first of a very long list of mistakes he was going to make in the imminent future.

A short time later, he woke in the night with his hard cock rubbing the curve of her ass. With a groan, he reached between them, fingering her slit from behind.

After that, there wasn't much thinking involved at all.

"You fucking did *what*?"

The shouted question froze every single person in the main station outside the conference room more effectively than a blast from a Taser. Captain Austin Rainey looked about two seconds from blowing a blood vessel in his brain as he slammed the door, cutting off the curious stares from the main squad room.

"I've got a hunch, Cap," Tonio insisted in his own defense. "This Rab character, he's looking to take on somebody with acquisition skills. And trust me, these guys aren't buying antiques or fine art. If they're into anything legal, I'll eat my badge."

"You might do that anyway when I shove it down your throat," Austin snapped.

Tonio's partner on the force, Chris Ford, shot him a look that said *I told you so.* Tonio ignored him. "Cap, I'm telling you, this group is dirty. They're—"

"I *know*."

Tonio hesitated. "What do you mean, you know?"

"Just what I said, shithead." Austin swiped a hand down his face and glared at him. "Do you have any idea what you've done?"

"Uh-oh," Chris murmured.

Dread seized Tonio's gut. "No. But I'm sure you'll enlighten me."

"You've just stepped on an ongoing investigation into Robert 'Rab' Silva and his merry band of thieves, drug runners, and killers," Austin said pointedly. "By the City of Langdon PD."

Tonio processed that, heart sinking. He'd seriously fucked up. "They're outside Langdon's city limits! How was I supposed to know?"

"Oh, let me see? Maybe *ask* first? They're outside *our* city limits, too, but it just so happens they've been wanting to take these guys down for a while. You just landed in the shit, and now I've got to fix it."

"I'm sorry, Austin," he said quietly, meaning it. "I just felt I'd stumbled onto something and my instinct kicked in."

"Which creates the question—what the fuck are *you* doing hanging out in that dump, anyway?"

Tonio shrugged. His reasoning seemed so stupid now. "I like going somewhere nobody knows me, fitting in with the crowd. Maybe even learning tidbits we can use. I've done that before, when I was with the San Antonio PD. Sometimes it pans out."

"Okay, let me think." Austin was silent for a moment. "This might work to our advantage. Maybe Langdon could use a man on the inside, something they haven't been able to make happen. Could be they'll turn over the case altogether."

Austin left the room without dismissing them, so they waited. In the meantime, Chris gave him shit.

"Smooth move, Ex-Lax," he said, snickering.

"Man, shut up. I'm not in the mood."

"You, like, *never* fuck up. But when you do, you really go for it."

"Chris," he started, getting pissed.

"Hey," his friend said, holding up a hand. "I've got your back, no matter what. You know that."

His partner was so sincere Tonio's anger evaporated. "Thanks."

About twenty minutes later, Austin walked back into the room and shut the door. "The chief at Langdon is seriously fucking pissed. But they let us take it, since they haven't been able to get an in with the group."

"Yeah?" Tonio said, brightening.

"Yep. Time will tell how lucky a break it was." He studied Tonio thoughtfully. "Tell me exactly how this meeting came about. Leave nothing out."

So he spared no detail. He wasn't embarrassed about hooking up with a woman. Hell, he was human. And it wasn't like he'd intended to fuck the gang leader's ex—it just happened that way.

"He doesn't think much of women, either," Tonio mused. "Going by the way he talks to them."

"Speaking of women, you still seeing this woman, Tess?"

Tonio shrugged. "Hadn't planned on it, especially. Why?" One look at the captain's face, and Chris's, and he knew where this was going. "Oh, no way. Fuck that, I'm not getting involved long-term with someone."

"You said yourself she's the way in," Chris pointed out. "She knows the group, and more important, Rab."

"Yeah, and he could kill me for touching her, even though they've broken up."

"Did he seem like it was a problem?" Austin asked.

"Well, no," Tonio admitted. "But—"

Austin snorted. "But nothing. You started this, and now you've got to keep your cover. Dumping her too soon will set off alarm bells we don't want clanging, you got that?"

"Yes, sir." *Shit and fuck!*

"Good. Besides, you can have your cake and eat it, too, in this case. Just don't blow this."

Resignation settled over him. With acceptance of the situation, excitement about bringing down a big player began to fire his blood. "Should I start tonight?"

"Might as well, if you're ready."

"I am, Cap."

"Good. Chris, you'll have his back. Monitor behind the scenes, keep your partner safe."

"I will, Cap."

"Okay. Get going and report in once a day to me and Chris, nobody else."

Austin left, and Tonio blew out a breath.

And just like that, he was undercover working for one of the most dangerous men in the entire state, with an unwanted girlfriend in his bed.

Tonio went to sleep that night, and dreamed of a woman with a Celtic tattoo and jade green eyes.

# 2

Angel paused in her work, leaned the handle of the mop against the bar, and wiped the sweat from her eyes.

God, how she wished she could afford a regular cleaning service. But that sort of luxury would have to wait, like everything else on her wish lists of *one day* and *maybe*. Glancing around, she tamped down a surge of irritation that Andy, her head bartender, had booked out last night after closing, leaving her to take care of it. She released a sigh, knowing she couldn't blame him.

Rab and his posse had hung around long after she locked the doors last night, something that was becoming an unwanted habit. Andy was terrified of the gang, but Rab most of all. And he should be.

Eight months ago, her brother had been paroled. She hadn't known he was out until forty-eight hours later, when he'd shown up on her doorstep begging for a place to crash.

*"Just until I get on my feet, sis. I'm a changed man, I swear."*

For all the mistakes he'd made, he was family. The

only family she had left, except their mother, whom she didn't talk to much. Less than two weeks after she allowed him to cross her threshold, his buddies had arrived—the ones that weren't still locked up. That had been the beginning of the end of her hard-won freedom from their parents' legacy. She saw the past repeating itself now, in her brother.

Rab hadn't been lying. He *was* a changed man—changed for the worse.

All their lives, he'd been a first-class fuckup. An apple right off Dad's felonious tree, and their mother had been too afraid to stand up to either of them. Rab's slide into delinquency had started when they were kids, with petty shit like pinching candy from the grocery store. He was the kind of kid who liked hurting small animals, too. Just for laughs.

By the time they were in high school, he'd graduated to stealing cars for the hell of it. Then on to selling them. That proved to be so profitable he and his buddies branched out into other goods Angel didn't want to know about.

But the cops got wind, and eventually busted them. Rab went to prison, as hardened and cynical as a man three times his age. If she'd held out a shred of hope that his time inside had resulted in a productive, law-abiding citizen, that prayer had been smashed to bits the instant Rab and his dogs made themselves a fixture in her bar and in her life. They harassed and terrified her employees, drove out the good customers, and attracted birds of a feather. Like that new guy, Tonio.

Their presence was becoming a big problem, because the stakes for her brother getting caught this time were much higher—Angel could lose her business. Her freedom. Worst-case scenario, her life.

She had to get rid of them. But how? Rab kept her in the dark about the dirty details of his dealings. The couple of times she'd tried to press him for answers, he'd told her in that cool, dangerous voice to mind her own fucking business and she'd be a lot happier. So she had nothing solid to tell the cops, even if she dared.

And getting help from the outside? She had no idea whom she could trust. Even cops could be dirty. Not that she knew of any on Rab's payroll, but still.

The scuff of heavy boots on the concrete floor jerked her to the present, and she looked toward the door to see the object of her fears and frustrations bearing down on her. Straightening, she raised her chin and looked Rab dead in the eye. *Never give him an inch. Never cower.*

"You're up early," she said, her tone direct. Unwavering. More often than not, it was the best way to handle him. "Did the world explode? Is the sky falling?"

He blinked at her, then barked a laugh, the sound rusty. He wasn't a man who made that noise often. "You think you're funny, dontcha? Get me a beer."

With that, he sat his ass on a barstool and gazed at her expectantly.

She snorted. "Get it yourself. Anyway, what about your drug testing? Fail that, and you're going back inside."

*Is it terrible of me to think that wouldn't be the worst thing to happen?*

"Not gonna happen," he drawled, sliding off the stool. Walking around behind the bar, he grabbed a glass and drew a beer from the tap. "I've told you before, it's all about timing. I'll be clean when the next test rolls around."

"If your timing was so impeccable, you wouldn't have been caught and put in prison in the first place."

He stilled and set the glass on the polished counter, eyes narrowing. For a couple of seconds, she thought she'd gone too far, but then his lips turned up.

"My sister's got solid brass balls. I've always admired that."

"Thanks. I think." Rolling her eyes, she headed for the back to put away the mop and bucket.

"Hey, it's a compliment," he called after her.

After putting away the cleaning items, she leaned against the wall with a sigh. Rab was in an unusually good mood, but it wouldn't last. Never did. The man was a ticking bomb, waiting silently for his moment to detonate.

Resigning herself to his presence, she walked back into the main area and busied herself behind the bar. Aware of him studying her, she did her best to ignore him until she couldn't stand the quiet any longer.

"What *does* bring you by before noon?" she asked, checking the liquor stock.

"Got a meeting with the new recruit. Tonio."

"Now?"

"Soon."

She frowned. "I thought that wasn't until tonight."

"I moved it up." He took a sip of his beer.

"How'd you get hold of him?"

"He called, left his number with Andy. Anyways, it's good to keep the men off guard. Plus, I want to feel him out when there's not a crowd distracting me."

"If you decide to take him on, what'll you have him doing?" She pretended not to be overly interested in his answer, but he still didn't bite.

"Not your concern," he said sharply. "You writing a book or something? You're always asking questions about my business."

She glared at him. "That's because you're conducting *your* illegal business in *my* place of business, and you could get me shut down. Not to mention all of us thrown in the joint. Then where would we be?"

"Relax. Nobody's going to blame you, especially if you don't know a thing. So stop asking and you'll be better off. I'd hate to have to make you." He winked.

*Is he serious? Would he actually harm me?* Forcing herself to remain calm, she tidied the glasses. "So, what about Tess? She's fucking the new guy, you know."

"So? I don't give a shit what that dumb bitch is doing, or who." But his words had taken on a dangerous edge, belying the truth of them. There was something in his eyes, a nasty gleam she didn't like. "She stays away from me, we'll be fine."

"And you don't care that your new man is with her?"

"She's not a problem, for now. She becomes one, I'll deal with her. And I'll make sure Tonio understands this, too."

*How will you do that?* Rab had never killed anyone—that she knew of. Angel forced herself not to shiver.

The door opened, and more footsteps sounded at the entrance. Angel swung her gaze toward the newcomer—and her breath caught in her throat, same as it had last night.

Tonio was a big man. All over. Well over six feet of pure muscle, a lot of which was emphasized by his snug black T-shirt. One with white letters spelling SLIPKNOT across his chest, and straining with the job.

His torso was flat, and she could see the hint of a six-pack. Long legs were encased in worn jeans with a hole ripped out of one knee, and he wore black shit kickers on his large feet. God, what she could see of his body was a dream, and she wondered what he looked like naked.

The very best of his features, however, were his sexy face and short black hair. Neat eyebrows arched over brown eyes so dark they almost blended in with his pupils. His nose was straight, not too big. His mouth was full and wide, his jaw strong and attractively peppered with stubble. He wore no bandanna today, leaving his hair free to feather back from his face.

He was the most gorgeous man she'd ever seen. And he was taken.

As he approached, his gaze flicked to Angel. Before he returned his attention to Rab, she could've sworn his eyes had warmed with male appreciation. If so, he quickly and wisely masked it.

"Rab," he said, holding out his hand. Her brother hesitated before he shook it, and then Tonio gestured to Angel. "I don't think we got a proper introduction last night."

Rab nodded and spoke in a clipped tone. "This is my sister, Angel. Angel, Tonio Reyes."

"Nice to meet you," she said. Belatedly, it occurred to her just how ironic those words were, coming from her mouth. When had it ever been *nice* to meet any of Rab's thugs? Hadn't she just despaired over how to get rid of them?

"You, too." Again, there was a flash of heat in his gaze.

She hadn't imagined it, then. Before she could come up with anything more to say, her brother steered the man away, into his usual booth in the corner. As she worked, she kept one ear open, but could only hear the faint murmur of their voices. An occasional word reached her, but no specifics.

Since there was no way of getting closer without pissing Rab off, she eventually gave up and took refuge in her small office in the back. Perhaps she could lose herself in making the accounts balance.

Anything to forget about salivating over the gorgeous man with the big dark fuck-me eyes.

Tonio was painfully aware of Angel moving around the bar and dining room. Every step she took, that tight round butt swaying in her jeans. A certain part of him took notice, and he hoped the table concealed his interest.

She wore her long dark hair loose again, and the strands brushed over the Celtic tattoo on her arm. To an unpracticed eye, she appeared busy. But he'd gained enough experience over the years in watching people, observing body language, to know that she was tense. And aware of his gaze tracking her every move. She wasn't unaffected.

With an effort, he forced his attention to Rab, who was eyeing him, expression stony. "So, tell me, what can I do for you?"

Rab paused. "First, keep your eyes off my sister."

"She's a beautiful woman," Tonio replied with a shrug. "I'm not blind."

"The last man who messed with her walks with a cane and is adjusting to life without his spleen." A cold, glittering gaze let Tonio know he wasn't joking.

"I'm with Tess, remember?"

"That slut's not the kind a guy stays with forever. Especially with a woman like Angel around to tempt him."

Tonio bristled a bit. True, the two women were completely different, but that didn't make Tess a bad person. "Did I come here to discuss business or are you going to waste my time?"

After a moment, Rab sat back in his chair and regarded him thoughtfully. "You said you acquire things but don't specialize. Give me some examples."

"I fill special orders. Cars, weapons, you name it. I get the merchandise from wherever it's located and deliver it to the buyer. Sometimes the stuff is boxed or crated and I don't know what's inside, but that's rare. I get paid either way, so I don't give a shit."

"You don't know what you're taking? How does that work?"

"Occasionally I'm a middleman. Somebody wants merchandise taken from one place, such as a warehouse, and delivered somewhere else. I just grab the goods. I don't care what it is."

"But most of the time you're the acquisitions guy?"

"Yeah. I prefer it that way, knowing what I'm after and what the risk is."

"So you specialize in cars. Weapons. What else?"

"I've run some weed. Coke. Even a few stolen paintings once." Settling into his role, he gave a laugh. "Don't care for art myself, but whatever. Money's green no matter what the load."

Rab nodded. "Anything you won't do?"

Tonio weighed his next words carefully. "Two things. First, I won't take on human cargo. No trafficking illegals. That's some sick shit, man. I mean, stuff is just *stuff*, like the art. But people? Forget it."

The other man took a draw of his beer. Set it down. "I don't deal in selling people. Too messy, and I like my green to flow from less complicated sources. Besides, I like to play with my toys so much I sometimes break them. It's how I decompress."

Tonio paused. "Whaddya mean? Break them, how?"

"Never mind that for now. What's the second thing?"

*Cristo*, what else was this crazy bastard into? Tonio let it go for the time being—but he would definitely keep in mind what the man had said. "I'm not a hit man. You got that kind of issue, I'm not the guy you call. I'm in acquisitions and delivery." Another calculated risk, but Rab didn't seem bothered.

"But I'm willing to bet you're armed, even now."

"I'm carrying," he confirmed. No reason to lie about that. "I'd be stupid not to protect myself if necessary, but I don't go around offing people for thrills."

One corner of Rab's mouth kicked up. "Me, neither. Hard as it might be to believe, I don't start that kind of trouble. But I don't mind finishing it, if I'm forced to."

"Good to know."

"I'm a businessman, like you. My goal is making money,

the fastest, easiest ways possible. And socking it all away for a rainy day, like when the government finally falls completely fucking apart and takes the banks down with it."

Sadly, Tonio couldn't totally disagree with that viewpoint. Just Rab's methods.

"Hell to the fuckin' yeah," he said. Apparently that response pleased his new *boss*.

Rab drained the rest of his beer, then said, "You get ten percent of the haul."

"When I take most of the risk?" He snorted. "Twenty."

"You're dreamin', man. No way. We all take risks."

"I didn't set up this meeting, you did," Tonio pointed out, tapping the table with one finger. "You're looking for someone to take the heat off. An acquisitions man who knows what he's doing, and that's me. I think you've got something in mind or I wouldn't be here right now."

Rab stared at him for a long moment. "Fifteen. I have a big job in mind, but I want to assign you a few trial runs first. See how things go."

"Sure. What do you have in mind?"

"What types of vehicles do you have access to for hauling?"

"Anything the job requires. Van, eighteen-wheeler, plane . . ." *Or I will, as soon as the department loans them to me. One more expense for Austin to get cleared, and won't he be happy? Shit.*

"Good. We're gonna need a semi next Thursday night. I'll give you the deets once I have them firmed up."

"No problem." Just then his phone buzzed—the one he'd acquired for the undercover job. *Tess.*

*U busy 2nite?*

He had reservations about giving her the number, because it meant a personal tie he didn't want. On the other hand, she'd given him an "in" and made his presence in the group seem legit.

"Something important?" the other man asked casually. There was the hint of an edge in his tone, though.

"Just Tess." Pocketing the phone, he looked up. "Her hanging around, that going to be a problem? Your sister seemed to think so, last night."

Rab considered this for a few seconds. "Hadn't been for you, I would've tossed her ass out. She can hang as long as she's with you. But keep the bitch out of my face. Got it?"

"Got it."

*Asshole.* He longed to punch the bastard in the mouth. How he kept the desire out of his expression was a mystery.

Rab stood, signaling an end to their discussion. After giving Tonio a knuckle bump, he headed for the door. What Tonio really wanted to do was give him a knuckle bump in the face.

"Gotta hit the men's room. See you," Tonio called. The other man gave a wave but didn't look back.

Once Tonio heard the man's motorcycle start up and drive off, he changed directions. Instead he grabbed Rab's beer mug and took it to the bar. Hesitating, he eyed the area behind the counter and then lifted the walk-through arm, going in search of the dishwasher. He found it under the counter and opened the stainless steel door just as a voice sounded next to him.

"What the hell are you doing back here?"

Straightening, he looked into Angel's annoyed face and held up the mug. "Your brother left without taking care of his glass. I was just putting it away."

Her eyebrows lifted. "Seriously? I pay people to do that, you know. You shouldn't be behind the bar." She crossed her arms over her chest, drawing his attention to her cleavage. "I'm up here, buddy."

He shot her a grin, meeting her less-than-amused gaze. "Sorry. Not about enjoying the view, but about trespassing. I just didn't think you should have to clean up his mess."

She ignored his comment about ogling her bust. "The last time I caught one of Rab's thugs standing there, he was trying to get the register open."

Thug? He winced inwardly. Of course that was what she saw when she looked at him—a felon and a troublemaker, like the rest of them.

"Stealing from you would be like stealing from Rab. I'm new, not stupid."

"That remains to be seen." She softened some, perhaps sensing he wasn't a threat. "Anyway, thanks. Rab and his friends aren't usually too considerate, especially when it comes to leaving a mess."

"It's no biggie." The silence stretched between them for a moment as he studied her. She stared right back at him, open and unafraid. Direct. He liked that, and found himself grinning. "You're the boss around here, huh? Somehow I'm not surprised."

"Boss and owner. I'll take that as a compliment." She looked pleased.

"It was meant as one. How long have you lived in the area?"

"All my life. Still live not far from the house where I grew up."

He'd lay down money that Rab had encroached on her space and privacy for a free place to crash. But he didn't say so. "That's cool. What about your folks?"

"Mom lives in an apartment across town. Won't stay with me, which is just as well." A sad expression flitted across her face, then vanished and her gaze darkened. She continued without explaining what she meant by that last comment. "Anyway, she deserves her peace after what our father put her through. And before you ask, he died in prison."

"I'm sorry," he said sincerely.

"Don't be. *I'm* not." She sighed. "He was a piece of shit, and Rab's turning out just like him. You'd have been better off heeding my warning last night. Unless you're too far down the same path, in which case, good luck."

He blinked at her, a little shocked at her bluntness. "Do you give that advice to all the guys who work for your brother?"

"Nope. Just you." She cocked her head, studying him. "Can't figure out why, though. You seem different from that bunch somehow, is all. Not as harsh around the edges."

*Crap*. This was *not* good. Gathering his alter ego around him, he gave her a cocky grin. "Not so different, *bonita*. I've got bills to pay, same as them. I've got a government who thinks I'm supposed to exist on barely more than minimum wage, and doubles my taxes if I dare to try to rise above poverty level by going into business for myself."

He stepped closer, into her personal space, stalking her. Crowding her into the counter, he leaned forward and took in her wide green eyes. The hitch in her breath. "So tell me how I'm a piece of shit for trying to survive."

"I didn't say you were," she said, voice husky. "But participating in my brother's crazy schemes will land you in prison—or worse."

He was almost pressed to her front, could feel the heat from her body. Smell her sweet scent. *Dios*, he wanted to touch. To know if she was as soft and silky as she looked. Her eyes darkened and her lips parted, and for a second he thought she'd press her lips to his.

Then he heard the distinctive sound—the *thwick* of a switchblade.

"Move back," she said coolly.

Glancing down, he saw the tip of the blade pointed at the bulge in his crotch. "Whoa. Easy there." Carefully he backed up a couple of steps.

"I should cut you like the pig you are." Whatever hint of desire had been building was long gone, at least on her part.

For a horrible moment, he thought she'd made him as a cop. "Pig?"

"You're with Tess. I don't have any respect for cheaters, so you can move on now."

Tess, again. God*damn*, that woman was going to put a serious crimp in his social life if he didn't manage to extricate himself from the situation soon. He wasn't doing either of them any favors by staying with someone he knew wasn't going to be "the one."

"Tess and I aren't serious."

"You're sleeping with her, though, right?"

"Well . . ."

She narrowed her eyes. He was guessing that didn't bode well for any hope of further conversation. "Out."

"For now." He winked. "I'll see you around."

"I'll be waiting with bated breath," she said drily.

Letting his face show amusement he didn't feel, he gave her a smile, then turned and left. It wasn't until he was outside that he let down his guard and cursed his damn luck long and loud. Why the fuck did he have to meet such a gorgeous, intriguing woman under these circumstances?

Trudging to his old beater car, he got in and slammed the door so hard he worried it might fall off the hinges. The rust bucket was barely holding together. He had a sweet ride at home, a 1978 Corvette Stingray, but didn't dare drive his baby and allow it to sit outside Stroker's for any length of time. That would just be asking for it to get stolen.

Driving around for a bit, he made sure he wasn't being followed. Once he was satisfied, he turned the car toward Sugarland. To his brother Julian's house, where he lived with his beautiful wife, Grace. The two of them were insanely in love, and Tonio was glad. It had been about time someone tamed his horndog of a brother, and Grace was more than woman enough for the job.

When the couple first met, Julian had been screwing

his way through the female population of Cheatham County. The guy's libido put Tonio's to shame. Tonio had been living in Texas, working at the San Antonio PD at the time, but he could hear the passion for the lawyer in his brother's voice long before the man would admit how much she meant to him. Then he'd gone after her, and she hadn't made things easy. Good for her.

Recently, though, they'd been dealing with some trouble. Not with their marriage, however. A few weeks ago, Julian and fellow firefighter Clay Montana had been running the ambulance to a call, with Clay at the wheel. A truck had run a red light and hit their vehicle broadside right in Clay's door. Julian's friend had sustained massive internal injuries and head trauma and had been in a coma ever since. The doctors still weren't sure if he'd survive, or ever wake up.

There had even been some discussion of taking the poor bastard off life support. But the barest detection of brain waves had tabled that, for now.

Julian's injuries had been less severe. Even so, Tonio had almost panicked to learn that his brother had a concussion, broken ribs, and torn ligaments in one ankle. He was almost healed, but still hobbling around the house and bitching about going back to work. His ankle was solid enough, though his ribs were taking more time.

However, the biggest obstacle of all was in Julian's head. He was having nightmares about the accident, wasn't sleeping well. Grace had to wake him from the terror almost every night, and exhaustion was taking a toll. Especially since Tonio's stubborn brother was refusing to take any antianxiety meds. He was seeing a counselor, though, thanks to FD rules. Tonio prayed it was helping at least some.

He hoped so, or Captain Howard Paxton wouldn't let him set foot in Station Five. Howard was Grace's brother-in-law, married to her sister Kat. He'd made no bones about Julian's head being screwed on straight before his return. Nobody wanted their rescuer to be the one with PTSD.

And that was what Julian was suffering from, whether he would admit it or not. Grace was worried about him.

A short time later, Tonio pulled into the couple's driveway and shut off the engine. With a sigh, he climbed out and was soon knocking on the front door. After a moment, footsteps sounded from the other side, and the door opened. Grace stood there smiling at him, long blond hair pulled back into a ponytail. Even dressed in jeans and a T-shirt, she couldn't hide her class. She was so far removed from Angel and her world, the differences were a bit disorienting.

Grace pulled him into a hug and clung tightly for a moment. "I'm so glad you're here," she whispered into his ear.

"I'm always here for you guys—you know that." Pulling back, he noted the sadness in her eyes. "Oh no. Did Clay die?"

"No, but . . . Come inside, we can talk where we're more comfortable."

"Something's happened."

"Yeah." She led him into the living room, where Julian was sitting on the sofa.

Across from his brother, in a stuffed chair, sat Howard. Both men looked up at his arrival, darkness shadowing their expressions. Julian started to stand, and grimaced in pain, wrapping an arm around his ribs.

"No, don't get up." Crossing the distance quickly, Tonio leaned down and gave his brother a one-armed hug. "Bro. Good to see you."

"You, too."

Tonio turned and shook Howard's hand. "Howard, good to see you again, too. But I get the feeling this isn't a social visit."

The big man appeared grim. "Not entirely, though I'd already planned to come today and check on Julian." He paused. "I came to give him and Grace the news that Clay woke up this morning."

"What? That's great!" A strained, unhappy silence met his enthusiasm. "Isn't it?"

"The brain damage, it seems, could be pretty severe," Howard said quietly. "He can't speak, doesn't seem to understand what anyone's saying."

"But he just woke up, you said. It may take a while for his brain to heal."

"Yeah. He was only awake for a few minutes, so of course the doctors will be able to assess him better once he's fully conscious. It's just that he wasn't able to respond to the simplest questions, like his name, his occupation, or who's the president. He seemed confused, then afraid. He got tired fast, and went back to sleep."

"That's to be expected, I guess. Gonna be a long haul for him." Tonio glanced at his brother, who wasn't making a sound. In fact, he was staring at the floor, the emotional pain on his face heartbreaking to witness. "Hey, he'll recover, bro. It'll take time, but he will."

"You don't know that," Julian responded dully. "He might wish he had died after all."

Tonio exchanged a worried glance with Grace and Howard. Grace scooted close to her husband and put a gentle hand on his knee. "Honey, why don't you go rest for a while? I know you're tired."

"I'm not an invalid," he snapped.

Her response was firm. "No, but you're exhausted from not sleeping at night. To be honest, so am I." His head jerked up at that. Clearly, he hadn't thought about how his stress was affecting her. "Yes, I'm tired, too. The best way you can help me out is to take care of yourself. Go take a nap, and when you get up I'll have some dinner in the oven."

"I'm sorry, baby. I wasn't thinking."

"It's okay." She folded him into her arms, then gave him a kiss. "Go."

Contrite, he pushed to his feet, sucking in a breath at the pain. Then, with a nod, he bade his good-byes and hobbled down the hallway, out of sight. Grace waited until the bedroom door clicked shut before she spoke in a low voice.

"I'm so scared for him. I've never seen him like this." Blindly, she reached over to the end table for a tissue, then dabbed at her eyes. "The accident, what happened to Clay, is tearing him up inside. Nothing I say or do seems to make it better."

"He's hurting, Grace," Tonio said softly. "Give him time."

"I know, and I am. It's just . . ." After hesitating, she shook her head. "I can't shake the feeling there's something more going on than I'm aware of. He's not just upset or sad—he's completely devastated. He won't talk about the wreck, and I don't know how to help him."

A few tears escaped to roll down her cheeks. Damn, he was no good with crying women. He hated to see her upset, and he had no idea how to help any more than Grace did. Come to think of it, she was right, too.

Wasn't it normal for his brother to react this way? Tonio knew Julian had regained consciousness before a second ambulance arrived at their mangled one. He'd also heard from a uniformed traffic officer who'd responded to the call that the inside of the ambulance was soaked in blood. One side of Clay's head had been a soggy mess, his face barely recognizable.

Julian and other witnesses had told the cops later that Clay had the green light and started through the intersection. They'd seen the big truck at the same time, barreling through the light, bearing down on Clay's side. Clay had whispered something, Julian couldn't remember what. Then they were hit.

"I'm sorry, guys," Grace said, bringing him back to the present. "This has been really tough to deal with."

Tonio gave her an encouraging smile. "No apologies wanted or needed. We're family, hon. You're not alone, and we'll do whatever we can to support you both."

"Damn right," Howard agreed, crossing his arms over his massive chest.

She gave them a watery smile in return. "Thanks. If you mean that, then please stay for dinner. And before you tell me you can't intrude or put me to the trouble, let me just say I could use the company. I love him so much, and this has been hard."

Tonio moved to sit by her, clasped her hand. "I can only imagine."

Grace had taken time off work to care for her husband. He hadn't realized until now that she was at the end of her rope doing it alone. He felt like crap.

"So, stay?"

Both of them gladly agreed, and visited with Grace, Tonio sipping beer and Howard a soda, since he wasn't a drinker. Later, she started preparations to make lasagna, and Howard ran home to fetch Kat and bring her back to eat with them. While the captain was gone, Tonio broached a subject that had been bothering him all afternoon.

"You know I'm here for you, but something's come up and it's really bad timing."

"What is it?" She divided her attention between talking and layering the noodles, cheese, and meat sauce.

"I just started an undercover assignment. That was part of the reason I came over, to tell you guys I won't be around as much for a few weeks. Now I'm having second thoughts, though."

"What? No. You can't put your work on hold because of us." Setting down her spoon, he wiped her hands on a towel. "If anybody understands how important your job is, it's me and your brother."

"I know. I just can't help feeling like I'm abandoning you both when you need me the most." He loathed that feeling.

"That's not true." She gave him a smile. "You've been with us every step of the way, and we appreciate it. Go do what you need to do and don't worry."

"After what you told me? Right."

"If it makes you feel better, can you somehow check in with us?"

"I can manage, just not too often. I don't want to get caught by these guys I'm going to be hanging with."

"True." She thought about that. "Your captain knows where you'll be, right?"

"Yes. Austin Rainey."

"Then if something happens and we need you, I'll call him and he can pass along a message. That way you'll know it's really important, and we won't be calling you and messing up your cover."

He blew out a breath. "Thanks. That eases my mind some."

"Don't worry. I shouldn't have dumped all that—"

"Don't apologize again or I won't eat all your lasagna!"

"Ha! Fat chance of that."

She was right, of course.

Howard returned with Kat and their baby son, Ben. Julian got up from his nap shortly before the lasagna was ready and they actually had a nice time. After dinner, Tonio held and played with the baby, giving his parents a break. He liked children. Good thing, because his mother was forever asking when one of her sons was going to give her grandbabies.

Ben squealed and he grinned at the thought. One day, for sure.

And he couldn't help wondering—no. He wasn't going there. Couldn't afford to right now. He had a theft ring to bring down.

Now if only he could figure out how to protect his heart from the leader's sister, he'd be gold.

# 3

Angel leaned against the doorway to the kitchen and studied the thinning crowd.

Rab and his cronies were in their usual corner, being louder than normal, drinking a tad too much. Especially since they had a job planned for tonight that they didn't want her to hear about. Truthfully she didn't know much. Just that they were going to steal something, and if they got caught they'd all go to jail.

Even Tonio. The man was there, too, sexy as hell, white teeth gleaming in the darkness against his tanned complexion. His bandanna was back in place around his head, tied at the nape of his neck, black hair poking up in spikes. His throaty laugh did strange things to her insides, and heated every part of her.

And Tess was sticking to him like a burr, spoiling the picture. The vapid blonde was leaning into his side, stroking his arm or chest now and then. Nibbling on his strong neck, the movement of her arm suggesting that her small hand was wandering south. From the way he shifted once in a while, she'd hit the target.

"Goddammit," Angel muttered, glaring at the other woman. "Skanky ho."

Watching the bitch rub all over him like a cat in heat made her blood boil. That she had no right whatsoever to be pissed didn't seem to matter one bit. She was jealous, plain and simple.

Why *him*, for God's sake? The man was a *felon*. Why couldn't she feel this insane attraction for the hunky, burly construction worker sitting near the door? Or the nice pediatrician who came in once in a while and had made his interest clear? But no. She had to do things the hard way. Long for the impossible.

"Wow, who's the laser glare of death aimed at? Your brother or Tess?" Andy appeared beside her, grinning.

She huffed a laugh. "Take your pick."

She studied Andy for a moment, unable to comprehend why even *he* didn't get her motor running. He was tall, lanky, and attractive with curly brown hair falling over blue eyes. A lover, not a fighter, from the way he avoided Rab like the Ebola virus—not that she deducted any points for that. He was younger than she was, but not by much, being twenty-five to her twenty-eight. Andy was cute, with a sweet personality.

But he just didn't do it for her. Seemed the dangerous types were the ones who did. Must run in the family.

This didn't bode well for her future love life. Disgusted with herself, she pushed away from the door and busied herself at the bar pulling beers, even though she had plenty of staff tonight. Anything to distract her from the temptation across the room. As luck would have it, however, her servers "suddenly" got very busy elsewhere when Rab's group started demanding more beer.

Gritting her teeth, Angel walked over to check what brands they were drinking. She did her best to ignore Tess. Really. But the woman was in the mood to be as big a bitch as possible, and was apparently determined to succeed.

"So, Miller for you two, one Corona, and one Dewar's for you," she repeated for each man, nodding at Tonio last.

"I said *I* wanted another Bud Light." Tess thumped her mug on the table, hard, sloshing a good bit over the rim.

"You haven't even finished half of that one," Angel said evenly.

"It tastes like shit. Either you or your lackey back there obviously didn't hook up the tank thingy right."

*God, give me strength. I can't choke her.* "There's nothing wrong with the beer, Tess. I've tasted it myself."

"Well, then there's something wrong with your taste buds. Get me another one."

"Ask me in a nicer tone and I'll consider it."

Tess's mouth curled into a sneer. "The customer is always right, remember? I'm the customer and I want satisfaction."

"So does Mick Jagger," Angel muttered. "Forget it."

She started to turn. Just when she did, Tess snatched the mug off the table and tossed the beer all over the front of Angel's T-shirt. Angel let out a shriek and then stood gaping at the other woman, arms held out from her sides. The liquid was cold, and now she was soaked and smelly.

"You rotten bitch." Angel lunged, fully intending to rip the grin off the blonde's face.

But Tonio interceded, leaping to his feet and placing himself between them. Laying a hand on Angel's arm, he gently steered her back, away from Tess.

"Hey, it's not worth it," he coaxed. "Your patrons are watching, waiting for a show. Don't lower yourself to her level."

That got her attention. There was no way Tess heard his words or she would've been royally pissed. That made Angel feel a little better. Didn't change the fact that she was still wet and cold, though.

She nodded, seething. "You're right. I've dealt with bigger problems than her before. What the hell do you see in her?" She shook her head. "Never mind."

Skirting Tonio, she ignored her brother and his friends laughing behind her. Effing jerks. Anyone else's brother would've jumped to her defense. And yet Tonio was the only one who wasn't amused by the scene. What made him so different from the others? He just didn't seem to belong with that motley group, criminal or not.

Back at the bar, she walked behind it and got Andy's attention. He turned after handing a man bottle of beer, and stared at her shirt.

"Jesus, what happened?"

"Tess, that fucking . . ." She blew out a breath. Calling a customer names in front of others wasn't cool, and she'd already slipped once. "I need to change. You're going to have to take their order to them and handle things out here for a few minutes."

"Oh man." He groaned but looked at her in defeat. "Sure. I'll take care of it."

"Thanks. I know you hate dealing with them. I won't be long."

"It's okay, I'm not *that* big a wimp."

Quickly she gave him the order—purposely leaving off a new beer for the bitch—and walked out from behind the bar. There was a hallway to the left that led to the restrooms. Beyond that was her office. She hurried there, unlocked the door, and let herself inside.

The space wasn't huge, but it was big enough to hold a desk with a computer and printer. Behind the desk in the corner stood a file cabinet and a separate tall closet where she kept her purse and a change of clothes. Against an adjacent wall was a full-sized sofa for when she wanted to rest for a bit—or take refuge from Rab. The paint and carpet were clean and fresh, as she refused to have the space look dingy. It hadn't cost much to fix up, and it pleased her.

With a sigh, she peeled off her shirt and tossed it onto the arm of the sofa. Her bra was a little damp, too, but it would have to do. She'd just walked to the cabinet and grabbed the handle when there was a knock on the door.

"Hang on—"

She'd barely got those words out when the door opened and Tonio strode inside, shutting the door behind him. Shit, she'd forgotten to lock it.

"What are you doing in here? I'm changing!" She glared at him, then turned her back to fish around for her extra shirt.

"Sorry."

Humor laced his apology, spoiling it. When she faced him again, pulling down the hem of the T-shirt, he looked contrite. But at the same time his gaze flared with interest. That wasn't cool, considering.

"Tess actually let you escape her claws for five minutes?" she asked in a derisive tone.

"We're not joined at the hip, Angel. Far from it. After what she did to you, I sent her home."

His voice stroked every feminine cell in her body. It was deep and smooth, and conjured images of him naked and sweaty. Just the picture she didn't need when he was with somebody else. "Is that so? Still doesn't explain why you followed me in here. You get off on stalking people? Or is it just me?"

For whatever reason, he seemed to take that as an invitation to get up close and personal. He crossed the short distance, determination on his face, and the heat that flared between them could've started a fire. Stopping, he left about a foot between them, as though careful not to crowd her like he had done before. Slowly he reached up and brushed her cheek with his fingers.

She froze, heart thumping madly in her chest. She didn't know what to do, whether to push him away or respond, but he didn't appear to have the same issue. His big hand cupped her face and then he bent down, capturing her lips with his.

It was just a kiss—and yet it was so much more.

His mouth was sin. Pure, one hundred percent wickedness that reached into her soul and made her want. His tongue parted her lips and she groaned, wrapping a hand around the back of his head to pull him closer. He tasted like whiskey, rich and smoky. His hair was free above the knot in his bandanna, and was silky to the touch. His body felt good pressed against hers, and he smelled so damn good, too.

She wanted him to take control. Bend her over the desk or sofa, rip her jeans down, and have her. Any way he wanted. In that moment of insanity, she knew this was a mistake. Urgently she shoved at his chest and broke the kiss. "No. You're sleeping with someone else."

"Not anymore. That ended before it even started."

"I don't believe you."

"I'm serious, Angel. It's not her I want." His expression seemed sincere, and his statement rang true.

But still. "Why? Is that how you operate, jumping from woman to woman as the mood strikes? Sorry. Not interested. I'm not going to be a notch on your bedpost."

He shook his head, brushed a thumb over her lips. "That's not what this is about. I feel the spark between us. Don't you?"

She did, down to her toes. "You don't get it."

"Explain, then."

"Even if I could trust you, which I seriously doubt, this can't go anywhere. For one, if you mess with me, my brother will fuck you up." She gave a sad laugh. "Not because he cares that much about me, but because you're one of his posse now. Nothing means more to him than making a good score and padding his bank account. If he feels anything is going to jeopardize that, including one of his men being distracted by fucking his sister, he'll put an end to it. Painfully."

Concern laced his voice. "But he wouldn't hurt you, would he?"

"I don't think so." She frowned, recalling his veiled threat to shut her up. "He's never laid a hand on me, but you? Different story. You have yet to prove yourself valuable to him, and he won't hesitate to make you pay."

"I appreciate your concern, but I'm not going to let that happen," he said, lips curving into a smile.

"Arrogant much? Or just stupid?"

His laugh was genuine, surprising her, the sight making her nipples tighten and the rest of her ache with need. He was beautiful in a way no man should be. Mesmerizing. It was no wonder Tess didn't want to let go of him. *Tess*.

Skirting him, she walked to the door and opened it. "This has been a fascinating conversation, but it's time for you to leave. I don't— "

"What the fuck is going on in here?"

Rab's voice behind Angel caused her to jump. Whirling, she cringed at the evil glare he was aiming at Tonio— who didn't appear the least bit fazed.

Quickly she tried to diffuse her brother's suspicion. "Tonio was apologizing for Tess's behavior. He said he sent her home."

Rab looked between them, skepticism written on his face. "Sounded like more than that to me. You harassing my sister, asshole?"

"Wouldn't dream of it," Tonio replied, appearing unfazed. "But I don't think she believes I'm sincere, considering how much she hates Tess."

"I don't hate her," Angel muttered. "I just wish she'd fly away on her broom and find another watering hole to land in."

That caused both men to snort, and Rab clapped Tonio on the shoulder. "Maybe nobody will have to worry about the airhead after tonight. Come on, let's go."

A look of reluctance flashed across Tonio's face, but it was there and gone in an instant. His smile was all easy confidence as he said, "Sure."

Before Angel could blink, both men were gone. Tonio didn't even look back. With a sigh, she left the office, locked it, and went to help Andy prepare for closing.

And she tried not to think about a certain criminal who made her *need*. On every level.

Tess unlocked the door to her shitty motel room and let herself inside.

Walking over to the equally shitty, lumpy bed, she sat and rested her elbows on her knees. Put her head in her palms.

She was tired. To the core. This wasn't working, and tonight she'd overplayed her hand. That group was never going to accept her into the fold. Not completely. She'd fucked up, and she was going to hear about it.

Glancing at the time, she grimaced. She would have to check in with the boss soon. Fuck if she knew what she was going to say. Taking off for parts unknown sounded pretty good right about now. Maybe Fiji. Or Switzerland. Anywhere she could blend in and never been heard from again.

Resigned, she grabbed her phone and punched in the

number. It was answered on the second ring. The voice on the other end was terse.

"Tell me some good news."

"The Ravens might win the Super Bowl this year?"

"Funny." He didn't sound amused. "Try again."

With an effort, she tamped down the sickness in her gut. "Yeah, that's about all I've got."

"I'm seriously not in the mood," he snapped. "You should have made at least some progress by now."

Faced with no other choice, she filled in tonight's events—and held the phone away from her ear as he launched into a tirade.

God, it was going to be a long night.

Sitting alone in the dark, Tonio leaned his head back on the sofa and tried to find his calm center. Zen. Or whatever the fuck it was called.

After days of waiting, tonight would be the first true test of his skills. Not to mention his loyalty to Rab. The gang leader hadn't let him in on what was going down, but from the preparations he'd been making, Tonio figured it involved car theft. The equipment included a "borrowed" eighteen-wheeler and a couple of slim-jims for opening automobile locks.

The temptation to call in a bust was strong. Grand theft auto would get Rab sent back to prison where he belonged, and he'd no longer pose a threat to Angel. But only for a few years, and then what? He'd be right back on her doorstep one day, trampling all over the life she'd made for herself.

No, he needed to hold out for the bigger score. Rab

had indicated this job was peanuts compared to the big one he was planning. The more charges those shitheads racked up, the better, and Austin agreed. Maybe if they played their cards right, Rab and his gang would never see the light of day again.

That would be best in the long run. Especially for Angel.

His thoughts drifted back to their kiss. She'd responded so beautifully, melting in his arms, even though she clearly hadn't wanted to. They were attracted to each other, that much was a given. Did she sense something good in him, or did she have a thing for alleged felons? He didn't think it was the latter. At least he hoped not.

Shifting, he tried to ease the pressure in the front of his jeans, but it was no use. He couldn't stop thinking about her, how gorgeous she was, with those luminous green eyes and fall of dark hair. That Celtic tat he wanted to lick—among other places.

As he unzipped his jeans, he recalled how warm she'd felt against him. How her breasts pushed against her T-shirt, the soft curve of her hips. Those long legs. Pushing down his jeans and underwear a bit, he freed his cock and imagined her on her knees. Licking and sucking him, tasting the pearls on the tip.

Slowly he jacked himself. Pumped the smooth flesh through his fist and pictured his dick sliding between her lips, down the hot, wet tunnel of her throat. Just the right suction, all the way to the root and back . . .

The electric tingle started in his groin and he pumped harder. Faster. Soon his hips were lifting off the sofa, his breathing harsh as he gave in to the sensations flooding him. His balls tightened, and then he gave three more strokes before coming in a rush, hot seed spurting onto his shirt and spilling over his fist. He kept up the action until the release died away to pleasant aftershocks, then faded.

*"Dios."*

He'd come that hard from simply envisioning Angel going down on him. The real thing might put him six feet under.

Pushing from the sofa, he walked into the bathroom and wet a washcloth. Wouldn't be cool to show up for the job smelling like jiz. He'd never hear the end of it. He cleaned up and went in search of a fresh shirt, settling on a plain black tee. A pair of navy blue tennis shoes completed his ensemble, perfect for a thief who wanted to blend in with the night.

With a grimace, he grabbed his keys and wallet containing his fake driver's license and headed for the door. As much as he hated that he was about to steal from some unsuspecting individual, he was glad to get out of the drab apartment.

Stepping outside, he locked the door behind him and jogged down the stairs. The neighborhood wasn't the worst the area had to offer, but it definitely sent the message that Tonio was a man who could always stand to make another buck. The complex had been built sometime in the 1970s, and sat in the landscape like a squat old woman with shabby clothes and missing teeth.

Tonio's old beater was right at home amid the scenery. Jumping in, he fired up the vehicle and pointed it toward the rendezvous site. The drive took more than thirty minutes, since the destination was on the other side of Nashville, out in the country. Rolling hills sped by, but he could hardly see them. It was darker than a coal miner's ass out here.

At last he reached the road he was looking for and turned down it. About a mile farther, he spotted a turn-about area, the eighteen-wheeler he'd signed out from the department's search-and-seizure lot parked off to the side. He'd dropped it off in another lot earlier, for Rab's men. There was a pickup truck behind the larger vehicle. Tonio pulled in behind the pickup, shut off the ignition, and got out. The door to the other vehicles opened. Rab slid from the driver's seat of the pickup, and another man got out of the passenger's side. Tonio recognized him as Stan White, one of the group of Rab's men from the bar.

Phillip Horton, from the same group, swung down from the big semi, and it appeared he was alone. Tonio met them halfway and grinned.

"Now, you boys going to tell me what we're after?"

Rab stepped close and clapped him on the shoulder, squeezing hard enough to leave a bruise. "Wheels, my man. Fancy ones that'll fetch a good price with my contact."

So he'd been right. They were stealing cars, selling them. Some went to chop shops for parts. "What's my cut?"

Rab's expression lost some humor. "It's a bit early for a newbie to be asking that question."

"Good thing I'm not a newbie, then." He let his tone harden.

After a pause, the other man said, "You pass the first test, you'll make rent. Trust me."

Right. "Fine, so long as you know I don't work for free. What's the plan?"

"There's an estate in the hills, about two miles up the road." He pointed. "In the four-car garage, the dude's got a Ferrari, a Shelby Cobra, a Jeep Wrangler, and a Ducati bike. Guess which ones we're taking."

"The Ferrari, the Shelby, and the Ducati."

"Got it in one."

"Guy must be loaded."

"And then some," Rab agreed. "But it'll barely make a dent in his wallet, so I don't feel real sorry for him."

Tonio was sorry enough for both of them. The owner's insurance rates would probably skyrocket. It didn't matter how much money someone had. People worked hard for what they got, and stealing was wrong. Damn, he wanted to arrest this asshole and his buddies.

"Cool," he forced himself to say with a smile. "Let's go get our Robin Hood on."

"Robin Hood? How's that?"

"Robbing from the stinking rich and giving to the poor and needy."

That made the other man laugh. "Yeah, I like that. I'm Robin, so I guess that makes you guys my merry men."

*On a cold day in hell.*

Rab went on. "Okay, we're gonna leave the semi here. We'll take your car and drive to the estate, park outside the gate. Stan will work his electronic magic to get the gate to release, and we're in. Then he'll do the same for the pass-coded garage."

Tonio frowned. "Who is this rich guy?"

"You'll see. Don't want to spoil the surprise."

God, he hoped it wasn't a bigwig from one of the nearby cities—especially his own. He couldn't think of anyone he knew who possessed that level of wealth, though.

He shrugged. "Whatever."

"Come on," Stan complained. "Let's get the fuckin' show on the road. I want to sleep at some point."

"Don't be such an old lady," Phillip said with a sneer. "Besides, ain't no amount of beauty rest gonna help you none."

"Fuck you."

Rab cut off their arguing. "Enough. Let's move."

They got into Tonio's car, Rab in the front seat next to him, the other two in the back. Tonio figured they were taking his car in case they were spotted. In that case, Tonio would be identified for sure. He almost smirked at the idea, but refrained. Getting caught would be messy.

The silence was thick as he approached their destination. Just before the gate, Rab ordered him to stop and cut the lights, and he did, shutting off the ignition as well. As they got out of the car, Tonio squinted at the large, grand entrance to the estate. The walls were brick on either side, the gate itself some sort of heavy metal, like iron. An ornate design was worked into the metal, and he finally made out several guitars with the letters *JT*.

The entry looked familiar. In fact, he was sure he'd seen it before—then it hit him.

He turned to Rab. "Wait a second. This is Joe Turner's place, isn't it?" The group snickered, giving him the answer. "We're going to rip off the biggest country star since George Strait? Are you all crazy?"

Shit. One day, the department would have to settle up with the man. And hope he didn't sue the hell out of them. Of course, if he or his bodyguards caught them, they might end up full of buckshot and then it wouldn't matter.

"Relax," Rab said. "Turner's just some rich asshole same as any other. No sense in getting all worked up over it."

Tonio paced some while Stan worked on the gate, trying to shake his nerves. He'd done some undercover work, but it had been more low-key. He and his partner in San Antonio had posed as buyers during a drug sting, and another time he'd dressed as a homeless man to do surveillance. Nothing as risky as this.

Abruptly he realized Rab was staring at him. "Adrenaline. I always get keyed up before a score." Thankfully the other man seemed to buy his explanation.

Attention turned to Stan as he fiddled with the electronic box near the entrance, the one visitors would pull up next to and buzz the house with. He had stuck some sort of wand device into the panel, and was dialing, much like the way a thief would do to crack a safe. While he did this, Tonio scanned the grounds beyond, toward the house, listening. Nothing moved.

Then a hum shattered the stillness and the gate began to open outward. It startled him like a shot from a gun, but really wasn't that loud. Still, no lights came on at the house, nor did any dogs start barking. Tonio thought they were fortunate the singer didn't have a couple of vicious dogs guarding the place.

Leaving the car behind, they made their way as quickly and quietly as possible toward the house, but kept to the trees on either side of the drive. That way if someone looked out a window, with any luck they'd see nothing.

The garage was situated in the back of the house, the driveway curving around to the side and leading to the structure. This was where things could really get dicey. A lot of open ground stood between them and freedom—if they could even get the vehicles from the garage without tripping an alarm.

Keeping his eyes and ears open, he followed the others around the back to the big structure. It wasn't attached to the house, except there was a covered walkway leading from the back of the house to a regular-sized side door. Tonio saw they'd try to gain entrance there, and then open the big doors from the inside.

Taking out his cell phone, Rab risked using the flashlight app to help Stan see what he was doing. Stan inspected the doorframe, running his hand around and over the top of it. Finally he grunted in satisfaction and murmured in a low voice.

"This is shit for security. Somebody ought to tell Mr. Fancy Britches Cowboy that—after we steal his shit, of course."

*Yeah, that somebody will probably be me.*

In a couple of minutes, maybe less, Stan had the alarm system disabled and they were in. Phillip took a slim-jim and immediately went to work on getting the Ferrari unlocked. Not a tough chore for a seasoned thief. The Shelby wasn't even locked, and Tonio couldn't help shaking his head.

"Turner probably thought his cars were safely tucked away," he muttered.

"His stupidity is our gain." This from Rab, who then walked to the garage doors and set about opening them manually rather than using the automatic opener. "Can't risk someone inside hearing the hum."

"How are we going to do this?" Tonio asked. "Hot-wire all of them and haul ass?"

"That would be faster," Phillip agreed.

"More risk of being heard, though." Rab laid down the veto. "I want to do this quiet. Push both cars down the drive and out the gate before we start 'em up. You and me will take the Ferrari. Then you'll come back for the bike. Stan, you and Phil take the Shelby."

Tonio didn't like it. "That means more than one trip. The longer we hang around, the more likely we are to get caught."

"You heard me, T. Let's do it."

Tonio gritted his teeth and stifled the retort that sprang to his lips. Both at the stupid orders and the shortening of his name. He guessed that meant he was becoming part of the group, for what it was worth.

Stan and Phillip pushed the Shelby out the door and down the drive as planned. Tonio peeked out toward the house, but there was still no sign of movement. His heart was pounding in his chest and he decided he wasn't cut out for this crap. He'd much rather be firmly on the right side of the law than what he was doing now, even if he was actually a good guy in disguise.

Once the Shelby cleared the gate, he and Rab went next. All progressed without incident and he left the three men with the cars. One more trip, solo, and then they were out of here.

Of course, Murphy's Law decreed this was the precise moment it should all go to shit.

He was halfway down the driveway with the Ducati when the lights on the front porch came on. A man's shout sounded from behind him, followed by the loud, angry barks of the dog the man had just turned loose.

"Fuck!"

Immediately he dropped the motorcycle and ran. Ahead of him, the Shelby roared to life and took off. The headlights on the Ferrari came on and its engine purred as well, the car idling. Rab was waiting, at least. Tonio poured on the speed, legs pumping, aware of the canine gaining. He heard the barks and snarls getting closer.

Just as Tonio lurched through the gate, strong jaws clamped around his calf, biting down hard. He yelled as the dog shook his leg like a stuffed toy, and turned, kicking to try to dislodge its hold.

"Goddammit, hurry!" Rab yelled.

"I'm trying—"

"Who the fuck is there?" the man screamed, gaining on them.

In a last-ditch effort to shake the dog, Tonio pulled one side of the gate closed. He was trying to drag himself to the other when Rab caught on, jumped out of the car, and closed the other side, effectively trapping the pooch on the other side. Tonio ripped his leg free, leaving bits of flesh and denim behind.

He and Rab dove for the car and Rab took off, fishtailing wildly. Tonio put his head back on the headrest, panting, and assessed the pain. It hadn't hit yet, thanks to the rush. But when it wore off, he'd be in a world of hurt.

He'd been snapped at but never seriously bitten by a dog and he heard the bite wounds sucked.

"You good?" Rab asked.

He had to chuckle. "Yeah. Fuckin' peachy." Then he let out a stream of curse words in Spanish that would've had his mama boxing his ears.

Rab thought that was funny and it seemed to put him in a good mood. *Asshole*. He was all smiles, eyes bright as they drove the car right up the ramp and into the back of the semi behind the Shelby. In short order, Tonio and Rab jumped out of the back, the ramp was lifted, and they were back in their respective cars.

"Stan and Phil will take care of the transfer," Rab barked. "Can you drive?"

"Yeah." *Barely*.

"Meet me back at Stroker's."

With that, he was gone, tearing out after the big semi. Tonio followed, aware of his calf throbbing in agony with each beat of his heart.

He'd escaped. But not unscathed. Somehow he had the feeling that was going to be his theme song on this assignment.

And if he was lucky, he'd keep right on escaping.

# 4

The bar had closed at two a.m., but it was almost three before the place was clean and ready for the next day.

In her office, Angel made the mistake of flopping onto the sofa to rest for just a minute—then realized she was so tired she'd never make it home. She'd just decided to stretch out right there and go to sleep when her cell phone rang.

Instantly she sat up, and tensed. Phone calls in the middle of the night were never a good thing. Especially when Rab was up to no good.

Groaning, she stood, reached for the phone she'd set on her desk. It was her brother. Great. "Hey, what's up?"

"You still at the bar?"

"Yes. Why?"

"Got one injured. Perkins is meeting us there in ten. Let us in the back way."

And there went her night, and any hope she'd see a pillow before sunrise. Dammit. "Who's hurt?"

"Tonio."

"What?" she gasped, before she thought the better of it. "What happened?"

"Not on the phone. Be waiting."

A click ended the call and she cursed. Both at her brother for getting her involved in his mess, and that Tonio had been injured. She probably shouldn't have reacted to the news where Rab could hear, but she hadn't been able to help it. The idea of him hurt in any way made her kind of sick to her stomach.

Unable to sit still, even though she'd been dead on her feet moments ago, she headed for the back entrance and hovered until she heard the cars arriving. Anxiously she opened the door and waited as the two men exited their vehicles and started her way.

Tonio was limping badly, and as he drew closer to the light, she saw his normally bronzed face was pale. Trickles of sweat were rolling down from his temples, and his teeth were clenched in obvious pain. Her gaze traveled down the leg he was favoring, and she saw the denim was ripped and bloody.

"Jesus, what did you do?" she asked as he stepped inside. Rab was on their heels as she walked with him to her office.

"I got the business end of a pissed-off dog. That's the short version."

"And the only one you're getting," her brother added curtly.

She shot him a glare before returning her attention to Tonio. "Sit."

He did, the action causing him a lot of pain. Now that

he was in brighter light, she could see that the blood had almost completely soaked his jeans from the calf down to his shoe. She knelt and gingerly lifted the material.

She couldn't help the hiss of breath that escaped on viewing the torn and mangled flesh, punctured with bite marks. "Damn, he really got you. That's a mess."

"Thanks. I couldn't have guessed that."

Looking up, she noted the wry twist to his lips. He had a sense of humor, even in a situation like this one? He was so unlike Rab's other men that it struck her anew. Before she had time to think on it further, Rab got a call. He answered and the conversation was brief.

"Be right there." After he rang off, he hitched a thumb at the door. "Perkins is here. Let him in, Angel."

There was no point in arguing and wasting time, so she didn't bother. As quick as she could, she let the older man in and locked the outer door behind them.

"He's in my office."

The doc merely grunted.

That was where most of Rab's injured men wound up, for one very simple reason—Rab didn't want Dr. Perkins to know who any of his guys were or where they lived. Nor did the doc want to know. A physician working for cash under the table didn't care about anything beyond what he needed to know to treat the injury.

People who asked Rab too many questions might have to disappear. Or so he'd said more than once.

In the office, the doc didn't bother with introductions. He simply knelt and retrieved a pair of latex gloves from his bag, then rolled up Tonio's jeans leg and removed his shoe and sock. Angel got a chair for Tonio to prop his foot on, and Perkins went to work. He cleaned the area thoroughly with antiseptic, muttering as he did.

"Hmm." He sighed. "Dog bite?"

"Yeah." Tonio grimaced as the doc scrubbed.

"I can't stitch the skin. The wounds here are punctured and the others are too ragged."

"Do what you can."

"That'll develop a nasty infection without an antibiotic. I'll give you a shot and leave you with some pills to take for a week."

"Okay."

After Perkins was done cleaning the area, he spread some salve over the wounds and then bandaged the calf. "Change this every day until the skin begins to heal. Watch for redness or oozing as signs of infection, but the antibiotic should take care of that. I'd also recommend you go to the hospital and undergo a series of rabies shots—"

"Not going to happen," Tonio said. "But thanks."

"Well, that's your choice." Digging in his bag, he produced alcohol, a cotton ball, and a syringe. He pulled up Tonio's shirtsleeve, swabbed a small patch on the upper arm, and then deftly delivered the shot.

"There. That should do. Try to stay off the leg for a day or two to allow it to heal. Rab knows how to reach me if you need me for anything else."

"Thanks, Doc. I appreciate it," Tonio said.

Perkins blinked at him, and it was apparent he wasn't used to any of Rab's thugs offering their gratitude. "Um, you're welcome. I'll see myself out."

He looked expectantly at Rab, who handed him a roll of bills. Flushing, Perkins nodded and then made himself scarce. Once the doc was gone, Tonio looked at Rab.

"I could've paid him."

"You will. I'm taking it out of your cut from the job."

Tonio snorted. "Really? On second thought, I think the price should be chalked up to hazard pay myself."

"Good thing I don't care what you think." With that, Rab stood. "By the way, keep your eyes open. We were followed back here tonight."

Tonio stared at him. "The hell you say."

"Interesting coincidence, too, you being new and all." Rab's eyes glittered dangerously.

"I never saw anybody. But if we were followed, I had nothing to do with it. Could be somebody you've pissed off."

"Maybe." He paused, then let it go for the moment. "Go home, get some sleep. I'll have your cut in a couple of days."

With that, he was gone as well. Angel studied Tonio, shivering inwardly at the thought of someone tailing the men. Could it be an enemy? Or could Tonio be responsible? Either way, she wondered at her brother leaving her alone with Tonio like this. Was it some sort of test for the new guy?

"Don't worry. He knows I'm in too much pain to take advantage of you," Tonio said, as though reading her mind.

"I didn't think that much pain existed for men."

He laughed, some of the tension around his eyes and mouth easing. "There are some conditions even I can't perform under. Try not to be too disappointed."

She grinned. "I can't decide if you're teasing or just being an ass."

"Being an ass. I have no sense of humor."

"I disagree. About the humor, I mean. I have no doubt you can be an ass. You *are* male."

"Ouch." He sighed. "On that note, I'm going to head home."

"Are you okay to drive?" she asked in concern.

"I'm fine." But he hissed in pain and wobbled a bit as he put weight on the damaged leg.

She made a sudden decision. "I'll drive you. Leave your car here and either I can pick you up tomorrow to get it or you can get a ride."

"I don't want to put you to any trouble."

"It's no bother. But we'd better go. It's getting late. Or really early, depending on your viewpoint."

She gathered her purse and phone. As they left the office and exited out the back, she noted his limp worsening with every step. She resisted the urge to help him, knowing how fragile male egos were, especially the ones she was used to. Once they were settled in the car, she dug around in her purse and came up with a bottle of Tylenol. She shook three out and handed them to him.

"Here. I don't have any water, but that should help some."

"This is great, thanks." He dry-swallowed the pain medication and let out a groan. "God, this sucks."

"What exactly were you all doing that you got attacked by a dog?" she asked as she pulled out of the parking lot.

"Like your brother said, it's nothing you need to know about. The less you can repeat, the better."

"Because you'd have to hurt me?" Her voice was thin as she voiced her fear.

"Yes. But not in the way you might think."

Glancing at him, she frowned. "What's that supposed to mean? Never mind. You're not going to tell me."

"Right again."

"You're a strange man, even for one of Rab's. I'm not quite sure what to make of you."

She felt his shrug as he replied, "There's not much to get. I'm a businessman, plain and simple. Unlike your brother, I don't get my kicks by playing the power trip for the locals."

Angel had no idea what to say to that. Finally she settled on, "Most businessmen don't steal."

"Don't they?" He was silent for a moment. Thoughtful. "I think you're wrong. A lot of people take from others. It's just that some wear better clothes than I do."

For some reason, that tugged at her heart, and it shouldn't have. Maybe it was the way he said it. Low and sort of sad. She glanced at him again, and he was staring out the window. His strong profile, the expression on his face, touched something inside her. The feeling was confusing. Like the pit of her stomach had been cold and empty for a long time, and his mere presence lit a candle deep inside.

"Who took from you?" she asked quietly.

"It doesn't matter."

It did, though. The truth was written on his face. "I know I've said this before, but you don't fit with those guys. Rab and his friends."

He turned his head to study her. "So you've said. What makes you think that?"

"There's something different about you. I can't put my finger on it."

For some reason, this didn't seem to make him happy. "Do us both a favor and don't dwell on that too much. I'm not out to be bosom buddies with them. I just need to make a buck. Oh, turn here."

She drove for a few minutes, going where he directed. The silence stretched between them, not entirely comfortable, but not in a bad way. The tension building between them was an awareness she hadn't felt in ages. A sexual one, but something more, too. Just being near him excited her on a primal level, like she wanted to look beneath the surface and find out what made him tick. An ordinary thief out to make a dollar? There was nothing ordinary about him.

Several minutes later, she pulled into the apartment complex he called home. Her own place wasn't fancy, but this area was depressing. Definitely no place she'd want to hang around alone, much less after dark.

"Thanks for the ride," he said, his white smile a slash in the gloom.

"Not a problem. You going to be okay?"

"Yeah. It's going to hurt like a bastard for a few days, but I'll be fine."

"If it gets worse, please let me or somebody know. I'll be glad to drive you to the ER."

"I'm sure that won't be necessary."

He shifted, but instead of getting out of the car, he leaned closer. Reached out and cupped her face, and her skin heated beneath his touch. His palm was a bit rough and felt good. Even better was the blaze that lit his dark eyes, the very real desire pouring off him in waves. Her body trembled in answering need, leaving her breathless.

This was the sort of bad boy mamas warned their daughters about. The dark, dangerous, seductive type who made a girl want to throw caution to the wind. Ride with the top down, take the curves too fast, get drunk on kisses and touch. Love being alive.

Their lips met, and she knew right away the first time was no fluke. This kiss was every ounce as electric, scorching her all the way to her soul. Setting every cell on fire. Moving closer, she laid a hand on his chest, relishing the muscle underneath his shirt. She wanted to feel skin.

He broke the kiss, though, and groaned. "God, you make me need. I shouldn't want you, *bonita*."

The lilt of his voice as he lapsed into Spanish made her shiver with pleasure. *Bonita*. She knew enough to remember it meant *pretty*. She wondered if he uttered endearments to all the women he fooled around with, and found she didn't want to think so. She didn't want to picture him messing with anyone, especially Tess. Who was supposed to be history.

"I'd better go inside before I do something we'll both regret," he said.

"Who says I'd regret anything?"

He shook his head, smiling a little despite the pain he must be enduring. "You have a man?"

"I wouldn't be kissing you if I did. I'm not like that."

"I didn't think you were, considering you made your position on cheaters clear before." His hesitation indicated his reluctance to leave. But finally he opened the door and eased his injured leg out, then the other. "Be careful driving home, and don't make any stops. Especially in this neighborhood."

"I won't." It was nice, his caring.

"I'll see you soon."

"Bye."

With reluctance, she watched him go. After he started up the stairwell, obviously having a hard go of it, she bit her lip. Maybe she should've helped him, but that might've led to her staying. And ravishing him, bad leg or not.

She left, turning the car toward home. As she did, her thoughts turned to Rab and she hoped he would be asleep. At this hour, he should be. He was unpredictable, though.

For one selfish moment, she wished her brother had gone to their mother's to beg for a place to stay. Then she felt horrible for thinking it. Mom didn't deserve to be saddled with him. *Neither do I, but he's family.*

When she arrived home, she was disheartened to see the light on in the living room. As she walked in through the kitchen from the garage, her worst fear was confirmed. Rab was still up, watching television.

"What took you so long?" From his spot in the easy chair, he gazed at her, expression unreadable. She hated the blank stare.

"I had to take Tonio home."

"Had to?" The hint of a sneer crept into his tone.

"He was in no shape to drive," she defended.

"I'll bet. What else did you help him out with?"

Stiffening, she glared at him. "That's none of your business, and you know what? Insinuations like that are pretty freaking disgusting coming from my own brother."

Slowly he rose from his chair, unfolding his considerable height. The look on his face was dark as he approached and stopped in her space. Her heart pounded, but she didn't budge when he touched her face.

"I told him to stay away from you," he said quietly. "Did he fail my test already?"

Her body was frozen. Like a bird in the thrall of a cobra, not daring to flinch. "I like him, Rab. It doesn't have to be a test."

"He's fucking Tess."

She shook her head and took a step back. "He says they're finished. And yes, I believe him."

"Then you're stupid. All men say shit like that when they want in someone else's pants."

"All men aren't like you," she said stiffly.

His grin made her nervous.

"True. More than you realize."

"What?" The shadows in his gaze were even more unsettling than usual.

He waved her off. "Nothing."

"Back to Tonio. Whether or not I see him is my business. I want you to stop interfering and scaring away every man who looks at me. I'm serious."

"Or what?" He looked so smug.

"I'm asking you as your sister. Your flesh and blood."

After regarding her for a moment, he said, "You know there's almost nothing I wouldn't do for you. Right?"

*Except find your own place to live.* "Right."

"Maybe I should pay Tess a visit. Make sure the bitch keeps her nose away from you and yours. Especially after what she pulled at the bar."

A chill washed over her, like ice water had been tossed over her head. "No. Leave her alone, Rab."

"Why would you stick up for her? She disrespected you in front of everybody!"

"Like you cared. You and your friends found it pretty funny at the time."

"Oh, I cared. Make no mistake about that." His smile was razor sharp. "Don't worry. I've got it handled."

"I mean it, Rab! Don't—"

"Give it a rest, okay? I'm going to bed."

Angel watched him head down the hall, and shivered. Replaying their conversation, she had the awful feeling he really would confront Tess. Perhaps even hit her, or God knows what else. Angel had no choice but to warn the woman, but didn't know where to find her.

Tonio might. As much as she didn't like it, she'd have to ask him.

She went to bed and dreamed of him wrapped around her, making love all night long.

Tonio went to bed with the hard-on from hell.

This despite the fact that his leg throbbed from just below the knee all the way to his toes. After tossing and turning until almost sunup, unable to get comfortable, he took the problem in hand to get some relief. If he kept that up he was going to rub the skin off his dick. Or start a forest fire.

As good as it felt to get off, it couldn't compare to the real thing. He found himself longing to know how it would be to have Angel's naked body against his. Sure, he wanted to make love to her, but he also thought it would be awesome to hold her, too. He thought of the happiness his brother had found with Grace, and a pang struck him in the chest.

Since leaving San Antonio and his cheating ex-fiancée, he hadn't wanted a repeat of that closeness. Unbidden, the memories assailed him. He closed his eyes against the onslaught, but it was no use trying to shut them out. It never was.

*Mama fussed with his tie while Julian and Maria looked on in amusement at their mother's antics.*

*"Do you have the tickets? You don't want to be stranded here when your plane leaves for the Bahamas."*

*"I have them, Mama," Julian said, patting his suit coat where the tickets rested safe inside. "Tonio has enough to think about."*

*"Good boy."*

*Tonio grinned at his brother over Mama's head, and Julian rolled his eyes. Their mother was a classic worry-wart, and making sure the wedding details were all handled had nearly driven her crazy. But she would hardly let anyone help, either, which was part of her problem.*

*He looked at his mother. "Have you seen Rachel? How's she doing?"*

*Mama's smile appeared strained. "She's fine. A little nervous, but that's to be expected. She looks gorgeous." At that, she brightened some.*

*"Yes, she does," Maria put in, glancing at Mama.*

*Was it his imagination, or was there something to the look that his mother and sister exchanged? With a mental sigh, he told himself to shut off his inner detective.*

"You look great, too," Julian said. "You're going to knock her dead."

"Thanks." He tugged at the tie. "I'm just ready to get this over with."

"And get to the honeymoon part." Julian waggled his eyebrows suggestively, which earned him an elbow from Mama.

"Behave. And go find Danny," she ordered him. "Where does that boy keep disappearing to, anyways? The wedding is going to start soon!"

"I'll go check, Mama." With that, Julian headed out of the changing room.

Tonio frowned. Daniel Sheffield, his best friend and best man for the wedding, had been acting weird the past few weeks. He'd tried talking to Danny about it a couple of times, but his friend shrugged off his concern, saying nothing was wrong. Tonio thought maybe he was a little jealous that his best friend had found a woman and was getting married. But he'd let it go.

Today, however, when Danny should've been celebrating right along with Tonio and their other groomsmen friends, he'd been absent more often than not.

It left a strange feeling in the pit of his stomach. Again, he put it aside. He had a beautiful bride waiting, and the thought made him smile.

"It's almost time," Mama said, bringing him out of his musings. She smiled, tears in her big brown eyes. "I love you, hijo. Now and always."

"I love you, too, Mama." He grabbed her and, for a long moment, squeezed her tight. When he let go, his mother dabbed at her eyes.

*"Maria and I will check on Rachel and then take our seats. We'll see you after the ceremony."*

*"Okay."*

*His sister took their mother's arm and led the reluctant woman out. Tonio took a deep breath, and tried to steady his nerves. This was it. Nothing in his life would ever be the same. Was he ready?*

*He'd better be, because he had a future wife waiting on him.*

*The music started, and Danny finally rushed in, appearing a bit disheveled. Sweat beaded on his upper lip, and he appeared somewhat out of sorts as he addressed Tonio.*

*"Sorry. Was in the men's room," he explained.*

*"Ah. No problem." Tonio slung an arm around Danny's shoulders. "You're here now, and that's what matters. You ready?"*

*Danny's smile seemed forced. "I should be asking you that question."*

*"I'm ready as I'll ever be."*

*They waited an eternity as the guests were seated. Then the wedding party started in, bridesmaids and groomsmen paired together. Tonio filed in and stopped to kiss his mother and sister, which produced a fresh wave of tears. He gave his mother a wink and then took his place.*

*This was it. The moment he'd waited for all his life. He was going to marry the woman of his dreams—gorgeous, smart, successful Rachel. He hadn't figured out what she saw in him, a regular guy and a cop to boot, but he was grateful she had said yes. His heart thudded in anticipation, excitement.*

*The music swelled with the first strains of the traditional wedding march, and the guests turned in their seats in anticipation of rising when the doors swung open to reveal the bride. But long moments passed, and the doors didn't open.*

*The guests began to fidget. And then whisper.*

*Still, Rachel didn't appear. Now Tonio's heart pounded for an entirely different reason as his cop's brain kicked into overdrive. What if something terrible had happened? He turned to Danny.*

*"I need to go check on her," he whispered.*

*"No, you stay here. I'll go see what's keeping her." His friend patted his arm, looking sick.*

*"Okay."*

*"Be right back."*

*Danny hurried down the aisle and disappeared out the double doors. Several minutes passed, and the guests began talking in quiet tones. Tonio shrugged off the comforting touches of the other groomsmen as he desperately tried to deny what was going on. Danny would be back soon with an explanation.*

*But Danny didn't return. Neither did Rachel.*

*Instead Rachel's father came through the doors and stood for a moment, looking haggard and swallowing hard as the room fell silent. Briefly his gaze met Tonio's before he addressed the guests miserably.*

*"I'm very sorry, but there will be no wedding today."*

*Those words burned themselves into Tonio's brain. He processed their horrible meaning, and his knees threatened to buckle. He was barely aware of his friends hurry-*

*ing him out of the chapel and into the hallway. On the way, he grabbed Rachel's father by the arm and dragged him along.*

*"What the fuck is going on?" he demanded. "Where's Rachel?"*

*He thought he'd throttle the man before he finally answered, sorrow etched on his face.*

*"She's left you, son. She and Danny ran off together."*

Opening his eyes, Tonio blinked back the tears he would no longer allow to fall.

That had been the worst day of his life. Nothing else, except his father's death, had ever come close. Rachel's and Danny's betrayal had been a death of a different sort.

And then they were gone for real, and his agony had compounded by leaps and bounds. No matter what they'd done, how badly they'd hurt him, his part in the tragedy was something for which he'd never forgive himself.

Someday he had to find a way to heal. How would he ever trust a woman again with his heart? His friendships with men had suffered as well, as he no longer trusted easily. Chris had learned that right away, even if he didn't know exactly why Tonio held back.

But he liked Chris, and the captain, too. Respected them both. They could become good friends if Tonio would allow them in. He'd work on it.

And Angel? She was nothing like Rachel on the surface. Nobody else, even his ex-fiancée, had ever made him react this way. Like he wanted to spend all his hours with the woman, learning all about her. What she liked and disliked. What made her laugh.

He also wished she could see the *real* him. But that just wasn't possible. Yet.

Dragging himself out of bed, he limped to the bathroom and washed his hands. Then he removed his bandage and hissed as the gauze tugged at the dried blood. He swallowed his antibiotic capsule with some tap water and started the shower.

He let the hot water beat down on him as long as he could, then washed his hair and body. The area around the wound was painful but had to be cleaned.

"Damn," he groaned. "That fucking hurts."

After stepping out of the shower, he dried off, dabbing the injury with a towel. Then he applied more topical ointment and wrapped it in a fresh bandage before dressing in jeans and a blue T-shirt.

Thinking of his brother, he sat on the bed and made the call using his real cell phone instead of the burner. But it was Grace who answered.

"Hey, brother-in-law. How's it going?"

"Been better," he admitted. "Got into a jam last night, but I'm fine."

"I hope so," she said, sounding worried. "Can you give me details?"

"Dog bite. That's all I can share."

"Ouch." Sympathy colored her voice. "I don't even want to think about how that happened."

"Yeah. How's Jules?"

"The same. Tonio, I'm really concerned. I know he's

keeping something from me, but he won't open up. He's supposed to see a department counselor because he survived a traumatic accident on the job. I asked when he was going to start his sessions so he could get cleared to go back to work, and he bit my head off. He actually said he didn't know if he was going to return!"

Shocked, Tonio whistled through his teeth. "*Dios*. That's not like him at all."

"I know."

"I get that he got hurt, not to mention witnessing what happened to Clay, but he should be improving emotionally. The accident wasn't his fault."

"Exactly. I don't know how to help him any more than I have since this began."

"I wish I could be there to help."

"Me, too, though I honestly don't know what you could do."

Tonio would lean harder on his brother than Grace would. So hard he'd make the man crack and share what was eating him. No point in mentioning it right now, though.

"Hopefully this case won't take too long," he said. "Then I can focus on Julian."

They chatted for another minute, and then she took the phone to Julian, who'd been resting when he called. His brother sounded cheerful, but Tonio could tell the good humor was forced; the man was on the edge of a cliff. The situation added a new level of stress to the undercover job.

"You take care, bro," Tonio said fondly. "Talk soon."

"Sure. Be careful out there."

Tonio hung up, and just as he did, there was a pounding on his apartment door. Reaching to the nightstand, he grabbed his gun and tucked it into the back of his jeans, then yanked his shirt down over it. Then he padded quietly to the door and peered through the peephole.

Angel stood on the other side, looking around. His pulse kicked up a notch and he opened the door, pleased to see her.

"Hey, come in," he said, standing aside. "Excuse the place. It's not much."

She walked inside, glancing around. "It's fine. You keep it clean."

"I hate clutter. Have a seat? Can I get you something to drink?"

"Water is fine, thanks."

Her eyes bored into his back as he hobbled to the kitchen. Digging in the fridge, he snagged two bottles of water and took one back to her. "Shame it's not something stronger."

She smiled at that. "It is a little early. Come by the bar later and we can fix that."

"I might just do that." He watched her take a drink, then fiddle with the bottle. "What's on your mind? I'm sure you didn't come all the way over here for bottled water."

"The pleasure of your company?"

He laughed. "I'd be more flattered if that wasn't phrased as a question."

"Oh. Well, it's true. I did want to see you."

"Then my day has already improved."

She studied him, smiling back. “Mine, too. But I also need to ask a favor.”

“Anything in my power,” he said sincerely.

“I need to get in touch with Tess.”

“O-kay,” he drawled, blinking at her. “That’s the last thing I expected to hear. Why, are you going to dump a keg of beer on her?”

“The thought did cross my mind. But no, I actually have something to discuss with her, something that’s bothering me.” She fell silent, biting her lip. Then she said, “Rab was waiting for me when I went home last night. And he said some things that were really disturbing.”

Tonio instantly went on alert. “What kinds of things?”

“First, he mentioned me and you. Asked if we’d slept together. He was really weird about it, and the way he was talking felt strange. Very inappropriate.”

“How so?”

“His tone, the way he looked at me,” she said, clearly unhappy.

“What did you say to him?” He didn’t like the sound of that. At all.

“Basically that it was none of his business, and that I like you. Whatever happens, if anything, he should stay out of it.”

“Good, because I hope something *does* develop between us.” Moving close to her, he pulled her down on the sofa beside him and put a hand on her thigh. “He has a problem, he can see me.”

She nodded. “Thanks. Maybe he’ll leave us be.”

He doubted that. “So, what does this have to do with Tess?”

"He brought her up, said he might pay her a visit and tell her to keep her nose out of my business. It was the way he said it that gave me chills." She took a shaky breath. "I think he'd actually hurt her. Or worse."

"You want to warn her about him?"

"Yes. I think someone should."

"I agree, but has she ever listened to you before?"

"No. She can't stand me." Angel made a face.

"Then she won't believe you're sincere. I could try to talk to her, pass along the message."

Her chin jerked up at that. "Oh, she'll get a message, all right. She'll think you care more about her than you do. Unless you *do* care too much, and then—"

Tonio covered her mouth with his, kissing her into silence. He moaned into their kiss, tasting, making sure she understood how ridiculous that last statement was. When he pulled back, they were both breathing hard. His cock was pushing against his zipper, needing, even though he'd taken care of that earlier.

No beat-off session could match the real deal.

"I'll talk to her," he said. "I'll make her understand the threat—and that she and I are off the table."

"Off the bed, you mean."

He chuckled at her almost militant expression. "You're beautiful when you're being a badass."

She flushed at the compliment. "I can be even more of a badass if necessary. I'm starting to feel a bit possessive."

"Me, too," he admitted. "Crazy, huh?"

"Yeah." She sighed. "I don't know what to do about Rab, either. He's weirding me out. He comes in and out at all hours, and his moods are becoming erratic."

"If it comes to it, I'll help you throw him out. Or you can stay with me if he gets too unstable."

"Thank you, but I hope it doesn't come to you having to intervene. He's dangerous when he's crossed."

"I'll worry about me." He paused. "Do you think he's on drugs?"

"I don't think so, but I couldn't swear."

"Okay. One step at a time. I'll go see Tess. I'll warn her and hope she listens."

Pressing against him, she slid a hand up his thigh, to his crotch. "All right. You can handle her—I'll handle *you*."

He liked the sound of that. But he loved the feel of it even better. This attraction was ill-advised. Giving in, dangerous.

But damned if he was going to stop now.

# 5

Angel couldn't recall the last time she'd wanted to touch someone as much as she wanted to touch this man.

The attraction between them flared hotter than ever, and was impossible to deny. His breath quickened as her hand crept to the heat at his groin, and the very good reasons she shouldn't give in to this flew out the window.

"Tell me to stop and I will," she said, voice husky to her own ears.

His chuckle was a bit hoarse. "Isn't that supposed to be my line?"

"Don't waste your breath on my account."

"Then I guess we know where we stand on the subject. Unless you have your switchblade handy and plan to cut off my dick after all."

"Nah, you're a free man now. Waste not."

His grin was devastating, a dimple gracing one side of his sexy mouth. The devilish gleam in his dark eyes called to her inner bad girl, and she planned to make the most of it. The man was simply intoxicating.

Sliding off the sofa, she parted his knees and knelt

between them. His gaze glittered as she pushed up his shirt and went for the button on his jeans. A thin treasure trail of downy hair led below his waistband and she couldn't wait to see more.

Lowering the zipper, she parted the material. Then he helped her work the jeans and boxer briefs down past his hips, and his cock sprang free. It was quite impressive, long and thick, proportional to his large body. Eager, she bent over and flicked the tip with her tongue, savoring the salty, pearly drop on the end. She enjoyed his quick intake of breath, the grip of his hand in her hair. She liked her lovers big and dominant.

Going down on him, she sucked in as much of him as she could. There was no way she could take the whole length, so she used her hand at the base to give him some dual action. Using her tongue to lave the silken rod, she sucked and pumped as he raised his hips to meet her attentions.

"Yes," he hissed. "Like that."

Smiling briefly, she didn't stop to reply. Instead she increased the tempo, using her other hand to play with his large balls. Of all the sensual touches she could give, this was her favorite. Because no matter how big or tough the man, this would bring him to his knees. Every single time.

"Angel, I'm gonna come!"

Pulling off, she whispered, "Do it."

A few more strokes and his body tensed, his grip holding her in place as he shot with a groan. She swallowed as fast as she could, milking him until he went still, relaxing into the cushions. Finally she sat back and wiped her mouth with a grin.

"Good?" she asked, raising an eyebrow.

His laugh was husky. "I'll let you know when my brain cells start firing again."

"That won't happen. Sucked them all out."

"Oh well. Who needs a brain anyhow?" He grinned as he tucked himself back in. "Let me return the favor. Please?"

She thought about it. Was *really* tempted. But her mother had always said it was good for a man to be left wanting just a bit more. For a woman not to be too easy—even if she *had* made the first move.

"Next time," she said, giving him a wink.

"I'm going to hold you to that." His voice, the hungry expression on his face, said he was serious.

"Counting on it." Unsure what to do next, she stood.

"You don't have to leave right now, do you?"

She liked that he didn't seem happy about it. "I have some stuff I need to do, but I can hang out for a little while if you want."

"Sure." He shrugged and schooled his expression, as if belatedly realizing he should be a bit more nonchalant. But not quickly enough.

She'd caught the pleasure written on his face before the mask descended. That knowledge gave her a little thrill.

Settling next to him on the sofa, she scooted close, letting their thighs touch. He laid a hand on her knee and turned to face her better, staring into her eyes. It felt as though she were being dissected, or he was trying to solve a puzzle.

"You don't have to work at it so hard," she teased. "I'm not that tough to figure out."

That surprised a laugh out of him. "Really? That would be a first where women and I are concerned."

"Had a rough go of it, have you?"

"You could say that."

"From your tone, I'm guessing this goes back before Tess."

"Way back." For a second, something like sadness shadowed his features and then was gone. "It doesn't matter. Ancient history, never to be repeated."

That told her more than he probably intended. If she had her guess, he'd been hurt somewhere along the way. She peered at him curiously, trying to imagine anyone getting under the big man's skin deep enough to wound him emotionally. It seemed impossible, if she went by appearances. But people were often not what they seemed.

"Care to talk about it?" she asked.

"Not really." He shifted the topic away from himself. "So, tell me more about your *madre*. Are you close?"

A tiny spear of regret stabbed her chest. "Not as much as I'd like. We get along, but . . . there's a lot of water under the bridge. All those years she didn't stand up to our father have taken a toll. As an adult, I understand about abused spouses. But back then, as a kid? Not so much. It sticks with you."

His gaze was sympathetic. "Parents are supposed to be protectors. When parents fail in that area, it can be hard for the kids to forgive them, even when they're grown and know the extenuating circumstances."

"You sound like you speak from experience." She stared at him, waiting.

"No, my mama is a good woman. Too good to end up with me as a son, I know. But I had *compadres* who came from some bad family shit. Some of them ended up in prison."

"Where you're going to go if you keep dealing with Rab and others like him," she pointed out.

He grinned. "Aw. I may start to think you really care."

"I do." She snorted. "God knows why."

"My charming and magnetic personality?" His voice deepened and his slight Hispanic accent gave her chills in good places.

"I'm immune," she lied. It didn't matter, he wasn't fooled.

"Sure. Whatever you say."

She returned his grin, then steered the conversation back to him. "You mentioned your mom. What about your dad?"

"He died years ago, killed in a drive-by shooting as he left a gas station."

"I'm so sorry," she said sincerely.

"Mama never got over it." His smile was sad. "But she had me, my brother, and sister to keep her busy."

"So you have siblings. Are you the oldest?"

"How'd you guess?"

"You seem like a take-charge kind of guy. I don't know, it just seems to fit you."

"Well, you're spot-on."

She eyed him. "What does your brother do?"

Tonio hesitated, then said, "He's a firefighter. Not

around here, though. My sister lives with Mama, who has all but given up hope she'll ever get married."

"What are their names? Do you guys all get along?"

"Julian and Maria. Yeah, we're pretty tight, though I'm closer to my brother."

"What's he like?"

Again, the pause. What was up with that?

"He's nothing like me." A slow smile curved Tonio's mouth. "He was a womanizer from the moment he learned what his dick was for, and real happy about it, too. A wild child. Drove Mama crazy when we were growing up. She was so sure he'd get some girl pregnant."

"And did he?"

"Somehow he dodged that bullet. Now he's happily married and . . ." He trailed off, an odd expression shadowing his face. "Anyway, those days are behind him."

"Reformed bad boy?"

"Definitely. Maybe there's hope for me, too?"

That made her laugh, because of the way he said it—like a naughty little boy who wasn't really sure he *wanted* to reform.

As they continued to talk, Angel found she really enjoyed spending time with Tonio. He was so easy to be around, the minutes just seemed to fly. Finally she checked the time and sighed. "I have to go. My liquor shipment hasn't come in yet, and I need to purchase some stock to hold me over."

"I get it. Things to do."

"Yep. By the way, how's the leg?"

"Still sore as hell, but I'll make it." He winked. "I'm tough to take down."

"Glad to hear it." Retrieving her purse and keys, she headed for the door. Tonio rose and joined her. They studied each other for a few seconds, the moment stretching taut. Then he reached out and touched her face.

"I'll talk to Tess. And talking is all I'm going to do," he reiterated. "I'm a one-woman-at-a-time kind of guy."

"That could be taken more than one way." She smirked, and he rolled his eyes.

"Why do women always look for hidden meanings in what a guy says?"

"Because there usually *is* a hidden meaning," she retorted. "Guess I'll see you around."

Reluctantly she turned to leave, but his voice stopped her. "Can I get your cell phone number?"

She nodded, a little thrill going through her. "Sure."

Opening her purse, she dug around and found the cell. "Tell me your number first." As he recited it, she punched it in. His phone rang and then she ended the call. "There. Now we have each other's numbers."

"Thanks. I'll let you know how it goes with Tess."

Stepping forward, he cupped her face in his hands and gave her a kiss. It started slow and gentle, a press of his full lips against hers, then quickly heated and became much deeper. More demanding. Opening for him, she allowed him to claim her, twirled her tongue against his. Tasted.

At last, he let go, lips curving upward. "That's so you don't forget where my interest lies."

After that kiss, she hoped a report on Tess wasn't the only reason he'd call, and that he was telling the truth about who he really wanted. Then she berated herself as stupid for thinking that way. Her brother's men weren't stellar examples of loyalty or faithfulness when it came to their women. Most of those relationships—and she thought of that term loosely—lasted about as long as a change of underwear. "Oh, I won't forget."

Despite that, however, a niggle at the back of her brain suggested maybe this man was different.

If that was true, she was going to solve the puzzle of Tonio. One way or the other.

After Angel left, Tonio wandered into the kitchen and leaned against the counter.

"Goddamn," he muttered. On one hand, he was disgusted with himself. Messing around with the sister of his target was not only unprofessional; it was dangerous to his health.

But, sweet Christ, he could only think it had been worth it. Watching the beauty on her knees, lips wrapped around his cock. Blowing his mind. And not just for the obvious reason, but because Angel didn't seem the type of woman who'd willingly get on her knees for just any man.

He didn't want to think what that could mean. He needed to get going, anyway. If what Angel said about Rab was true, and he had no reason to think otherwise, Tess needed to know that man had focused his potentially brutal attentions on her.

On the way to the motel, he mulled over Rab's attitude toward women. More than once he'd made his regard for the fairer sex pretty transparent. Meaning he had little to none of it. How much of that stemmed from their mother? Even Angel had admitted to having a tough time forgiving the woman.

Certainly the thief had a bond to his sister. But it seemed more like one of possession than the love of a brother. Plus, Angel was his meal ticket right now. What happened when he didn't need her anymore?

That chilling thought spurred him to drive a bit faster. Because Rab didn't need Tess anymore, either.

A few minutes later, he pulled his car into a space outside Tess's motel room and shut off the ignition. Blowing out a breath, he steeled himself. Their last parting hadn't exactly been friendly. Still, he hadn't been lying when he claimed he had a better shot at getting her to listen than Angel did. Putting those two women together now would be like putting two rabid cats in a sack and tying it closed.

Getting out of the car, he walked to the door and knocked. A television could be heard through the thin door separating the room from the outside world. The volume lowered and footsteps halted in front of the door. After a few seconds, the door opened and the blonde was scowling at him.

"What do you want, Tonio?"

He took in her appearance, and a frown of his own creased his forehead. "You look different."

It was true. She was a pretty girl, but normally her hair was teased more. The makeup heavier, especially the eyes. Gone were the jeans with the strategic holes in the curvy places, as well as the eye-popping tank tops that were in danger of wardrobe malfunction.

Instead her hair was shiny and straight, her face almost bare of war paint. She wore a soft blue fitted T-shirt and plain jeans.

"You mean I don't look like a slut?" Cocking her head at him, she dared him to clarify.

He blushed, since that had been his next thought. "You're not dolled up to go out," he said instead. "You look like the girl next door."

"I'll take that as a compliment. Us gals don't always sit around all dressed up, waiting for a man to call, you know." She gave him the stink eye. "Again, tell me why you're here or I'm closing the door."

"Can I come in? This won't take long." He caught how her gaze strayed past him, to the parking lot. "I'm alone."

"I guess," she hedged. "For a minute."

Her reluctance made sense, he supposed. After all, he'd dumped her, and she'd responded by accusing him of using her to get an in with Rab. Which he'd denied, of course, pointing out that it had been *her* idea to introduce him. But he *didn't* deny that he intended to make a play for Angel, hadn't gotten the words past his lips fast enough, and that had earned him a resounding slap in the face.

Once they were inside, she faced him, arms crossed over her chest. "I assume you didn't come here to charm your way back into my pants?"

"Sorry, no." He held her stony gaze. "But I did come to pass on a warning."

Tess laughed. "From Angel?"

"Yes, but not for the reason you might think."

"So you're not fucking her yet?"

"No. Not that it's any of your business."

"I don't believe you," she said, scoffing.

"I don't much care. What matters is what she told me about her brother."

The woman's attention sharpened, and she became all business. So unlike the carefree barfly he'd first picked up. "What about Rab?"

"I don't think it's escaped your notice that he doesn't like women that much."

Her eye roll was accompanied by a snort. "That's supposed to be news?"

"Not exactly. What *is* news is what he told Angel. She was going to come see you and warn you that Rab was acting unstable."

"Also not news, the unstable part."

"But he threatened you specifically, Tess," he emphasized, letting his frustration show. She was being a bit blasé for his comfort. "He was going on about how you disrespected Angel in front of his posse. About how that can't be allowed to go unanswered. Do you get it?"

Her already pale face whitened, and she blinked at him. "Are you serious?"

"Yeah. Rab already doesn't respect women, so his anger isn't about Angel. Not really. What it *is* about is giving him an excuse to hurt a female. Any excuse."

"Why are you telling me this?" she asked, voice fearful. "You're one of them. *His* men. He'd see you coming here as a betrayal to him."

"If he finds out. You going to tell him?"

"No. Of course not." She sounded sincere, and he detected no lie in her expression or mannerisms.

"My advice is to make yourself scarce for a while. You got family somewhere, go visit. Let the asshole cool down and forget about you."

Sitting on the edge of the bed, she rested her palms on

her thighs. She studied the floor for a few seconds before raising her head again. "You didn't answer my question. Why did you come here?"

"Hey, I do what I have to do to survive. But hurting women isn't part of the deal, that's all." He shrugged. "I don't give a shit if Rab doesn't like it."

"Well, thanks. I guess I owe ya."

"Nah. Just do yourself a favor and head out for a few weeks. Months, whatever."

She nodded. "Thanks for the advice."

"Sure."

There wasn't much else to say, and the sudden silence was uncomfortable. Giving her a nod, he turned, opened the door—

And came face-to-face with Rab. *Shit.*

Surprise flashed across the man's face. Then suspicion. "What the fuck are you doing here, Tonio?"

"What do you think?" He adopted a casual pose while keeping himself between Rab and Tess. Behind him, the woman was quiet. "I was just impressing on my former lay the importance of leaving town. Especially after what she pulled with Angel."

Rab narrowed his eyes. "How is that your concern?"

"Man, really?" He gave a grin, hoping it appeared real and not strained. "What did you come here for? To put her in her place—am I right?"

"That's not your biz," he growled in a low voice. His fists clenched at his sides.

Damn, the jerk had a serious issue with his anger. Tonio stepped closer, not backing down. "It *is* my business. Literally. You beat up a woman, you break parole. You break parole and your PO finds out, you get sent back to the pen. Is that what you want?"

A tic in Rab's jaw, the simmering heat in his eyes, showed that Tonio's message was slow to get through. He really wanted to hurt someone.

"Think, amigo," Tonio went on. The Spanish word for *friend* burned on his tongue like acid. "Is one very satisfying act worth losing out on the money we'll bring in? You can run the operation from inside, but you can't spend the *dinero*."

Casually he stepped out the door of the motel room, pulling it closed behind him, and forcing Rab to back up. Then he walked past Rab, hoping the other man would give in to the impulse to follow. Thankfully he did. Though he clearly wasn't happy about it.

As they reached Tonio's car, Rab paused. Then he grabbed Tonio by the shoulders, spun him, and slammed his back against the driver's door. Hard. From nowhere, Rab brandished a large knife and held the sharp edge against his throat.

"Easy, man," Tonio said calmly. He met the other man's gaze steadily, careful not to betray a hint of fear.

"Let's get one thing straight. I won't be handled by one of my men," he snapped. "Not ever. Especially not the newbie. You got that?"

"Sure. Whatever you say." Rab badly wanted to cut him. Craved it. The desire to let the blade sink in radiated from his soul. *Dios*, the fucker was crazy. And in this neighborhood, nobody would stop him, or call the cops.

"You're damn right, whatever I say."

"I'm a businessman, that's all. Told you that from the start."

"Yeah, you did." Some of the sanity returned to the other man's gaze, and he tucked away the knife.

"I want to get paid, same as anyone. Come on, let's go get a beer."

"Yeah." But Rab didn't budge. "You got a thing for Angel."

A statement, not a question. This was dangerous territory. But he knew Rab a bit better now, understood more about what made him tick. And it certainly wasn't love for his sister in this case. It was an exercise of power, pure and simple.

"Who wouldn't?" he asked. "She's gorgeous, and she's a successful businesswoman. You can see where that would appeal to a guy like me."

"I told you to stay away from her." His knife hand was twitching.

Leaning against the car door, Tonio crossed his arms over his chest. "I know. But here's the thing. Angel's not gonna stay single forever, and she's got a mind of her own. She's not going to let you run off all her lovers. Even you can't deny that."

"Your point? And get to it fast."

"Wouldn't you rather her hook up with one of your men, instead of someone you don't know at all?" At Rab's skeptical look, he pressed on. "That way, he could keep an eye on her."

That got the man's attention, and he chewed on that for a few seconds. "What for?"

"For you. Look, Angel's not thrilled about our line of work. What if she got it in her head to report us?" *Sorry for throwing you under the bus, sweetheart.*

"She wouldn't dare," Rab spat.

"You sure about that? Willing to stake your freedom on it? From what I can see, she's a conscientious lady with a good work ethic. She's honest. Am I wrong?"

Rab shook his head and responded grudgingly, "No, that's spot-on. She always was the Goody Two-shoes in the family."

If Tonio had harbored any lingering doubts that Angel wasn't squeaky clean, Rab's candid words dispelled them. "How long before she can't stand what you're doing anymore?"

"But she doesn't know the details of what I do. I make sure of that." But doubt was beginning to creep in.

Tonio went for the kill. "Yeah, but somehow she'll find out. Women have a way of doing that. There's a way to minimize the damage, though, if she's involved with me. She won't turn if her heart's involved with someone in the group."

He felt like a complete piece of shit for playing his hand like that. But it would give him a legit reason to be around her without Rab coming unglued. And maybe he'd learn something to help his investigation, though he didn't know what.

"Makes sense. I don't like it, though."

"What's not to like? Angel gets a man, and you get someone to keep her on a leash. Trust me, a woman will do stuff for her man that she wouldn't do for anyone else. Love is blind, amigo," he said in a conspiratorial tone.

"Once I reel her in, even if she does accidentally learn something she shouldn't, she won't say a word."

Rab was silent for a long moment. Finally he nodded with visible reluctance. "All right. Keep her on that fuckin' leash and off my back."

"Will do." He paused. "One more thing. It'll be easier to do that if you're not living in her house, keeping her concerned all the time about what you're up to."

"What the fuck?" he snarled. "Where am I supposed to go?"

"Stay with your mother?" That went over just about as well as expected. Rab simply stared at him as if he'd suggested living with Satan. "Or not. Crash with one of the other guys. They owe you, right?"

He considered that. "Yeah, that might work. Be nice not to hang around my nosy sister so much, anyhow."

"There you go." Thank God. Two birds with one stone. He hated Rab being anywhere near her on a daily basis, especially in the same apartment. "How about that beer?"

"Got some stuff to do first. See you at Stroker's in a couple of hours."

"Okay."

Rab gave him a fist bump and then walked to his motorcycle. Straddling it, he revved the motor and sped away without looking back. Tonio didn't breathe a sigh of relief until the noise from the engine had faded into the distance. Next, he glanced around and pondered where to park his car for some surveillance. Finally he settled on a side street, back among some trees, that afforded him a view of the motel.

He watched for a while, half-afraid Rab would circle back around when he was sure Tonio had left. That he'd return to harass Tess, or worse. But the area remained peaceful, nothing happening until he spotted Tess leaving with a couple of bags. Sitting up, he was glad to note that she walked to the office and appeared to check out, because she came back outside folding a sheet of paper that was likely a receipt for her stay.

He wasn't sorry to see her go. The last thing he wanted was for something bad to happen to her because Rab was pissed and had something to prove.

Mind eased some, he put the car in drive and headed for the bar.

The knowledge that Angel would be there had him pressing on the gas a little harder.

"I'm changing motels," Tess said to her boss.

"Why? Have you been compromised?"

"I don't know. I don't think so, but it's a precaution."

Quickly she gave him the rundown on her interesting visit from Tonio Reyes.

"He actually came to *warn* you?" her boss asked in surprise. "And you're sure he doesn't have feelings toward you?"

"Positive." She gave an inward sigh. Time would tell whether Angel Silva was the lucky one.

"Then what the hell was that about?"

"You've got me. What I do know is I need background on Reyes, yesterday. I want to know who this guy is, *really*."

"He's not who he says?"

"I'd bet my life on it."

"Okay. I'll find out what I can."

The boss hung up, and Tess hoped they learned some answers soon. Felons like Tonio did not go out of their way to rescue their former fling from their boss's wrath. Especially when she was Rab's ex as well. Nor did she believe the line of bullshit Tonio had fed the man.

Tonio had protected her. She wanted to know why. Could be the answer was simple, but in her experience that was rarely true.

She had a feeling anything concerning the big Latino was far from simple.

It was her job to find out exactly who she was dealing with—and she would.

Very soon.

# 6

Yeah, he had stuff to do, all right.

First, he had to let off some steam. Goddamn, that bastard Tonio had pissed him off. *Nobody fuckin' handles me and gets away with it.*

He'd wanted to wring that bitch's neck. He itched to feel her throat underneath his fingers, her muscles strain as she gasped for air. Maybe he'd slip her a little cock, too, just to make things even more fun. Ride her while she bucked and twitched.

Until she stopped.

Then that self-righteous *I'm all about business* wetback had to stick his nose in where it didn't belong. Money was great, and necessary, sure. But sometimes a man had to let his demons loose. Stop the noises in his head, just for a while.

Rab shut off his motorcycle outside a bar on the outskirts of Sugarland, the Waterin' Hole. Driving to the place took longer than getting to Stroker's, being across the county, but he didn't come here often and enjoyed the anonymity. It was a good place to have a drink or three and pick up some willing company.

Strolling inside, he bellied up to the bar and took a seat. The bartender wandered over and he ordered a whiskey, neat. When it was placed in front of him, he downed it fast and then ordered another, this one on the rocks. He'd savor this one some. Bide his time.

After an hour or so, the crowd thickened somewhat. The women were mostly in groups or pairs, with a very few who appeared to be alone. Bitches were more cautious these days, more hesitant to hook up with a stranger. As they should be.

He grinned to himself at that. There were always one or two bold ones. The ones who knew who they wanted and had no problem going after him. It was a game to them to see if they could land the biggest, baddest dude in the place. Take him home or to a motel, fuck his brains out. Yeah, nothing but a game, but that was okay.

Because it was one he played like a master.

He didn't have to wait all that long. A body slid onto the recently vacated stool next to him, and a feminine voice ordered a whiskey sour. Rab curled his lip in disgust. Who the hell ruined good whiskey by putting sweet shit in it? But he turned his head slightly to eye her and decided the drink didn't matter.

The woman was a brunette, hair the color of melted chocolate falling just to her shoulders. She was a bit busty, breasts battling to escape the tight red tank top, but that was fine with him. Her body was full, just shy of plump, rounded ass filling out her faded jeans where it was parked on the stool. After a few years and a couple of whiney kids, that compact body would turn to fat. But right now she'd give a man quite a ride.

Their eyes met, and he gave her a ghost of a smile before turning his attention back to his drink. He wouldn't speak first. That wasn't the way it worked.

"There must be something mighty interesting in the bottom of that glass," she said. Her voice held the hint of a flirt.

*Bingo. Time to reel her in.*

He raised his head. Let his smile widen. "Well, not really. Hasn't been anything interesting happening all night. Until you walked in, that is."

She beamed at him—and there it was. That click of mutual attraction sliding into place, heating fast. Like water boiling on a stove. Spilling over.

She had a pretty enough face. Sexy blue eyes rimmed heavily with liner, lashes thick. She took a sip of her drink, then traced the rim with one red fingernail. "Can't imagine why you don't have a girlfriend in your lap."

"We broke up. You know how it goes."

"Yeah. Sadly, I do."

"Now, that's just wrong," he said with a grin. "He must be blind and stupid."

"Thanks." She flushed with pleasure.

"I'm Rab."

"Sharon."

They made small talk for a while, and he bought her a couple of drinks. He wasn't paying much attention to their conversation and didn't care. He wanted her loosened up so he could get her away from here. Find out if her ass made as good a double handful as it looked. If her titties tasted as good as he thought they would. His cock was aching to sink inside tight, wet heat, take his fill.

"Wanna get out of here?" he interrupted. She paused in the middle of telling him about a friend who was sleeping with three different guys, and eyed him up and down.

"Thought you'd never ask."

He paid the tab and said, "Gotta hit the men's room. Wait for me out front?" Then he gave her a wink, keeping up the facade of charm. She bought it, sliding off the stool and pressing her lips to his in a brief touch before heading out.

He did have to go, but that wasn't why he sent her ahead. This way, nobody inside the bar would actually see them leave together. This wasn't his first rodeo.

After taking a piss, he exited out the back way. Patrons weren't supposed to leave through that door, but the fire alarm was broken. He knew because he'd broken it himself, not long ago. It was always good to have a second avenue of escape.

Outside, he rounded the corner of the building and spotted Sharon waiting for him on the walk near the front.

"Hey, over here," he called.

She turned and smiled when she saw him. "How'd you get over there?"

"I'm parked back here," was all he said by way of explanation. This was where things got tricky. "I'm on my motorcycle, though. You ride?"

"Not much," she admitted. "Only once or twice."

"I can follow you. That way neither of us will have to come back for our ride."

"Sure." She shrugged. "Where we going?"

"How about that little motel off the interstate, by the river, Sleep Inn?"

"Works for me."

Digging in his pocket, he took out his wallet and handed her a fifty. "Get us a room, sugar. I'll be there as soon as I stop for supplies."

She gave him a playful smile. "Not planning to ditch me, are you?"

"Not a chance." Stepping real close, he dragged her against him, let her feel the outline of his hard cock in his jeans. "That say I'm planning on ditching?"

"Nope." She waved the money, stepping back. "See you soon."

"How do I know you'll be there?" he asked.

"You don't. But I will be."

"We'll see."

That was a risk—her taking the money and leaving him high and dry. But women, for all their caution, could still be fooled into believing in a man's best intentions. After all, he'd given her the money. He had trusted her; therefore he must be trustworthy.

What dumb bitches.

After watching her leave, he waited a few minutes, then started out of the parking lot. He didn't need supplies, he just wanted to give her a head start. Nobody would be able to connect them.

A short time later the motel came into view. He spotted her car at the end of a row of rooms, but instead of parking next to her, he drove to the all-night diner next door. Leaving the bike in the shadows at the back of the lot, he walked to the motel. The night was quiet, no one out. Just how he liked it. In seconds he was knocking on the door closest to her car, hoping it was the right one.

Immediately it opened and Sharon was letting him in, all smiles. She was already half-undressed, wearing only her lacy white bra and matching panties. Her fingers were wrapped around the neck of a bottle of tequila.

"Want some?" she offered with a giggle.

"Sure, why not?" Easing inside, he took the bottle and closed the door. "Let's get the party started, sweet thing."

What a party it was.

The tequila went down easy, giving him a good buzz. It lowered what few inhibitions Sharon had left, too, and she giggled as he stripped off her bra and panties. His clothes were next. Soon they were both rolling around on the bed, drinking and making out. Her mouth was soft, her body inviting. She was filled out in all the right places, rosy-tipped breasts and hips full.

Setting the bottle on the nightstand, he decided it was time to get down to business. Women were good for a couple of things at most—cooking and sex—and he wasn't here for a meal. Not the kind that involved food, anyway. He wasn't leaving until he enjoyed the vigorous fuck he'd been looking forward to.

"You like it rough, sugar?"

She giggled. "What? Oh, sure."

Her fingers were wrapped around his dick, stroking. He hissed, closing his eyes for a minute and reveling in the touch. But it wasn't enough, and impatience overcame him. Quickly he flipped her onto her stomach, ignoring her protest at the sudden manhandling.

"Hey, wait—"

"Shut up."

This wasn't about the dumb bitch. He needed to get off, and she was going to help him with that. Spreading her legs, he crouched between her thighs and used his fingers to open her up. She giggled some more and squirmed, unaware of the raw need of the beast she'd let in to the room.

Reaching for his jeans on the end of the bed, he fished a condom from the pocket and sheathed himself. Then he gripped her hips and lifted her to a kneeling position. "Stay like this."

Lining himself up, he pushed inside. She took his big cock like the whore she was. He didn't know whether her moan was from pain or pleasure. Didn't care.

"Fuck yeah," he hissed. God*damn*, the slut was tight. Snapping his hips, he pounded into her without mercy. Their skin slapping together was almost the ultimate high. Almost.

"Hey, take it easy." She tried to crawl forward a bit.

Fuck that. It felt too good, and there was one way to make it even better.

He fisted a hand in her hair. Yanked her head back. Continuing to pound into her tight sheath, he let go of her hair and wrapped his fingers around her neck, thumb at the nape and the other four digging into her throat. Right at the windpipe. His hand was big, her neck small. A perfect fit.

Slowly he began to squeeze. At first, she got into it. *Shit yeah*, that was so fine. The bitch bucked underneath him like a wild pony, and started squealing like a little piglet being skewered. Loving every minute of it, same as him.

He wasn't sure when her movements changed. When the struggle began in earnest. He was too far gone, riding the wave of ecstasy to the finish line. Finally he crossed over, the tingling in his balls giving way to the inevitable explosion. With a shout, he pumped into her on and on until his orgasm tapered to spasms that he milked for all he was worth.

At last he let go of her neck—and she flopped face-first onto the bed.

"Hey, thanks. I gotta go, though."

No answer.

"Sharon?"

Pulling free, he removed the condom, tied it off. Then he set it aside on the covers and leaned over to peer into the woman's face. "Well, fuck."

Her eyes were open, and her expression was one of disbelief. Like she couldn't quite grasp she was going to die, her throat crushed while her evening pickup pounded her into the mattress.

Damn, he hadn't meant to ice the bitch. But what a way to go, huh?

Shit, he wasn't going to feel guilty. Contempt washed over him. It was her own stupid fault for hooking up with a stranger in the first place. In the bathroom, he used a few tissues to wipe himself. Then he took fresh tissue and padded to the bedroom, wadding up the used ones and the condom inside them and tucking them into his pocket to discard later.

A sweep around the room and he was out the door, pulling it shut using his shirt. All was still and quiet as before, so he made it back to his motorcycle without incident. Unseen and unheard.

Adrenaline pumping, he turned the bike toward Stroker's and his mind toward the upcoming score.

Time to proceed with the planning. The question was, could he trust Tonio?

The answer was easy—if not, Tonio would end up as dead as the woman he'd left in the motel room.

Just one more enemy, crushed in his fist.

Tonio sat nursing a beer and thought about calling it a night. Wherever Rab had gone, he was taking too long. Tonio wanted to get going on whatever business the gang leader wanted to conduct and then get out of here. In the meantime he was stuck with Phillip and Stan, and another man who hadn't been with them during the botched job the other night. A mean-looking SOB named Enrique Torres.

The men reclined in their seats, bullshitting about everything from the latest football scores to the last woman they'd fucked, and how hard. They were full of shit. They'd made a few passes at the waitress and a handful of other women, and had no takers so far.

Tonio couldn't imagine touching one of them even if he was a lady and they were the last dudes on earth.

Tuning them out, he entertained himself by watching Angel work. He wasn't the only one, either. Plenty of eyes followed her as she filled orders, chatting amiably with customers. She looked hot, as always. Tonight, her long dark hair was in a ponytail. She wore formfitting jeans and a snug black art deco T-shirt with sparkly silver angel wings drawn on the back. He figured she liked the play on her name. Tonio did, too.

*And I like everything about her—except her brother.*

As if his thoughts had conjured Rab, the man came through the door and worked his way to their corner table. He didn't sit. Instead he jerked his head toward the door.

"Let's go."

"What? I just started this beer," Stan complained.

Rab sneered. "Take it with you, dipshit. Who's gonna stop you?"

Shrugging, Stan picked up the bottle and carried it out. Tonio imagined how satisfying it would be to arrest the sleaze for an open container violation, or for public intoxication. But he and the department had bigger fish to fry. On the way out, he caught Angel's stare, saw her lips thin in disapproval. It wasn't aimed at her brother, but at him. It caused his heart to sink a little, but there was nothing he could do about it. For now.

Outside, they gathered around Rab's bike. The night was cool, and Tonio hunched his shoulders, having forgone a jacket. Enrique was the first to speak, his tone mildly curious.

"What's going on, amigo?"

"We need to have a meeting," Rab said.

"About the big job?" Phillip asked.

"Yeah." Looks were exchanged, and a few grins. "Don't count your money just yet, assholes. There's a lot of risk."

That deflated them some. "So, what's the plan?" That from Stan, who squinted at Rab in the darkness.

"Not here. Enrique, we'll head to your place."

The man nodded, though everyone knew he was going along with Rab's order rather than giving permission.

"What about him?" Phillip jabbed his thumb in Tonio's direction.

"He goes, too. We'll see what he's made of, yeah?"

"You sure we can trust this guy?"

"Maybe, maybe not." Rab grinned. "But you know what I do to players who don't measure up."

"Standing right here," Tonio snapped. "Can we just get on with it? I'd like to get home at some point tonight."

The others snorted and they dispersed to their vehicles. It was a damn good thing being undercover on this gig didn't require him to like or get along with these slimeballs, because his acting skills weren't *that* good.

Tonio let them pull out ahead of him and then reached between his knees, carefully digging his fingers into a slit in his seat cushion. Gripping the smooth casing of his personal cell phone, he slid it free and laid the device on his lap. Driving while attempting to appear as though he wasn't doing anything suspicious wasn't easy. But he managed to unlock the screen, punch in his contact, and hit SPEAKER.

Chris answered on the second ring. "Hey. What's going down?"

"We're driving to Enrique Torres's house to discuss the big job. They're letting me in."

"Could be a test. Just be careful." The other detective

was concerned, with good reason. "I've got your back. Got the listening equipment ready to go, and I gotta tell you, this stuff had better be worth the price tag. Rainey blew the whole freaking budget on it."

"I'll bet the chief is shitting kittens." He smirked at the thought.

Chris chuckled. "You could say that."

"Well, with any luck, we'll get evidence on the recording to accompany the sting. Federal charges would go a long way toward earning forgiveness."

"True that."

"Gotta go."

"Okay. Watch your back, man."

Ending the call, he slipped the phone back into its hiding place. They wouldn't risk putting a wire on him, but his cell and his burner had tracking devices on them, and so did his car. Along with having Chris on surveillance using the long-distance listening device, the department was taking as few chances as possible with his safety, which was something of a reassurance. Not foolproof by any stretch, but at least they were making an effort.

Enrique's small house was in one of the most dangerous neighborhoods in the county, even worse than the one where Tonio's fake apartment was located. And that was saying something. Tonio's was run-down, shabby, and aging. But this area was a gang-infested, drug-riddled slice of hell that wasn't safe no matter what time of day or night.

Pulling into the weed-choked driveway, he shut off the ignition and got out, scanning the area quickly. Across the street on a dilapidated front porch, several young men and women were hanging out, swigging from bottles. Smoke curled in the light from a single bulb, and the sickly sweet odor of marijuana drifted from the rowdy group. One of the guys called a rude greeting to Enrique in Spanish, making an observation about his lack of a woman and the limp state of his dick, to which the other man responded with a one-fingered salute.

Everyone laughed, not particularly bothered, so Tonio guessed this was normal discourse between Rab's henchman and his neighbors.

Nothing else moved, the night otherwise quiet despite the party across the way. Chris was out there somewhere, probably on a side street, monitoring their meeting. The knowledge took the edge off some, and he managed to relax slightly. He wasn't alone.

The inside wasn't much of an improvement over the outside. The minimal furniture was stained and torn, as was the carpet. The walls were yellowed, dull, and there was a foul odor in the air as though someone had forgotten to take out the garbage for weeks. He curled his lip but didn't comment as they made their way into the tiny kitchen. Enrique fetched beers from the fridge, passed them out, and they settled around a rickety table situated in a small space past the end of the counter. Tonio made a show of twisting off the top and pretending to take a healthy swig. He had to start watching his intake. If he wasn't careful, he'd be drunk twenty-four/seven hanging with these losers. Many an undercover cop had been lost to substance abuse while trying to cope with the pressures of the job.

Rab leaned back in his chair, eyeing each of them. Finally he got to the point, addressing Tonio. "The quickest, easiest way to make a pile of cash has always been cars. Vicious guard dogs aside."

"Yeah, I don't know if I agree about the easy part," Tonio said curtly. His healing calf throbbed as if in agreement. "Anyway, now you've got something new in the works?"

"Something big."

"Why fix what isn't broken? Stealing and selling cars to chop shops is profitable," he pointed out. *Chris, I hope you're getting all this.*

Rab nodded. "It makes us money by the tens of thousands, no lie. That's not too shabby for a night's work. We do a deal, we're set for two or three months."

"So, what's the problem with that setup?"

"Nothing, if we want to keep doing it for the rest of our lives. Who the fuck needs that shit when we can do one job that'll net us millions instead of thousands? Then we can retire to wherever we want. Screw the goddamn government and everybody else."

Tonio stared at him. "And where the hell are you going to get your hands on a product that will rake in that kind of green? Crack, marijuana, meth, all the shit that can bring in the kind of cash you're talking about is so tightly controlled by the major drug cartels you'll *never* get your hands on it. And you'll get us all killed trying to move in on their business."

The man couldn't possibly be that dumb or have that large an ego. Could he?

But Rab just grinned and shook his head. "I didn't

take you for a stupid motherfucker. We're going to steal something valuable from a target that won't fight back after we strike."

Tonio waited, annoyed at the smirks on the faces at the table. "We're going to play guessing games?"

Rab jerked a brief nod at Enrique. The man rose and disappeared for a few moments while Tonio stared hard at the other three men at the table. The mood between them was tinged with excitement, their expressions almost smug. Right there, he knew that didn't bode well for whatever this gang had in mind.

They were about to bite off way more than they could chew, but that was all right. He'd be there to arrest their asses when the shit came down.

Enrique returned with a battered old map and a handful of snapshots. He unfolded the map and spread it out, then placed the four pictures on top of it in a rough square. Tonio peered at the map and noted that it was of the state of Missouri—not exactly a hotbed of criminal activity. Then Enrique tapped the center of the square with the tip of an index finger, on a general area north of St. Louis.

"The warehouse in these pictures is located here," he said. "It's in a rural area, off the grid, for a very good reason."

"The millions of dollars' worth of shit inside?" Tonio guessed.

"Right."

"So, what's the mother lode? Drugs?" Silence. Tonio glanced at Rab. "Illegals? I already told you I don't—"

"Yeah, yeah, I know," Rab interrupted. "You don't deal in live cargo. It's nothing like the sex trade, so get your boxers out of a knot. Even *I* don't need the kind of hassle that involves dozens of whiny lowlifes we have to keep alive while we truck them from one place to another. Too big a risk of somebody getting loose, too."

Tonio resisted the urge to choke him until he stopped breathing. But it wasn't easy.

"And people wouldn't be worth millions anyhow," Stan put in.

"So what is?" Tonio glanced between them. Clearly they didn't trust him enough to give him all the details just yet. "Look, I need to know what I'm getting into here. If the payday is worth the potential disaster."

"It is," Rab said. "You'll have to trust me on that, for now."

Son of a bitch! He had no choice but to go along. See if he could pump the bastard for a bit more information. "Fine. What about distribution? If this haul is as big as you're implying, we're going to need a big street team to move the score."

Rab shook his head. "No. No way am I bringing in more guys. Somebody will talk, and then I'll have to shut his mouth but it'll be too late. Anyway, this is what I wanted to tell you: I've got a buyer."

That perked up Tonio's interest. "Yeah? For the whole shebang?"

"Yep. Lock, stock, and barrel. We take our cut and the shit's off our hands."

Tonio leaned back in his chair, crossed his arms over his chest, and made a show of frowning. Thinking over Rab's plan. "But that means we'll walk away with a lot less."

"We'll still clear a million each," Rab said eagerly. His eyes were lit with excitement. Greed. "Once we lift the cargo and deliver it to the buyer, the cash is ours, free and clear. None of the risk or hassle of selling the stuff ourselves."

Tonio took a sip of his beer. Paused. "This buyer. Is he with the mob?"

Rab's pause was even longer. Stan and Phil looked decidedly uncomfortable. Then Rab said, "Paulo Giancarlo."

Tonio whistled through his teeth. "Well, shit. Let's not do anything halfway here. You've already made this deal with him?"

"Yeah."

"Then you'd better hope we can deliver, man, because if not, that crazy bastard will cut off our balls and feed them to his Dobermans. And that's just for the first act."

He would, too. The Mafia boss had been on the FBI's Most Wanted list for years. They just couldn't catch him at anything red-handed. Giancarlo had a team of excellent lawyers, and the few times the FBI had managed to arrest him, the charges wouldn't stick. It was beginning to look like they were going to eventually be forced to nail him with something as mundane as tax evasion, like Al Capone.

"We'll deliver. That's not going to be as huge of a problem as you might think."

Tonio eyed him in disbelief. "You can't tell me that millions of dollars' worth of product is just sitting around unguarded, ripe for the picking."

"Not quite, but close. The building is owned by a big corporation and their security is pretty standard. A few guards around the perimeter, a couple inside. The place has been there for years and nothing's ever happened. These guys are soft, if you get my meaning. Rent-a-cops sitting on a big product."

"Okay. Even so, there's still the logistics of getting in and out without getting caught. There's only five of us."

"We'll talk about that later," Rab said, scowling. He was becoming irritated, obviously didn't like being questioned. "Like I said before, there is risk and we'll have to be on top of our game. The important thing is, we'll need three trucks to haul the product out. We'll set up a rendezvous point and make the transfer to Giancarlo."

"All right." Tonio tried hard to keep the disbelief out of his voice. "So, how did you find out about this warehouse full of money just waiting to be taken?"

"I knew a guy in the pen, who knew a guy."

Awesome. *Dios*.

"And Giancarlo didn't require some kind of proof before the deal?" he asked.

The gang leader scoffed. "He can't demand proof of something I don't even have in my possession yet."

*Oh, you poor, dumb fuck*. Well, really it wasn't that Rab was stupid. He was just a different breed of criminal than Giancarlo. Some Mafia bosses had honor, such as it was. Some, like this one, would make the rules, then change them. Fuck you over just because he could. In his case, he was simply nuts, according to the feds.

Guys like Rab would always chase the fast buck. And eventually want more and more, leading to his downfall.

Tonio let out a deep breath. "When's this going down?"

"Soon. Just got to arrange for the equipment we'll need."

"What do you need from me?"

"You line up the trucks. Then lie low and keep your mouth shut. Especially around Angel." Rab gave him a steely glare.

"I'm not new at this, amigo. I know how women blow things out of proportion."

The others snorted and a round of agreements ensued, followed by more drinking. The discussion of the Missouri job was apparently at an end for the time being. Tonio sat back and listened to them shoot the bull for a while. There was no more information to be gained, it seemed, and he was ready to get out of here.

He stood. "I'm going to call it a night."

"Me, too," Phil said. Stan and Rab followed suit, and the four of them headed for the door, trailed by Enrique.

They continued out into the front yard, where they paused, Rab bragging about some mods he'd made to his bike. Tonio glanced across the street to see the neighbors had moved the party inside at some point. Faint laughter drifted on the air now and then from inside the house, and an occasional shriek of revelry.

Tonio bet the guys in Narcotics would love to raid that place right about now.

He was just about to turn and tell Rab he'd see him later when a loud screech of tires filled the air. Whipping to face the noise, he saw a dark sedan fly around the corner about forty yards away, racing toward them fast.

Pure instinct had him reaching for the gun tucked in his jeans, at the small of his back. When an arm stuck out the passenger's window and the barrel of a gun glinted in the streetlight, Tonio dove for the nearest person next to him with a shout.

"Get down!" he yelled, shoving Rab to the ground.

The *pop, pop, pop* of gunfire peppered the area as Tonio shielded the other man. Lying half over Rab's back, he pointed his gun at the back window of the fleeing vehicle and fired a few rounds. At least one shot hit the car before it careened out of sight.

"Fuck!" Tonio spat, sitting up. "You okay?"

"I think so, yeah." Rab sat up, too, looking to the others, and snarled. "Shit, we got one down."

Stan was sprawled on the ground, Phil and Enrique crouched over him, cursing. Phil stripped off his T-shirt, balled it up, and pressed it against Stan's chest, but Tonio suspected it was no use. Blood was soaking the material and pooling on the ground at a rapid rate. The poor bastard's eyes were already glazing over, and the telltale death rattle sounded from his chest.

In seconds the motion stilled.

"Fuck!" Rab exploded, bolting to his feet. Fists clenching and unclenching, he looked up the street, and then at Enrique. "Who the fuck were those assholes?"

The man in question shook his head. "I don't know, man. Random drive-bys are pretty normal in this part of town. I'll find out, though, and they'll pay."

"Damn right they will," Rab said, voice stony.

"What do we do now?" Phil asked shakily. "Call the police?"

"No," Tonio said emphatically. "No police. Stan's already dead and the police will only get in our business. We can't afford that."

The responding officers wouldn't be from Tonio's city, much less his department, so the chances of his cover being blown were slim. But there was still a chance, and if he were to be recognized, Stan wouldn't be the only one down.

Rab ran a hand over his bald head in frustration. "We'll take his body and leave it somewhere it'll be found. That's the best we can do for the guy."

Tonio wanted to be sick. Stan hadn't been the brightest bulb, and he was a felon, but he was a person. He didn't deserve to be dumped like garbage. Tonio was stuck not being able to say a word as the others put the plan in motion.

Enrique fetched a tattered old quilt from the house. When he returned, he and the others rolled Stan's body into it and then Rab carried it to Enrique's car, placing it in the trunk. Tonio winced inwardly when Rab slammed it closed.

"We got this," Rab said to Tonio. "Go on home. We'll talk later."

"All right. Where are you dumping him?" He gestured toward the trunk.

"Probably out by Cheatham Dam. Somebody will come along and find him in the morning." Rab eyed him. "Why?"

Tonio shrugged. "Just don't like the idea of him rotting somewhere. Doesn't seem right."

"He won't, poor fuck." With that, the subject of Stan was closed. The gang leader's sympathy only extended so far. "Oh, by the way."

"Yeah?"

"That was quite a ninja move you pulled back there.

Pushing me down and popping off a few rounds at those headbangers."

"It was nothing."

"It was more than *nothing*. You saved my life. I won't forget that." Rab's gaze drilled into his, dark and serious.

Irony was a hell of a funny thing sometimes.

It was on the tip of his tongue to respond with something like *You would've done the same for me*. But he couldn't voice the lie. So in the end he just settled for a nod of acknowledgment, and that seemed to satisfy the other man.

There was nothing to do but get the hell gone. As he climbed into his car, he noticed the front door of the house across the street was opened just a crack, and there was a shadow of someone standing there peeking. It quickly closed again. Nobody wanted to get involved. No cops would be called, and no witnesses would emerge even if any showed. Same story in every neighborhood like this one.

Little did they know.

On the drive back to his apartment, the pull to go to Angel was strong. He had the urge to come clean about who he really was and what he was doing. He wanted to feel her arms around him, hear her soothing voice telling him everything would be all right. That he was doing the right thing.

He could imagine her body tight against his, breasts pressed against his chest. Hips grinding into his. Lips exploring his skin.

"Ugh." Thinking like that was getting him nothing but a hard-on he couldn't relieve at the moment.

And he didn't dare go to her tonight. His emotions were too raw, and that was something he wasn't used to. Truth be told, he was feeling so alone. Adrift. He might slip, give in to the temptation to tell someone who might understand his anger. His fears. The risks he was taking. Not just for himself, but for Angel, too.

And what if she didn't understand? What if she was angry, and turned on him? Rab was her brother, and blood, as they say, was thicker than water. Family ties were often the strongest.

Right then he missed his own mama something fierce. But he couldn't talk to her about any of this, either. It wasn't safe or smart to involve her in police business, so he rarely discussed details of his job with her.

Yeah, it would be nice to have a special someone to share his burdens with, and to love. Fat chance of that happening any time soon, right?

He waited until he was back at the apartment and locked inside before he took out the cell phone he'd retrieved from the seat in his car and called Chris. His partner answered on the second ring, sounding a bit out of breath and more than concerned.

"Are you all right?"

"I'm fine. How much of all that did you get?"

"Most everything," his partner said, excitement coloring his tone. "This equipment rocks. Only a couple of spots are going to need enhancing by the tech guys, I think. But what the *hell* was that at the end? Was Stan White really shot?"

"I'm afraid so. Looks like a random drive-by at this point."

Even though Chris had been listening in, Tonio spent the next few minutes going back over the meeting and the shooting, making sure his partner had heard everything. Including where Rab mentioned dumping Stan's body.

"It's a shame we can't pick him up for dumping White," Chris said.

"True. Charging him with obstruction won't accomplish much except piss him off."

"I'll get with the captain, see how he wants to play it. So, what about this big heist Silva's planning?" Chris laughed. "Does this guy have a set of balls on him, or what?"

"*Dios*, he's crazy. This is an oncoming cluster fuck of epic proportions," he told his friend. "These guys are mean, and they're good at stealing cars. But this? It's way out of their league. They'll never pull it off, especially now that they're down one man. What are the odds there's nothing of value in that warehouse at all?"

"Pretty good, I'd say. Or at least not the millions they're expecting."

"What could it be? Drugs?"

"If there's real money to be made, that's as good a guess as any. Could be weapons, too. Or, hell, it could be something as innocuous as furniture or pipe fittings. Let me make some calls, see what I can find out about corporate storage houses in northern Missouri. If I get a solid hit, I'll let you and Rainey know, and then we'll put the owners of the warehouse on alert."

"Sounds good."

"Be careful, Tone," Chris said, worried. "It killed me not to send in backup when the shooting happened. If I hadn't understood you when you said *no police*, I would have."

"I know, but that could've blown my cover. Like I said, I'm fine," he said gruffly. He wasn't good at the emotional stuff. He was suddenly, unpleasantly reminded of a few weeks ago when he'd discovered Chris almost dead on his living room floor, and the feeling of helplessness that had nearly crushed him. It didn't sit well that his friend had to go through anything even remotely similar.

"And you'd better stay that way."

"That's my plan. Gotta go."

"See ya."

He hung up and relaxed into the sofa, staring at the drab interior of the empty apartment. It was too damn quiet. Too lonely. He longed to call his brother. Grace. His mama or Maria.

Angel.

It was too late—or early—to bother anyone. They would become alarmed, getting a call from him in the wee hours. So he sat and peered into the shadows until his lids began to droop and he lost his battle against consciousness.

*A few weeks after Tonio was left heartbroken at the altar, he saw them.*

*Rachel and Danny were coming out of the diner on the town square, hand in hand. His ex-fiancée was smiling at his former best friend, her eyes only for him. She laughed at something Danny said, and the man bent and kissed her soundly.*

*It was more than Tonio could take. The anger that had been writhing in his gut since that awful day boiled over, found its target.*

*"Hey, asshole!" he shouted. Danny's gaze snapped to where Tonio stood down the sidewalk, and his eyes rounded. Tonio broke into a jog, making straight for the startled couple, keeping his rage focused on Danny.*

*"T-Tonio," the other man stammered. "Wait a minute! I can explain—"*

*He never got the chance. Tonio unloaded his fist right into the motherfucker's mouth, enjoying the way the other man's head snapped back, blood spurting from his split lip. Rachel screamed and immediately threw herself between them, trying to push Tonio off her lover.*

*"Tonio, stop! Whatever you think, he's still your friend!"*

*He stepped back and stared at her as a nasty laugh erupted from his chest. "Really? Did he tell you that when he was buried balls deep in your pussy, you lying little bitch?"*

*"Don't call her that!" Danny got in his face. "She doesn't deserve—"*

*"Don't tell me what she deserves," he yelled. His head pounded along with his heart and he felt seconds from stroking out. "She's a cheating bitch and you're a fucking loser. You know what? You two deserve each other. I hope you both rot in hell."*

*They stared at each other for long moments. Finally Danny said, "I hope we can all get past this one day."*

*"Don't count on it."*

*The couple's faces were filled with sorrow as they*

*turned away and got into Danny's car. Danny started the engine, revving it hard. Then he peeled out of the parking spot and down the street, driving much too fast. Much too upset to be driving just then.*

*That was the last time Tonio saw either of them alive.*

Tonio jolted awake, heart hammering in his chest. Swallowing hard, he swiped a hand down his face and struggled to force the horrible memories from his head. The awful guilt. His anger, no matter how justified, hadn't been worth two lives. He wasn't sure how he'd ever live with what had happened. For sure, sleep would be almost impossible now.

Just then he heard the insistent knocking at the door. With a groan, he pushed up from the sofa that definitely wasn't made for sleeping and stretched. A glance at the curtains showed the light was just beginning to slip through, and a quick check of his phone revealed it was just past six thirty.

Christ, not even four hours of sleep. Who the hell? After shoving the phone under the sofa cushion, he stalked to the door and looked out the peephole. His heart gave a little lurch and he opened the door.

"Angel. What are you doing here?"

# 7

One look at Tonio told Angel the man was exhausted. And wound tight.

His black hair poked in every direction. Lines bracketed his mouth, and his eyes were dark and shadowed in his face. Grim.

"You want to come in?" He stepped back and gestured toward the sparse living room.

"Yes, thanks." She took in his appearance—sexy as always, but his jeans were hanging low on his hips, shirt wrinkled. "I woke you up."

"It *is* the ass crack of dawn," he pointed out, rubbing his eyes.

"I can go if I'm too early. I feel bad now about waking you."

"No, it's okay. I'm already up now." He gave her a crooked smile that made her heart stutter. "Sorry. I'm just being grumpy. Have a seat and I'll start coffee. What brings you by?"

She followed him to the tiny kitchen instead, watching as he grabbed the pot and began to fill it with water.

His movements were tense, though he didn't seem irritated by her presence. "Rab told me what happened last night."

He whipped around, coffeepot banging on the counter so hard she was surprised it didn't crack. "He *what*?" Abandoning the pot, he stalked over and grabbed her wrist. "What exactly did he tell you?"

The murderous expression on his face caused her heart to give a kick of alarm. Even so, his grip wasn't hard enough to hurt. "He said there was a random shooting outside Enrique's house and Stan was killed. That's all he told me. Is there more to it?" She studied him closely for any sign that he was lying as he shook his head and released her arm.

"No." Running his fingers through his short hair, he blew out a breath. "It really does appear random. I don't think it's related to anything your brother is involved in."

"My brother? You're part of that group, too." What an odd way for him to phrase it, as though he was on the outside of whatever Rab was doing. But maybe that was because he was new on the scene?

"Right. But I know it can't have anything to do with me, because I haven't had a beef with anyone lately. Anyway, none of the guys could identify the car or the shooter. All signs point to random violence. What?"

She shook her head, at a loss. "I don't know. A *beef*? Who says that? Do people really say that anymore?"

"I say that. So?" He busied himself with making the coffee.

"And *all signs point to random violence*? Sounds like it came out of a textbook."

"Christ, Angel." He rolled his eyes, scooping grounds into the filter. "I was trying to make you feel better."

"A man is *dead*. You and my brother were standing just a few feet away from him. I'm having a tough time feeling comforted right now, Tonio."

She heard the hysteria rise in her voice and hated it. Nor could she stop the sudden tears that welled, blinding her vision. Immediately she found herself embraced and folded against his strong body, pressed against his chest. Her arms went around him and it felt so right to be there. So much like they just fit together.

She pushed her face into the curve of his neck and breathed in his scent. Manly with a hint of musk. Sweat. Exactly what a man should smell like, in her opinion. She gave an experimental lick, and he shivered, arms tightening around her.

"That could be a dangerous game, *bonita*."

"Tasting you?"

"Tempting me."

"What if I don't see it that way? As dangerous?"

"You should."

He was probably right. But she felt safe with him, as she'd never felt with any man. Ever. Best not to scare him away by telling him things like that, this early in their acquaintance. Instead of replying, she raised her face to his and took his mouth.

The kiss was electric. The feel of him wrapped around her, intoxicating. Every time they were together, the attraction grew more potent, like a drug she couldn't resist. There were plenty of reasons she should—and she chose to ignore them all.

His tongue invaded her mouth, explored. Tasted. His hands skimmed up her arms, then cupped her breasts, brushing her nipples lightly through the fabric of her blouse and the bra beneath. She wanted the barriers gone. For now, though, she let things progress at their own pace, naturally.

She did some journeying of her own, palms sliding down his waist to his hips. She liked his trim, firm muscle, the taut abs of his cut stomach. Lifting his T-shirt a bit, she observed that dark little treasure trail and was reminded how much she *especially* liked that, as well as where it led.

Her fingers dipped south to cup his sex through his pants, and she smiled when he sucked in a sharp breath. Was there a more powerful feeling in the world than nearly bringing a man to his knees by simply giving him pleasure? If so, she didn't know what it could be.

Tonio sure wasn't complaining. His hips moved forward, into her touch, and his length hardened under her hand. He groaned, the sound deep and rumbly. Full of want. Need.

"Angel, you're playing with fire," he rasped.

"Oh yes. I certainly am." She squeezed the thick, rapidly heating rod to emphasize her point.

"*Dios!* If you don't want me to drag you to my bed right this second, I suggest you stop."

"I suggest we have coffee later. *Much* later."

The man needed no further encouragement. Leaving the coffeemaker burbling away cheerfully, he pulled her down the short hallway to his small bedroom. Dominating the space was a queen-sized bed that couldn't possibly be comfortable enough for his large frame, but she supposed he had to make do with what he had.

Stopping by the bed, he turned to face her and pulled off his shirt. When he did, her gaze went to the beautiful silver cross hanging from a chain around his neck. The cross rested between his pecs, and for some reason, the sight touched something deep inside her.

"Your cross is gorgeous," she whispered, reaching out to finger the delicate symbol.

"Thanks. My brother wears one just like it."

"Your brother Julian, the firefighter."

"You remembered."

"Of course."

Tonio helped her off with her cotton blouse, painstakingly working on each button until he slipped the garment off and tossed it aside with satisfaction. Then he reached around and unhooked her bra and it followed suit, joining the blouse on the floor.

"You're beautiful," he said in a low voice. His palms cupped her breasts, thumbs stroking the nipples to attention.

"Thank you. So are you."

"Men aren't beautiful," he said with a smirk.

"You don't see yourselves like we see you."

"I'll say." Quickly he unzipped his jeans and shucked them down and off. His cock was firming up against his thigh, ready to play.

She took a moment to appreciate his large, fine form—all over—before ridding herself of her jeans and underwear as well.

Backing up to the bed, he pulled her down with him.

She crawled over him and straddled his lap, a position he seemed to enjoy very much, if his expression and the hardening against her butt was any indication.

Then he placed a sweet, gentle kiss on her lips. He started slowly, a brush of skin. An exchange of breath. Paused in between, giving her the chance to change her mind about their morning romp. But she wanted him every bit as much, wasn't about to say no. She wiggled against the hardness, wanting more.

"I think you're trying to kill me," he said with a short laugh.

"I wouldn't dare. That would be counterproductive." God, the man was sexy as hell. He pushed every button she'd ever possessed straight to *red alert*. His dark eyes were glittering with desire. With need.

"Tell me what you want." Reaching out, he caressed her cheek. "I have to hear it."

"Fuck me so hard I can't see straight. Tell me what *you* want."

His pupils dilated and she swore he almost went up in flames. "I want to lick every inch of that Celtic tattoo and *then* fuck you so hard you can't see straight."

Capturing her lips again, he flipped her and gently lowered her to the bed. Then he proceeded to make good on his wish. He kissed her quite thoroughly for several long moments. He had the best mouth and he knew how to use it—as he proved by using that talented tongue of his to trace every swirl of the design on her biceps, making her giggle.

Then he moved on to her breasts and spent some time with each one. Licking and sucking. Squeezing.

"Are you a breast man, by any chance?"

"Mmm."

She gasped as his teeth grazed a sensitive nipple. *The answer is obviously yes.*

His mouth latched onto the nub, suckling, and she moaned, burying her fingers in his hair as she'd itched to do since she'd arrived. The short black strands were as silky as they looked, just thick enough to get a good grip. She enjoyed the feel of his hair as much as she loved him lavishing attention on her nipples.

He moved south, kissing her belly. When he moved lower, she had to relinquish her hold on his hair and moaned in protest.

"I want to taste you first," he said, setting between her thighs. "I want to give you everything."

"Yes. Please." It had been way too long.

He looked satisfied. "You're so pretty. I want to see you spread for me, baby."

Pushing her knees apart, he lowered his head. Flicked out his tongue and lapped at her sensitive nub. With a sigh of bliss, she spread for him as wide as she could. Yes, it had been much too long, and she wanted Tonio. Like this, or any way he would have her.

His mouth was every bit as talented in this area, too. He licked her sex, delved his tongue in between the folds to fuck her sheath slowly. Driving her a little crazy. Then he'd withdraw and suckle the little clit, taking her to the edge. And withdraw again. Lick and suckle. Over and over until she was mindless, writhing.

"Oh God!"

"Are you ready for me, *bonita*?"

"Yes! Fuck me," she begged. "I need you."

That was all he needed to hear. Fishing in the nightstand, he wasted no time retrieving a condom and gloving up. Then he settled between her legs, placed the head of his cock to her opening, and pushed inside.

They came together like an explosion of lightning. Raw. Primal.

Rocking his hips, he began to thrust inside her. Deep, to the hilt, and out again. Though the movements were slow at first, there was no mistaking the passion. There was nothing gentle or easy about their first lovemaking session—this was pure heat. Lust.

This was a man stoking the fire in his lover, searing her to the depths of her soul. She buried her fingers in his hair again, watched his face as he made love to her. His eyes were half-hidden by his thick lashes, and smoldered with passion. The muscles of his shoulders bunched with each thrust, his cross hanging from his neck, dragging between her breasts.

"Harder," she urged. "Faster."

Increasing the tempo, he did as she asked, moaning. Driving them higher. She knew he was close when he gathered her to his chest, hips pumping furiously. She clung to his back, her own release building until—

She shattered with a cry, pulsing around his length. Her release triggered his and he came with a hoarse shout, sinking himself as deeply as possible. He stayed there, convulsing, holding her close, until at last they were spent. Then a bit longer as they came down from the high, kissing the curve of her neck.

*"Dios mio,"* he whispered.

"I'll say." She hugged him close. "Damn, you're good."

"You're much, much better."

Carefully he pulled out, wincing a little. Afterward, he got up and went to the bathroom. She heard the water running and assumed he was cleaning up, disposing of the condom. She was pleased when he came back carrying a warm washcloth for her to clean herself. When that was done, he tossed the cloth back into the bathroom and returned to the bed.

What made her even happier was discovering that Tonio was a postcoital cuddler. Rolling to his back, he gathered her to him and she laid her head on his shoulder, content. Why was that so surprising? Oh yeah—because he was supposed to be this big, tough felon. That, she still didn't get.

So she decided to go on a little fishing expedition. Minus the line and the hook.

With her fingertip, she drew circles in his chest hair. She waited until she felt him start to relax before she asked, "So, where have you done time?"

Instantly he was tense, his voice guarded. "That's your idea of pillow talk? If so, I gotta say, you suck at it."

"Where?"

He sighed. "Huntsville, down in Texas, for a few years. Got caught transporting stolen copper wiring and pipe fittings."

Her eyebrows rose. "Stolen copper? That's a thing?"

"A huge thing. That particular metal fetches great money, and it's easy pickings off vacant houses that are for sale, restaurants, that kind of target." After a pause, he said, "Just got out a few months ago. Moved here to start over."

"And you fell in with my brother," she said drily. "I have to say, that's in no way an improvement if you hope to better your life."

"It's not going to be forever."

Well, that was cryptic.

"How so?"

"I have plans." He studied her, expression unreadable. "Soon I'll be out of this business and make a normal life."

Her heart squeezed. "How? Hanging with Rab and those losers, how can you make that happen? Look what happened to Stan."

"It won't be like that."

"Everyone says that." Sadness pricked at her. She decided to steer away from that futile topic for now. "How's the leg, by the way?"

"Good. Just a bunch of scabs on the calf now."

"I didn't notice." She grinned, resting her chin on his chest. "I was too busy checking out other attributes."

"I did a fair amount of checking of my own."

His lazy smile made her wet all over again. Still not quite up for round two just yet, however, she kept on with her mission to find out more about him. "Where's your brother a firefighter?"

"In, uh, Chattanooga."

"You two are close?"

"Yeah. He's the best." A shadow crossed Tonio's face and his smile dimmed. "He's had a hard time of it lately, what with the accident . . ."

"What happened?"

"He and another firefighter were hurt on the way to a call. A truck ran a red light and hit their ambulance."

"I'm so sorry," she whispered. "Is he going to be okay?"

"Julian is recovering, but his friend has a long road ahead of him."

"But his colleague will heal, too?"

"With time, we hope so. I just thank God, or fate, or whatever saved my brother that day."

"Well, I'm glad, too, for your sake."

They snuggled for a while longer before Tonio finally made a move. "I need to get a shower and take care of a few things. Coffee first?"

"Sure, naked coffee sounds great."

Laughing, he slid from the bed. "How do you take yours?"

"My coffee? Naked. Just like my man." She leered at him and liked that she made him chuckle all the way to the kitchen.

In moments he returned with two steaming mugs and handed her one. They sipped their brew for a few minutes before he finally started the water in the shower, letting it heat.

"Shower with me?"

That was an invite she wasn't about to refuse. Setting her mug on the nightstand next to his, she joined him under the hot spray and had lots of fun getting dirty before they got clean again. Afterward, they dried off and got dressed.

As they did, she spent some time mulling over the things he'd told her. Again and again, she kept coming back to the conclusion that this man had a heart. He cared for his family and friends. And Rab and his drones weren't among those. Tonio was composed of puzzle pieces that didn't fit.

Angel was going to find the missing links.

"I need to make a couple of calls," he said. "Check on some things for your brother."

Ugh. Rab and his schemes. "That's fine. I'll take these mugs to the kitchen and then sit in the living room until you're done."

"Sure." Giving her a quick kiss, he plucked his phone off the dresser.

Gathering the mugs, she went to the kitchen and put them in the sink. The bedroom door closed, but she could still hear his muffled voice talking on the phone. To kill time, she walked into the living room and sat on his sofa, then reached for her purse on the coffee table. As she did, her body shifted and something dug into her butt cheek.

Something hard. Frowning, she looked down but couldn't see what it was. Reaching between the cushions, her fingers brushed what felt like a square piece of plastic. Curious, she pulled it up and blinked at it.

A black iPhone. What appeared to be the newest, sleekest model. But Tonio had a phone already—he was talking on it in the bedroom. A chill snaked down her spine and she glanced toward the bedroom. The conversation was still going, so she had time to punch the button below the screen.

Of course the screen was locked. That would've been too easy. But the newest text was visible when the screen lit up, and she peered at it, punching the button three times all together in order to read the whole message, from someone named Chris.

Found White where you said he would be. Can you believe this, there was another DB in the area?! Not even 50 yds away. Female, strangled. What to make of that shit? Call me when you get this.

Angel blinked at the message. DB? "Dead body? Jesus." She read it again. What the holy freaking hell was going on here?

Down the hall the bedroom door clicked open, and Angel shoved the phone between the sofa cushions, heart in her throat. Quickly she grabbed her purse and snatched her own phone out of it, unlocked the screen, and pretended to be thumbing through her pictures.

"Oh, there you are," she said, looking up. Putting away her phone, she dug out her keys and stood. "I just wanted to tell you good-bye. See you later?"

"Count on it," he rumbled in that deep, sexy voice of his.

After kissing the shit out of her, he saw her out the door. She floated on that for as long as it took the doubts to creep in—all of five minutes. That text was emblazoned on her brain and wouldn't leave.

Tonio had told someone named Chris where to find Stan's body? That meant Rab had dumped the guy somewhere? Sounded like her brother. God knows he wouldn't call the police, even if the shooting wasn't his fault. But what was that about a woman's body being found nearby? The implication—that Rab might have something to do with that, too—was scary as hell.

"Oh, God, please say he didn't."

And, more important, who was Chris? Why had Tonio contacted him for help in the first place?

More unanswered questions. She was going to get some satisfaction.

Once she arrived home, she was relieved to find that Rab was gone. She'd expected him to be sleeping half the day, but having him out of her hair was always welcome. And lately . . . She was more than a little afraid of him, though she tried not to let on.

For a bit, she paced the living room, puzzling over how to get some answers about Tonio. The best way she knew?

The Internet.

In her bedroom, she booted up her computer and started with a basic search. She thought about going to one of those sites where a person could pay for a quick background check, but she didn't know Tonio's birth date, which was a major drawback.

She'd have to check other facts. But what? Typing in Tonio Reyes, she hit the ENTER key and got more than one hundred thousand hits. The very first entry was about a popular, long-running fictional soap opera character by the same name. How odd.

No information was going to be forthcoming from that route. Nor did she have the connections to find out whether he'd been in Huntsville in recent years, or on what charges.

But he had a brother. Julian. What was the saying? Many a truth was told in a lie. Was Tonio lying about anything he had said? Or even part?

First, Angel tried typing in Julian Reyes and that was

just as vague as Tonio's name, scoring too many hits. Then she thought for a few seconds. She tried Firefighter Julian Reyes and partner hit by truck, Chattanooga. Enter.

Nothing that she could find.

Firefighters Julian Reyes and partner hit by truck in ambulance, severely injured, Chattanooga. Enter.

Still no hit. She hated to think it, but what if Reyes wasn't his last name? What if Chattanooga wasn't the correct city? She tried again, taking those items off the search.

Firefighters Julian and partner severely injured, ambulance hit by truck, Tennessee. Enter.

This time, there was an article, several weeks old, at the top of the page, in bold. Sugarland, Tennessee. Eighteen-Wheeler Runs Red Light, Firefighters Injured.

Sugarland, which was a nearby city. Not Chattanooga. Hand trembling, she clicked on the link.

> Two firefighters were injured this week when a fifty-four-year-old man driving an eighteen-wheeler ran a red light at an intersection and smashed into the driver's door of the ambulance driven by thirty-one year-old firefighter/paramedic Clayton Montana. Montana is listed in grave condition and is currently in a coma at Sterling Hospital. Doctors are guarded about his chances of survival.

Sucking in a breath, Angel fixed her eyes on the rest, heart pounding.

> The second firefighter/paramedic, Julian Salvatore,

sustained non-life-threatening injuries and was released to the care of his family. His brother, Detective Anthony Salvatore of the Sugarland PD, commends the quick response of the rescue unit and the team of doctors at the hospital for taking such good care of both men.

*Detective Anthony Salvatore. Anthony. Tonio.*

Detective Salvatore also stated that while he was not the arresting officer, the driver of the truck is in custody pending charges for vehicular assault and driving while intoxicated. If Montana does not survive, those charges will almost certainly be upgraded to either manslaughter or murder.

Angel skimmed the story again, then clicked the *X* to close it and sat stunned for a long while. She told herself that just because Tonio had lied didn't mean *he* was the detective in the article. After all, there was no picture of Anthony Salvatore with the story. Tonio could've come across that story himself and fabricated his whole identity based on it. He told her he had come here for a fresh start.

So his name might not be Anthony, or Tonio, at all. But the only way to know for sure was to see a picture of the detective. She went back to work, typing in Detective Anthony "Tonio" Salvatore, Sugarland PD.

She got two hits. The first article had no picture. But the second solved two mysteries at one time.

First, it lauded Detectives Tonio Salvatore and Chris

Ford for solving a string of poisoning murders—in which Ford himself was very nearly one of the victims. Tonio had actually saved his partner's life at one point. So that explained who Chris was, and it cleared up the mystery of Tonio's identity.

Because the article included a black-and-white but unmistakable picture of Detective Tonio Salvatore, tall and handsome in plainclothes, badge clipped to his belt, working the crime scene after the murderer was apprehended.

Her Tonio.

The undercover cop.

# 8

The second Angel was gone, Tonio crossed the room and fished his phone from between the sofa cushions.

Was this how he'd left it? He'd shoved it there in such a hurry, he wasn't sure. If she had found the device, wouldn't she have asked about it? Said something? Maybe, maybe not. Checking his notifications, he saw there was a text from Chris, and the time stamp showed it had come in well before she left. A sense of foreboding curled through his gut. If she'd found the phone, no way had she missed this. Angel was smart and she would put the pieces together quick.

The question was, if she *had* seen, what would she do about it? Would she rat him out to her brother? He didn't think so. But could he stake his life on it?

Punching in Chris's number, he waited. The man answered and he said, "Talk to me. What's this about a second body?"

"Man, that's some messed-up shit," Chris muttered, sounding tired. "We found Stan White's body near the dam, right?"

"Yeah . . ."

"So, we're doing a search through the area and *bam*. Down in the tree line near water, about forty yards from White's body, is a dead woman. No ID on her at the scene, but the cleaning staff at the Sleep Inn found her purse and the manager called the cops when they couldn't find *her*. Her name was Sharon Waite. They said she checked in alone, paid in cash."

"Interesting."

"Very. Especially since it's obvious she didn't remain alone for long. An empty bottle of tequila was found on the floor under the bed, probably knocked to the floor and forgotten when the killer cleaned up."

"Why do you say that?"

"Because the rest of the room was wiped clean, according to our CSI guys. There are a few prints on the bottle, but they're pretty smudged, so we'll see what they can get."

Tonio's blood quickened. "Any word on the whereabouts of Rab Silva? I'd love to skip the rest of this theft bullshit and hang that asshole for murder."

"That makes two of us." A sigh reached Tonio's ears. "I'm working on it. No witnesses so far."

"Shit." Resting his head on the back of the sofa, he stared at the cracked ceiling. "I hate being out of the loop like this. I need to be investigating."

"You're close to a dangerous criminal. You're where you should be right now. Maybe you can wrangle a confession?"

"Maybe. Rab is rough stock, but he's not stupid. I'll see what I can do without raising his suspicions." He paused. "Speaking of suspicions, his sister may have hers about me."

His partner's voice sharpened. "In what way?"

"That I'm a cop. She might have seen your last text message on my phone."

"Dammit, Tonio!"

"Hey, I had the phone hidden," he defended. "I can't be sure."

"Will she tell her brother?"

"I honestly don't think so. She barely tolerates him and doesn't approve of his choice of profession to say the least. She's a little afraid of him, too."

"Tonio," his friend cautioned. "As cops, we know how family members tend to stick together like glue no matter how much one disapproves of the other's actions. Turn on the news any day of the week and you'll see a sobbing mother or sibling claiming their poor baby boy couldn't possibly have done such a terrible thing, blah, blah."

"I get it. But I think I'm getting to know Angel some, and she's stronger than that."

There was a heavy pause before Chris replied, "That sounded sort of defensive. Tell me you don't have something going on with the hot sister."

He meant to tell Chris what he wanted to hear. Really, he did. But what came out instead was "I don't care if I get fired. I'm not backing away from Angel, or leaving her twisting in the wind. That's not how I'm made."

"Oh, holy hell." His partner barked a laugh. "That sounded very much like a guy who just jumped off the bachelor train feetfirst."

Some of the tension he'd been holding in seeped from his muscles, and some humor crept into his tone. "You think? I don't know, *amigo*. From the moment I first saw her, it was like being hit in the head with a baseball bat."

"Could be simple, healthy lust."

"Maybe." Tonio hesitated. "Feels like more. For the first time in ages."

"Wow. Wait—there's been a special woman before? When?"

"Back in San Antonio, few years ago. She left me at the altar. Literally never showed up, left me standing in front of a church full of guests, and ran off with my best friend."

"The hell you say! Man, why haven't you ever told me this before?" Chris exclaimed.

"Are you kidding? That was the lowest point of my life. Even my family knows better than to bring up the subject." Only, it didn't seem quite so painful anymore.

"Well, just be careful. If you think for one second you've been compromised, get the hell out. You got a place to lie low for a while if that happens?"

He thought about that. "I've got a cousin who owns a lake cabin in Texas. Nobody would find me there. If things go to shit, that's where I'll head until I get the all-clear."

"Sounds good."

He gave Chris his cousin Vincent's name and phone number and the location of the cabin. Hopefully he wouldn't need to use the getaway, but it never hurt to be prepared. "I may not be able to let you know if I have to get out of town fast, but I'll call as soon as I can."

"Watch your ass. Talk soon."

After hanging up, Tonio sat for a long while, contemplating Angel and what to do about her. Whether he should stay away from her for a while. The instant the idea entered his head, he knew he wasn't about to do that. Stupid as he might be, he wasn't giving her up. Not yet. He had the distinct feeling he should see where this could go between them.

Perhaps nowhere. Could be he was setting himself up for another big fall. But wasn't all of life the same in regard to the risk? He hadn't truly let himself be happy with another woman in years. The irony of his interest in *this* woman didn't escape him.

With a self-deprecating laugh, he pushed up from the sofa. Time to get his day started. He knew he ought to stay away.

But a certain crime scene was calling his name.

Tess hunched down in her car, watching her quarry as he puttered in the motorcycle shop. Looked innocent enough, but she knew Rab well enough by now to know better.

He was talking up his contacts. Planning something. But she wasn't in the loop any longer, so she didn't know *what*. That was frustrating as hell. Months of work down the toilet, for what?

The phone buzzed on the seat beside her and she answered. "Watcha got?"

"You sitting down?"

"Yep."

"Your boy, Tonio."

"Not my boy, but yeah?"

"Get this—he's a cop."

For a second, she swore the world stopped. Then she sucked in a breath and let out a loud laugh. "What! Who is he, really? What city?"

"Detective Anthony Salvatore, Sugarland PD. Goes by Tonio. They sent him in to get close to Rab." Her boss made a noise of frustration. "The dickhead who was supposed to let the local cops know to steer clear of his gang fell down on the job. What were the odds anyway, right?"

"Right. Now what?"

"We wait and watch. I bitched out all the appropriate folks, but if we yank his ass now, Rab might pull a runner. At the very least, he'll know his group was infiltrated again, and we know how the last time turned out."

Her lips pressed into a thin line. "I can't wait to nail this son of a bitch to the wall. He's such a fuckin' sleaze."

"Hang in there. We'll get him."

"Do I approach Tonio? Tell him who I am?"

"Not yet. Let's hold that to our vest for now. His boss might tell him, but he was worried about his detective having too many distractions in the field."

"Oh, he's got *distractions in the field*, all right," she muttered.

"I'm pretty sure Rainey was referring to him covering for a fellow law enforcement officer, not who he's fucking."

In spite of herself, Tess's face flamed. It took a lot to embarrass her these days, but damn. "I hate your ass, Harold."

"Good. I wouldn't let you near it."

"Bye, you jerk."

She punched the OFF button, smirking as it cut off his hearty laugh. Smug bastard. She couldn't fucking wait until retirement. Too bad that wasn't for another thirty-five years or so.

If she lived that long.

Rab rolled the buttery leather of the motorcycle jacket between his fingers and checked out the cool red stripes running down the arms. God, that was sweet.

Came with a sweet price tag, too. Soon, though, he wouldn't have to even glance at things like price tags. He could buy whatever he wanted, when he wanted. It was about time he got what he deserved out of this shitty-ass life.

Sam ambled over, took a look around. "Finding what-cha need?"

"Not yet, but soon." He let his smile say it all. The man knew; he helped hook up Rab with a lot of his equipment. Sometimes information, too.

"Good. Let me know if there's anything else." The man didn't leave, though. He kept looking past Rab, out the window.

"What's up?"

Sam's thick eyebrows drew together. "You see that car parked across the street?"

Turning around, Rab squinted. The vehicle was far enough away that he could tell it was a dark sedan with tinted windows, but not much else. "So?"

"It arrived when you did. Hasn't moved since."

Rab studied it a few more seconds, then shrugged.

"Might not mean nothin'. Thanks for giving me the heads-up, though. I owe you."

"Sure thing."

When Rab left, he kept a close eye on the sedan without making it obvious he'd noticed. He wasn't really expecting it to follow. So when it did, pulling neatly into traffic a few cars behind him, a chill broke out on his spine for the first time since prison.

Someone was watching him. Following him.

Someone with the means and the time to take away what he was trying so hard to build. They wanted to rip from him any chance at a good life. Just like it always was, someone trying either to take what was his or to knock him down.

Glancing back again, he noticed that the sedan was gone. Almost as though the driver had sensed him noticing, which was dumb. No way had they known.

Was it the feds? Giancarlo? Or some of Giancarlo's enemies? Whoever it was, if they thought they would get away with screwing him over, they were wrong.

He'd catch them unaware, soon.

And when he did, he'd send a message even the dumbest asshole couldn't miss.

A knock on his apartment door interrupted the dismal task of cleaning the tiny bathroom. Not that there were enough chemicals in the world to really clean this dump.

Tonio was surprised, but happy, to find Angel on the other side of door. She'd changed clothes, and looked smoking hot in snug black jeans and matching leather boots. Her top was pretty, with a black-and-white pattern. Not the usually kick-ass logo shirt she'd typically wear to Stroker's.

"Back again so soon? Don't you have to open the bar in an hour or so?"

"I got my other bartender to open for me, and someone else to close. I, um . . ."

"Hey, come in. Where are my manners?"

Letting her inside, he stepped back and then pulled the door closed. Then he gathered her into a warm embrace, nuzzling her hair. "You were saying?"

"I was kind of hoping you were free tonight."

His heart gave a hopeful lurch. "Free? Like, for a date?"

"Exactly like that." Her grin was shy, which was so unlike the normally take-charge woman he was getting to know.

It also hit him that she'd taken the night off. To spend time with *him*. Something his ex had never done. "I think that sounds like fun. What would you like to do?"

She brightened. "Well, there's this nice Italian restaurant downtown that has the greatest spaghetti and lasagna. I mean, it's nice but not expensive or anything."

"Hey, I'm not completely broke," he teased. "I can afford dinner."

"Well, it was my invitation, so I should be the one to pay."

"I'm not even going to dignify that with a response, other than to say my mama would beat my ass black and blue if she ever found out I let a date pay for dinner. So, it's a plan."

"Okay." She beamed at him.

That smile went through him like a million volts. "Let me change into clean clothes and we'll go."

Quickly he headed back to his room and dug through the small closet. There wasn't much to choose from, but thankfully he was able to come up with a nice button-down shirt and a dark pair of jeans. Last, he tucked his wallet in his back pocket—the one with his false ID.

"I'm ready," he said, walking back to join her again.

"Great! Let's go."

Outside, they climbed into his car and set off. Angel gave him directions, and on the way he liked how she sat real close, hand on his thigh. It was almost possessive and it made him feel good. Made him want to shout out the window at the world that she was his, and hands off!

That feeling had been absent for too long. It was highly possible he'd never felt anything at all but a faint echo of what he wished would be, and now recognized the real thing.

In minutes, he was pulling the car into a parking spot outside the restaurant. It looked to be a cozy place, red-brick with a neon sign that wasn't yet lit in the late afternoon. Climbing out, he hurried around to her side, reaching her door just as she was opening it. He relished her look of surprise when he opened her door the rest of the way and helped her out.

"Thank you," she said. "I didn't think men actually did that anymore."

"You'd be surprised."

"Oh, I'm surprised all the time, trust me." Her lips curved upward, and the look she gave him could only be described as mysterious.

*Huh.* What was that all about?

Placing his hand at the small of her back, he forgot all about it as he guided her inside to the hostess stand. A pretty, dark-haired young woman greeted them cheerfully and showed them to a table in a private corner. Then she handed each of them menus and left.

"This is nice," he observed. "But not overly fancy."

"My kind of Italian. Plenty of pasta, rich sauces, and portions big enough to fell a rhino."

Tonio laughed. "That's my kind of place, too. What's your favorite?"

She opened her menu. "Mmm. Too many to list. The spaghetti and lasagna are great, as I said. So is the linguine carbonara, the eggplant, whatever. Take your pick. I've never eaten anything here I haven't loved. Oh, and the garlic knots are to die for."

"Jeez, now I'm starving."

The waiter came and took their drink orders. Tonio stuck to iced tea and Angel got water with lemon. Then they took a few moments to make their choices, and by the time he decided, he was practically salivating.

"I think I'm going for the spaghetti with Italian sausage," he said.

"Good choice. Today it's the linguine for me. Nothing like a little cream sauce to clog the old arteries."

He smiled. "I think your arteries are years from being endangered."

"I'm careful, but I indulge now and then."

The waiter brought their drinks and took their food orders. Once he had disappeared again, Tonio reached out and laid his hand on top of Angel's. He stroked the soft skin, observed how her lips parted and her face showed her pleasure at his touch. No way was he imagining that.

"I like spending time with you," he said.

"The feeling is entirely mutual." She paused. When she spoke again, her voice held a note of confession. "Tonight is about us getting to know each other better. *Really* getting to know each other, if that's what you want."

His breath hitched. His pulse pounded with excitement he had no right to feel—especially with the weight of guilt her last words leveled on his soul.

"I have to get it clear in my head, what you're asking. You want more than hookups?" Her face colored and he cursed himself for not being a little more sensitive.

"Yes. That's what I'm asking. I want more than that, but if you don't—"

"Hang on. I never said I didn't, I just wanted to be sure I was on the same page." He'd never let go of her hand, and squeezed it gently. "I want that, too. But the life I lead—"

"Let's talk about some other things first."

"Okay. Like what?"

"What do you like to do in your spare time? What makes you happy?" She looked at him, really truly interested.

He thought about it. "I like to build stuff. Work with my hands. I like to build cabinets and shelves, and I like to tinker with my car some."

"I didn't notice any woodworking type stuff at your place, though," she said.

"I don't have any right now," he said quietly. Because

it was all at his real house. He missed being outside, among his *stuff*.

"Well, you'll get more. I can't wait to see some of the projects you do in the future."

"Thanks." He shrugged, pleased. "I'm no expert, but I do okay. What about you? When you get away from the bar, what sorts of things do you enjoy?"

"Reading, water-skiing, hiking. I want to travel, but I've never really been anywhere big." She snapped her fingers. "Does going across the border to Juarez to buy tequila count?"

That got a laugh from him. "As a vacation? I guess we do what we gotta do. But I'm sure you'll swing a real vacation one day. Where's your dream spot?"

"Anywhere there's a beach, preferably tropical, with clear blue water. But my number-one dream getaway is Italy. One of these days I'm going to eat pasta and drink wine in Italy in some gorgeous Tuscan village on a crooked little street. I'm going to see all the sights and come home ten pounds heavier."

"That sounds awesome. Can I come?"

"If you're good."

"As long as I don't have to be *too* good. That would cut down on the fun."

"True. What else gets your blood pumping?" She smirked a little.

"Besides sex? Let's see. I like all the things you said—skiing, hiking, pretty much anything physical. Except extreme sports. You won't see me free-falling off cliffs into puddles of water or jumping out of helicopters without parachutes."

"Well, darn. I had shark-diving off the coast of Australia scheduled for tomorrow at two."

"I'll have to pass."

The waiter interrupted, bringing their orders. Tonio dug in, and groaned. "This is so good."

"Told you."

They spent a few moments eating, making small talk about their favorite movies and books. Finally Tonio got the courage to brave a subject they'd barely touched on. "Tell me more about your mom."

Taking a sip of her water, Angel held it up and said, "I'd need a vodka for that conversation." Setting the glass down, she sighed. "Our relationship is strained. That makes me sad, but it is what it is."

"Does it have to stay that way? Can't you change it?"

"It's not like changing clothes. Our relationship is tarnished, and we can't just throw a coat of gloss over it." Toying with her fork, she grew thoughtful. "Dinners with her are painful. Oh, we're polite, but there's this weird undercurrent of anger and resentment between us. Truthfully I think most of it is coming from me, and she feels she deserves it and just sits there."

"And what? You want her to get angry back?"

"Maybe. I don't know. Anything seems like it would be better than her just sitting there taking it like a whipped dog, you know?"

"You want her to show feeling," he said. "Spirit."

"Yes." Slowly she nodded. "I want to see a spark. But she's dead inside."

"Or scared. Guilty." Pausing, he considered his next words carefully. "Tell me to butt out if I'm overstepping, but have you considered going to counseling with your mom?"

"Are you serious?" Her eyes widened and she gaped at him as though he'd suggested she build a rocket and fly to the moon.

"Totally. Together, you could have a breakthrough that could repair your relationship."

"There you go again with that textbook thing."

"Sorry. I'm just trying to help."

"I know," she said softly. "And I appreciate it. But what money tree did you imagine we would use to pay for this counseling? My basic insurance doesn't cover that, and I'm sure Mom's doesn't, either."

"There's always a way. Trust me on that."

She cocked her head at him. "Let's talk about you some more. Or rather, your family."

*Oh, shit.* "What about them?"

"How's your brother doing?"

"Julian is fine. Recovering."

"Chattanooga Fire Department, you said?" She took another bite of her linguine.

Suddenly his spaghetti was hard to choke down. "Yeah. He had a messed-up ankle that's still healing, some broken ribs, and was banged up pretty good all around. But it's his mental state his wife, Grace, is worried about."

At that, Angel appeared very concerned. "He's not dealing with the accident?"

"Not by a long shot. He's keeping something inside, but we're not sure what."

"Well, his partner almost died and he was in the ambulance with him. That's got to be enough to mess with anyone's head."

"I'm sure it's a huge factor, but that's not all. I can feel it, and so can my sister-in-law. We'll get to the bottom of it, sooner or later."

"I'm sure you will. You seem like you're very good at getting to the bottom of things."

There. Her tone. What was that? A shadow passed over her eyes, too. There and gone so fast he was sure he imagined it, because in the next moment she was smiling at him and asking about his mama.

"She drives me crazy, but I love her madly. You'd love her, too. Everyone does."

"What's she like?"

"Nothing like me. She's short and round, and pretty. She laughs all the time, at least when she's not scolding one of us in Spanish so rapid-fire even I can't keep up. Mama is one of the happiest people I've ever known, and loves with her whole heart."

Angel blinked several times and dabbed at her eyes with her napkin. "I'd love to meet a mother like her. I wonder what that must be like, having one so wonderful."

His throat grew a grapefruit-sized lump. For a few moments he felt like an asshole for leaving San Antonio and moving away from Mama and his sister. But he'd needed his fresh start. If he hadn't done it, he never would've met Angel.

He couldn't be sorry about that. "Someday perhaps I'll get to introduce you to her."

"Maybe so."

They finished off their meal, but were far too full to go for dessert. Tonio paid the tab with a minimal amount of fuss from Angel, and then they were on their way.

"I don't really feel like going home just yet, do you?" he asked.

"Not really. Any ideas?"

"Why don't we drive out to Ashland Park on the Cumberland River? There's a really nice place to park, and I've got a blanket in the trunk we can use to spread on the ground. The weather is getting cooler in the evenings, too, so it should be pleasant to sit for a while."

"Best idea I've heard all day."

Pleased with that plan, he drove with Angel tucked next to his side. It took a few minutes longer to reach that park rather than the one by Cheatham Dam, but he didn't want to go near the recent crime scene. Rather, he didn't want Angel anywhere close to that taint.

When they arrived, he found a parking spot close to a green grassy area beside the river. Perfect for an early evening of river-gazing and lounging with the most beautiful woman in the county. Or more like the state of Tennessee.

Taking the blanket from the trunk of the car, Tonio carried it tucked under one arm and held her hand with his free one. It didn't take long to find a good spot, and he spread the material out, then took her hand and helped lower her to the blanket.

Once he was settled, he spread his legs and pulled her between them, her back resting against his chest. Tucking his chin down onto her shoulder, he decided he liked that position very much, and just might never leave it.

They snuggled together for a long while, making small talk. Pointing out birds or boats. People-watching. Tonio was feeling happy and hazy, drifting in a sea of bliss, when Angel turned on the blanket to face him and laid a hand on his thigh. Her face was open, her voice soft as she spoke.

"From the time we first met, you were a puzzle I couldn't quite put together."

A chill broke through the warmth. "What do you mean?"

"You're so nice, not like Rab or his men. At least to me."

He tried a laugh. "Don't let that fool you, *bonita*. You know what I do to make money. I can't change what I am—"

"Yes. I know what you do."

The statement rang between them. But did she mean . . . ?

"I know what you do, the kind of man you are."

His heart thundered in his ears. She took a deep breath, looked straight into his eyes.

"And I know exactly *who* you are, Detective Tonio Salvatore."

# 9

Angel watched the shock flash across Tonio's face. He covered it quickly, but it was there all the same, and any lingering doubt she might've had was erased.

"It's okay," she reassured him. "I'm not going to tell anyone, least of all my brother. You can trust me on that."

After a brief battle with himself, he let out a sigh and gazed at her from under thick black lashes. "Guess I suck at undercover work, eh?"

"No. Rab isn't looking at you through a woman's eyes."

He snorted a laugh. "Well, there's something to be thankful for."

She couldn't help smiling. "For sure. Anyway, I always thought you were a bit too civilized to be part of that group."

"What did it? How did you find out my name?" he asked, curious.

"The story about your brother. An Internet search revealed the news story, and you were included. There was a quote, but the picture of you was with a different article."

He groaned, closing his eyes briefly. "I knew that would come back to bite me in the ass. The second I told you, I thought the accident was too recent. I shouldn't have told you so much of the truth of what happened, and I worried you'd figure it out."

"Do you realize how weird it is to hear my lover say to me he should've been better at lying?" She arched an eyebrow, and he winced.

"Sorry. But my case, and my life, is on the line here with your brother and his thugs. I didn't know for sure if I could trust you, at first."

"You know you can, right?"

He gazed at her for a moment, then nodded. "I do."

"Good. The real danger here is my brother, and making sure he doesn't run across something like I did that will give you away. Can your boss get that story pulled off the Internet?"

"Maybe." He frowned. "Damn, I thought they'd taken care of everything. That kind of mistake gets cops killed, and this case has been mishandled from the start."

Sadness pricked her heart. "He's planning something really big, isn't he? And really stupid?"

"I'm afraid so. I can't give you any details, but he's bitten off way more than he can chew with this one. Just the attempt will get him put away for a long time."

"As much as I hate to say it, that's probably for the best. Rab on the loose is a danger to himself and everyone else, eventually. His stint in prison didn't teach him a thing."

"That's often the way it goes with career felons. I'm sorry."

"He's made his choices. I'm not living my life for him."

"But it still hurts."

"It does. I always wanted one of those really cool brothers who was smart, well liked, and protective of me. A brother who'd take me places and spend quality time, you know? That's just not our reality and never will be."

They fell quiet for a moment. Tentatively he reached for her, opening his arms in invitation. She knew what he was asking without actually saying the words. He wanted to know whether they were moving forward, together, as they had been. Or if she had been setting him up for some sort of fall after finding out his identity.

Without hesitation, she scooted between his legs more firmly, and snuggled into his arms. His embraced tightened around her gently and his sigh of relief came from deep within his chest, making her smile. He'd been more worried about her reaction than he'd let on, and that warmed her inside.

"What's it like, being a cop?"

He took a few seconds to think about his answer. "It's not like any other job—that's for sure. Even though we're ultimately there to help people, many aren't happy to have us around or see us coming. We often have to do things or follow rules the public doesn't understand, and the media also skew things for the sake of ratings. I'm sorry, but not every procedure, no matter if we follow it to the letter, looks good on a cell phone video. Some days it's hard, almost impossible, to do our jobs."

"I can imagine," she said, nodding. "I heard a saying

once—it's tough to play the game when you're playing the referee, too."

"Being a cop is a lot like that. Too many refs in the game, all trying to call the shots. Add the media to the shit storm, and someone's getting a reprimand. Maybe even losing their entire career, many times unfairly." He paused before continuing.

"But it can be incredibly rewarding. When we catch a murderer or some other criminal, and the case is solid because we've tied every single detail with a neat bow, and we put him away? There's no feeling like it. Knowing that piece of shit is off the street for years, sometimes forever, because of our hard work."

"I admire what you do, Tonio. Don't doubt that. I believe in you, and I trust you."

"Thank you, *bonita*. That means everything to me." He squeezed her briefly, kissed the top of her head. "I'm not concerned about me at the moment. Are you going to be okay around Rab, keeping a secret like this?"

"I'll be all right. I don't see him much, and when I do, he's so wrapped up in himself and being as unpleasant as possible we don't really talk about anything important."

"You've talked about me."

"True. But he doesn't suspect anything. If he did, he'd be all over me, I'm sure of that. He's been acting totally normal, or what's normal for Rab, anyway."

"Okay. But if you detect the slightest hint of change in his attitude, call me. I have a number for my actual cell phone and I'll make sure you have that today." He fell quiet, and she could almost hear the wheels turning in his brain.

"What are you thinking?"

"I think you should spend more time at my place. The less you're around your brother, the better."

"And the more I'm around you, even better still?" she teased.

"There is that." Humor rumbled in his low voice. "What can I say? I'm stingy and I want you all to myself."

"Well, you're not going to get an argument from me."

"Good."

They sat for a while, and she enjoyed having Tonio's big body wrapped around hers like a living blanket. She wasn't the only one appreciating their position. It wasn't long before evidence of how very much he was also enjoying their interlude was pressing into the crease of her rear. Even through their clothing, his arousal was impressive.

Bending, he nuzzled into her neck and started to nibble the sensitive skin at the curve above her shoulder. A place she loved. His kisses and nips made her nipples tighten, and warmth gather between her legs.

"It's pretty deserted out here," he murmured, one hand cupping a breast through her blouse.

She sucked in a breath, becoming more aroused by the second. "Tonio. There are a couple of boats out there."

"They're too far away to see anything, baby." His roaming hand went under her shirt.

"What if they have binoculars or something?"

"They'll get a thrill?"

"Tonio . . ." Instead of an admonishment, his name came out as a plea.

Chuckling, he took her hand and pulled her to her feet. "Let's go for a walk, baby. I want to show you some nature."

"I'll just bet you do."

"Let's leave the blanket. We'll get it when we come back."

Excited, she clasped his hand and let him lead her away from their small lounging spot. He took them toward a trail about thirty yards from the riverbank, and they started down it. The evening was beautiful and clear, the lowering sun making pretty dapples through the trees and illuminating a forest of green. When Tonio came to a place that apparently pleased him, he stopped and pulled her against his chest.

He kissed her thoroughly, slowly. Legs spread, he held her against him from chest to groin, making sure she felt how much he wanted her. His body was hard, yet comfortable, and it was so right to be here, in his arms. Finally he pulled back and smiled. "I plan to have my way with you, right here. You have a problem with that?"

Her heart beat faster. God, he was the sexiest man she'd ever seen, big, dark, and gorgeous, and he wanted her here. In the open. The scenario was a fantasy come to life. More than a little naughty. "Not one that I can think of."

Grinning, he stripped off her shirt, then placed it on a nearby rock. Next went her bra, which he deftly unsnapped and tossed over the shirt. When he reached for the button on her jeans, she held up a hand.

"Wait. Isn't it your turn?"

His grin resembled a feral wolf, and his eyes practically glowed with an unholy light. "Nope. I'm stripping you naked for my pleasure, *querida*. You're my personal wood nymph, and I've captured you. I can do anything with you I want."

She shivered, nipples tightening in the air. She'd never played this kind of game before, and it was wicked. In a good way. "You can do what you want. It's only fair, since you caught me."

His dark eyes were hot as they raked her body. "Good. First, let's take care of the rest of this."

Her shoes and jeans were next. The panties went last, and he crouched by her feet, easing them down. As she stepped out of them, he ran a palm up the inside of one of her thighs. Upward, until his fingers brushed the folds of her sex and rubbed, spreading the moisture that was already gathering there.

"Beautiful," he said, voice husky. "Come on, let's go over there."

Standing, he led her to an outcropping where one of the rocky hills so prevalent in this area of the state rose from the earth. It formed a massive, stunning wall, and Angel couldn't help wondering what she must look like as Tonio turned her to face it, hands braced on it, with her legs spread like a sacrificial offering to a god. "I love that even more. Stay just like that for me."

She didn't have to tell him that she wouldn't dream of moving at this point. A flock of hikers coming by couldn't have budged her. Thankfully that wasn't an issue, because her lover spent the next few minutes bringing them both to the boiling point. She was hot, ready to explode.

Kneeling behind her, he spread her ass. Soon his warm tongue was lapping at her hot sex, spearing in and out. Driving her crazy with the need for more. She couldn't believe the whimpering noise was coming from her, but she couldn't stop. Her hips moved in time with his tongue. She began to feel almost feverish.

"Tonio! Please."

"You need my cock, *bonita*?"

"Yes. Fuck me!"

He stood. She heard his zipper and a rustle of denim. The sound of him taking care of the condom wrapper. Then he was spreading her again and pushing into her slick channel, gradually. He went inch by inch, letting her adjust, rotating his hips and moving deeper. Deeper still until he was all the way inside.

"God, you feel so good. So hot and tight around my cock. Do you like this, baby?"

"I love it." Reaching around him, she dug her nails into one of his naked cheeks and urged him on. "Give it to me. Don't hold back."

He practically purred like a big cat. "You want a good, hard fucking?"

"Yes, dammit!"

His laugh rumbled against her back. He pulled his length almost all the way out, then plunged inside firmly. Not hard enough to hurt, but enough to let her know what was coming. Then out, and in again.

Grasping her hips, he set up a rhythm, thrusting inside her heat. Plunging again and again until she swore the delicious slap of their bodies coming together, their moans of pleasure, could be heard for miles. He fucked her until she was nothing but a fiery blaze of flesh. Torn between staying in that twilight state of lust and wanting to blast over the edge.

Release finally won. Her body coiled and she began to shudder. Giving up control, she surrendered to the orgasm that rocked her to the core. Tore her apart and mended her back together. Distantly she was aware of Tonio plunging deep one last time, and holding steady, spasming inside her.

Coming back to her senses was gradual. It was like a veil lifted from her ears, and she suddenly heard the birds again. The whisper of wind through the trees. A few small rocks skittering from above, perhaps dislodged by some small animal. In the distance, a boat on the river.

"Oh my God."

He kissed her temple. "What?"

"I just had outdoor sex. In public."

"Well, yes," he said, laughing. "We both did."

"I guess I can cross that off my bucket list."

"What, you wouldn't do it again?" he asked, pulling from her gently.

"I wouldn't say never." She turned to face him, watching as he stripped the condom, tied it off, and stuck it in his jeans pocket to throw away later. The man was completely open and uninhibited when it came to making love. "If you were caught, you could get fired, though."

"I'd likely just get a reprimand from our captain, unless someone made an issue out of it." He winked. "Don't worry. I'm always careful."

"Always? You bring a lot of women out here to screw their brains out?"

"Um, no. Not at all. Never have before, until now. Guess I stepped into that one, huh?"

"With both feet."

Angel got dressed again, with no time to spare. She was just pulling on her second shoe when a couple of hikers, a man and a woman, walked briskly past them without stopping, giving them a wave and looks of curiosity.

"Wow," she said. "That was a close call. Getting caught doesn't sound quite as much fun once the heat of the moment is gone."

"I'll say. Let's get going before you get us into real trouble."

"Hey!"

He laughed again and led them back down the trail. The sun was sinking toward the horizon by the time they reached the spot where they'd left the blanket. Tonio shook it out and folded it, then carried it to the car.

Once they were on their way, Tonio took her hand as he drove. "Stay with me tonight?"

"That sounds like a good plan."

She really didn't want to be alone in the house with her brother. Not after what she'd learned about her lover. It wasn't that she couldn't keep a secret or thought she'd project any sort of guilt, but she needed time to process what she'd found. To let the truth settle before she faced Rab.

But things didn't go quite according to plan. When they arrived at her place, Rab was home. He glanced up from his spot in Angel's easy chair when they walked in, his interest sharpening as he saw that her companion was Tonio.

"Hey," he said.

"What's up?" Tonio walked over and gave him a knuckle bump.

Angel saw their interaction in a whole new light now, and she wondered how much it cost Tonio to pretend to tolerate her brother. Hell, she could barely do it and they were related.

Leaving them to talk, she went and gathered some things to shove into a bag. A change of clothes, some toiletries. Her phone charger. When she had the few things she needed, she walked back into the living room and braced herself. She had learned to read her brother's moods long ago, and tonight was one of his strange ones. He wasn't pissy, exactly, but sort of smug. Cutting. He liked making her uncomfortable.

"Guess I don't have to ask where you're going," he said.

She wanted to wipe the smirk off his face. "Guess not."

"Weren't you going to fix us any dinner?"

"We already ate, and you're capable of making your own dinner."

"You care about your lay more than your own flesh and blood, huh?" He snorted at the expression on her face.

"Come on, baby, don't give your brother a hassle. We're not in that big a hurry, so be a good girl and make him something to eat." Tonio delivered a resounding slap to her ass and winked.

Yelping, she shot him a burning glare. Rab hooted with laughter, expression radiating approval at his friend's actions.

"That's how you handle a woman," Rab said, chuckling. He waggled his beer at Tonio. "Sit. Take off a load. Angel, get the man a beer."

She knew what Tonio was doing, but that didn't make it burn any less to cater to Rab as though she were totally insignificant. Stewing, she resolved to play her part and stalked into the kitchen. After fetching a beer for Tonio, she got started making sandwiches for the men. Giving in didn't mean her asshole brother was getting a five-star meal.

Heading back into the living room with two paper plates, she handed them to the men and took up a spot next to Tonio on the sofa. The two guys were already into a conversation when she settled in, and Rab hardly acknowledged her offering as they ate and continued their talk.

"My old man was in for sixteen years before he was iced inside," Rab said, apparently in answer to Tonio's question. "Someone bigger and meaner than him shanked him in the heart." Angel winced, but Rab wasn't the least bit bothered.

"You ever get retribution?" Tonio asked.

Rab laughed, but there was no humor in the sound. "Knowing me, you'd think that would be my first course of action, right?"

Tonio's answer was careful. "I'd think so, yeah."

"It would've been, if my father had been in my corner, on my side, even once," he said in a low, deadly voice. "As it was, I wish I could've sent his killer a thank-you card."

"That's cold, Rab."

Her brother's eyes glittered with malice. "My father

was a cold man. Except when he was using me as his whipping boy—he was pretty heated then. Whenever he was pissed about something, he'd take it out on me. Angel remembers, don't you?"

Angel stared at him. "I remember him using his belt on you sometimes."

"His belt?" he repeated, incredulous. "That's all?"

"What did he do, man?" Tonio's expression was neutral.

"He'd take me to the basement, strip off my shirt and pants. Whip me bloody," he said quietly. "A few times he chained me down there in the winter, made me sleep without heat or a blanket. Sometimes he forced me to drink weird shit, but it was the antifreeze that almost killed me."

"What?" Angel gasped.

"You didn't know, did you?" Her brother eyed her, then nodded. "But good old Mom did, and she didn't do anything to stop him."

Angel was speechless. Never had she heard these stories from Rab before. He'd never opened up about the abuse their father had heaped on him, until now.

"She was afraid of him," Angel said helplessly.

"So was I." Rab gave a shaky laugh.

Scooting over, she reached for her brother for the first time in years. "I never knew it was that bad, I swear."

Standing, he avoided her touch. "Fuck this caring and sharing shit. Go on, both of you. Get lost."

She really didn't appreciate the tone, considering it was her house to leave or not as she chose. But Tonio's hand on her arm gave a gentle warning not to tangle with the bastard, and she backed off, though it chapped her ass to do so.

On the way out, she shut the door harder than she intended and fumed all the way to Tonio's car. "It's not his fucking house."

"I know. Just a little longer and he'll be back in Club Fed before you know it."

"It's really sad that I'm glad about that."

"You know what I think? That you're more upset about finding out what your father did to him than you're letting on."

Tears pricked her eyes. "Could I have made a difference?"

"You were just a kid," he said. "Your mother is the one who could've made a real difference, had she found the courage."

"It makes me sad," she whispered. "Rab could've turned out to be a better man."

"I know, sweetheart." He took her hand, squeezing it.

A short time later, he parked in front of his place. As he unlocked the door and let them in, something occurred to her. "This isn't really your place at all, is it?"

He made a disgusted face. "No, thank God. I have a house in Sugarland, and while it's not fancy, it's much nicer than this."

"This apartment never struck me as you. There's nothing personal, like rugs and pillows or soap dispensers or knickknacks. The stuff that makes it a home."

"Well, that's something it'll never be. I can't wait to take you to my real place. I think you'll like it."

"You talk as if that will actually happen."

"Why wouldn't it?" His lips curved into a smile. "If you want, I'll show it to you one day soon."

"I'd like that, very much."

"Want to watch a movie? I'll make us some popcorn."

"Snuggling with my favorite lawman? Sounds like fun."

His expression morphed into worry. "Angel, you have to be careful not to say those kinds of things. One slip and—"

"I know. I'm sorry. I just thought since we're here alone, it was okay to speak freely."

"First, never assume you're alone. There can always be someone watching and listening, through a bug or some other method."

A chill slithered through her. "That's a bit too cloak-and-dagger for me to believe."

"But true whether you believe it or not."

Walking into the kitchen, he dug a bag of microwave popcorn out of the pantry. In no time, they were on the sofa watching *Die Hard*, Angel curled into Tonio's side. In spite of John McClane swaggering all over the screen and blowing the building to pieces to take out the bad guys, her eyelids grew heavy.

It wasn't long before the day caught up with her, and sleep dragged her under.

Tonio felt Angel relax against him. Was it selfish of him to breathe a sigh of relief? Because the fact that she trusted him so completely blew his mind. He didn't know what he'd done yet to deserve it, but she did. He was going to work hard to make sure he earned it.

His cell phone ringing was almost drowned out by the movie. Lowering the volume on the TV, he answered the second he saw it was from Chris. "Hey, man. I was going to call you soon. There's been a development."

"Yeah, there's been one here, too."

"You first."

He sighed. "Angel Silva knows I'm a cop."

"What? How the hell did that happen?" his friend said, voice rising. "Was it the text you were afraid she'd seen?"

"That, and I had told her something about my brother's accident. She found the actual story on the Internet—along with this great picture of me in a different article. Whoever was in charge of making sure that stuff stayed buried obviously fell asleep."

"Goddamn. Is she going to be a problem?"

"No."

A pause. "You're sure about that?"

"Yes. I'd stake my life on it."

"Let's hope it doesn't come to that."

"So, what's your news? I hope it's a hell of a lot better than mine."

"I found out what's in that warehouse your dubious leader has such a hard-on about hitting. It belongs to Global Life Pharmaceuticals. It's stocked floor to ceiling with prescription drugs, and because of that, it's only slightly less impenetrable than Fort Knox."

"Jesus," Tonio muttered. "So Rab's sources were wrong about the lack of guards."

"Pathetically. There is absolutely no freaking way he's getting into that building and out again without getting all his men killed."

"Fantastic."

"There may be a bright spot, though," Chris said cheerfully. "If we can get a witness and some DNA, we may be able to get him on murdering Sharon Waite."

"That would be a better bust," Tonio agreed. "But just because she was found near Stan's body doesn't mean he killed her, and dumped her near him."

"Come on, Tone. He returned to the scene. Probably didn't even think about it twice, just did it."

"Maybe. Fingers crossed."

"Yeah. All right, that's all I've got for now. Touch base later."

"Later."

Chris hung up and Tonio relaxed some. They were going to get Rab and throw his ass back in prison. Angel would be free of that scum.

One way or another.

Tess wasn't thinking about dying when she answered the motel room door.

She was supposed to be safe there. She'd changed motels as she'd told Harold she would, so it made no sense that Rab was standing in her doorway, staring at her. And this time she didn't have Tonio as a buffer between them.

She was well trained, self-sufficient. Far from helpless. Yet there was something that froze her in front of this man now, like a rabbit in front of a snake. There was something horrible in his eyes, and as she tried to close the door in his face, he stuck his foot in it to stop her. Then he pushed inside and shut it behind him.

Her sidearm was in her hand in an instant as she yanked it from the waistband of her jeans, but he was even faster. Lunging forward, he grabbed her hand and twisted, overpowering her easily and taking the weapon. His grin was vicious as he waved the gun in front of her face.

"Was sitting around watching a little television tonight," he said. "One of those cop shows."

"Yeah? So?" Her smart-ass persona didn't work on him tonight. Her heart was pounding.

"The cop was following the suspect around. You ever do that?" He began stalking her. Backing her up slowly.

"I don't know what you're talking about."

"Don't!" he shouted, making her jump. Then his voice softened. "Don't lie to me. I saw the SUV following me."

"I don't know what you're talking about, or why you'd think it was me—"

"'Cause it occurred to be that I've seen an SUV just like that parked outside this motel in the last couple of days."

*Oh God.* "What the hell, Rab? Everyone drives those nowadays."

"But not all of them keep expensive guns on them." He crowded in close. "What else will I find? Hmm?"

Grabbing her arm, he dragged her to the nightstand, then let go of her arm. With his free hand, he tangled his fingers in her hair, yanking it painfully. "Open the drawer!"

She did, and when he found nothing but the motel Bible, he became even angrier. "Your suitcase. Dump it. Everything."

"Okay! Stop pulling my hair!"

A resounding smack in the cheekbone with the gun hand made pain explode in her face, and her ears ring. She dumped the contents of the suitcase, and then her duffel. Her heart pounded as her electronics were spread out on the bed. Zipped up in her Kindle case was the one thing she absolutely couldn't let him find.

But disaster happened anyway.

"Open that."

"No."

"Do it!" Another smack, and her head snapped to the side.

Tears welling, she unzipped the case and flipped it open to reveal the black leather wallet inside. With clenched jaw, Rab leaned down and fingered open the wallet—to reveal her shield from the Federal Bureau of Investigation.

"Well played, Agent. But I like my plays better."

With that, he shoved her onto the bed and began hitting her face, ribs, anywhere he could reach. Her best defense moves were like trying to swat an elephant, he was so big. Strong. He used that against her now, and the pain was all that was keeping her conscious.

At last he drew back. Cracked his knuckles and stretched as if nothing had happened. She was sprawled on the bed, unmoving. Watching him through bleary eyes. He went through the rest of her stuff and found her notes. As she lay there barely able to suck in a breath, she knew the exact moment he'd found the other thing she never wanted him to know. Cold rage washed over his face.

He looked as though he was turning to leave.

But then he turned around and raised his arm. And fired.

The bullet struck her chest and seized her breath. Flames of hell engulfed her as he casually wiped his prints from the weapon, dropped it onto the bed, and then walked out the door.

She had to get help. Reach the phone.

Rolling was agony. Blood was pouring from the wound in her chest. Reaching, she knocked the motel phone off the hook. She used that one instead of her own cell phone—if she passed out, or worse, then the cops would find her quicker.

Finally she wrapped her fingers around the receiver. Lifted it and punched 9-1-1. A man's voice answered, asking her to state her emergency, and she rasped, "Been shot."

"Where on your body have you been shot?"

"Chest. 'M at the Bent Tree Motel, r-room one twenty."

"What's your name?"

"Agent Tess Riley, FBI."

"Just stay with me, Agent. Help is on the way. Remain on the line, okay?"

"Listen," she whispered, struggling to make each word clear. "Detective Tonio Salvatore . . . warn him."

"Detective Salvatore?"

"Yes."

"Warn him? What about?"

"Rab knows."

"I'm sorry. Who's Rab?"

"Rab Silva . . . Just tell him . . . to run. Hurry."

She'd done all she could. Message delivered, she surrendered to the darkness.

# 10

An insistent buzzing woke Tonio. When it wouldn't go away, he spied his personal cell phone by the bed, lit up with an incoming call.

For a few seconds he considered ignoring it. But middle-of-the-night calls never boded well, and years of experience had him instantly awake and sitting on the side of the bed. He only hoped he didn't wake Angel.

"What is it?" he asked his partner. Chris responded with a few simple, terrifying words.

"Rab knows! Your cover is blown, get out of there now!"

Bolting to his feet, he turned on the bedside light and shook Angel as he barked into the phone, "What the fuck? How?"

"He paid a visit to Tess. Did you know she's a goddamn FBI agent?"

"What the shit? And nobody told us?"

"Right? Listen, he beat the fuck out of her tonight and then shot her in the chest. They don't know if she's going to survive. She had notes at the motel, and some of them were on you. At some point she found out you're a cop, and Rab saw the notes."

"Okay. I'm getting Angel out of here. Plan A like we discussed."

"Stay safe and call me when you get clear of the city."

He hung up to see Angel sitting up, yawning. "What's going on?"

"Rab knows I'm a cop. We've got to get out of town." Quickly he started pulling on clothes. "Get dressed and grab your overnight bag."

"Where are we going?" she asked, jumping out of bed.

"To my cousin's lake cabin in Texas."

"Why not just go to another cop's house or something? I'm sure you have plenty of police protection."

"And endanger their families? No way. We just need to get gone right now, but we'll come back when he's caught and things have cooled off."

In less than five minutes, they were ready to go, because Tonio had kept a bug-out bag ready. He did a quick check of his weapon, then tucked it into his jeans. Shouldering his bag and hers, he took her hand and pulled her outside. They jogged toward his car in the wee hours, only their footfalls making an eerie echo in the night.

But the noise of a car engine was fast approaching. Tonio shoved her toward his car as Rab's flew around the corner and skidded to a halt a few yards away. The driver's door opened and Rab jumped out, yelling.

"Angel, he's a cop! Get away from him!"

But Angel dove into the passenger's side of Tonio's

ride, and Tonio saw the moment it became clear in Rab's head.

"She knew?" he screamed.

"Rab, leave her out of this!"

"And you! I thought you were my friend!" His expression was truly anguished. "You weren't like the other guys. I told you shit I've never told anybody, and you betrayed me!"

"Rab, let's talk about—"

The other man opened fire, and the bullets pinged off the metal of the old car. Cursing, Tonio lunged for the driver's seat and started the vehicle, revving the motor once. Then he took off, rubber squealing, Rab in hot pursuit.

More bullets hit the car. A couple cracked the back window and he swerved, trying to keep the bastard from scoring a direct hit to the back of his head. Tonio raced up I-49 as fast as he dared, trying to navigate the winding road through the hill in the dark, certain he'd drive off a cliff any second.

The chase went on. Rab was relentless. Tonio managed to put some distance between them at times, but Rab would always catch up. The bullets were flying less frequently as Rab waited for better opportunities to use them.

As bad luck would have it, he found one.

There was a pop, and Tonio swerved, trying to regain control of the car. But a ton of steel was skidding sideways and he couldn't get it corrected. The tires left the road and the car shot down into a ditch, bumping violently until it slammed to a stop.

"Are you all right?" Immediately he felt for Angel in the darkness, touching her arm.

"Yeah, I think so."

"Okay. Let's go before he gets down here."

They jumped out and Tonio took a second to grab his bag, slinging it over his shoulder. In it was a flashlight, but he wouldn't risk using it until he was sure he'd lost Rab. Crashing noises sounded from above them and he grabbed her hand, whispering, "Hurry."

There was just no being totally silent when fleeing through the hilly forest of Tennessee. But he guided them as quietly as possible, deeper into the woods, careful where he placed his steps. Out here, one wrong move could mean plunging a long ways to your death. Or at the very least, twisting or breaking a limb.

Every so often, he stopped them and they would listen intently. It seemed the sounds of Rab's pursuit were getting farther away, but Tonio still couldn't risk the light from his phone or flashlight yet. So he pushed on, his goal to find them a good place to bunk down for the night.

"Do you think he gave up?" Angel whispered.

"Maybe, for now. But only temporarily. We can't be sure, though, which is why we need to find shelter and wait for our chance to circle back to the car in the morning."

"Won't he be waiting for us to do that?"

"I don't know. If he is, that might not be a bad thing."

"What? Are you crazy?"

He smiled, even though she couldn't see him. "My car and my bag both have tracking devices in them. Even now, my partner can see that we've gone off course and my car isn't moving. They'll be out here investigating soon, and if he hangs around, Chris will catch him."

"God, I hope so."

*Before Rab gets to us.*

They had walked for more than half an hour when Tonio spotted a dark place in the side of the hill. Leading her along the slight incline, he saw what he'd been hoping for—a cave. The entrance wasn't too overgrown, and they easily stepped inside, though they had to stoop a bit. Here Tonio finally had to break down and use his flashlight. But not before listening to the night sounds return to normal outside the cave for a good long while before digging it from his bag and switching it on.

"It's pretty clean," Angel said.

"Yeah. It's perfect for tonight. Let's make us a place to sleep."

He didn't think either of them believed for a minute they'd get much sleep, considering how nervous they were. Tonio was exhausted, but wired, too. Resting just wasn't an option for a while.

From his bag, he pulled out a thermal blanket. It wasn't much, but it would keep them warm in the chilly, damp cave overnight. There wasn't anything to use for pillows, so he provided a couple of his rolled-up shirts for that.

"This won't be the height of comfort, but you can sleep on top of me if you want," he said.

"Don't tempt me. If I do that we might not hear danger approaching because I'll be ravishing you."

Snorting a laugh, he settled in and then lifted the

blanket for her. She crawled in and he covered them, then settled her in his arms. The hard ground was less than ideal, but for now they were safe. He switched off the flashlight, plunging them into darkness.

They were quiet for a time. Tonio thought she must've fallen asleep, and soon he did as well. The next thing he knew, the world was coming awake outside their small hideaway. The sun was just barely up, and the birds were starting to chirp. Angel was a solid lump on his chest, and he didn't mind. But the hard-packed dirt floor under his back was another matter.

Shifting a bit, he eased her off to the side and left her under the blanket while he went to check out their surroundings. In the light of day, he saw they were in a beautiful valley, with rolling hills, rock, and forest stretching all around. He had a rough idea from which direction they'd come, but they'd have a long walk back.

Stirring came from behind him, then arms wrapped around his middle. "It's beautiful out here."

"It is. We're going to get to enjoy it a little longer as we hike through there trying to figure out where we left the car."

"Awesome. Not."

He turned to face her. "Are you up for the walk?"

"I'll be fine. It wasn't that bad last night."

"We were running on pure adrenaline then," he pointed out.

"I'm good. Just lead the way."

Quickly he packed the blanket and flashlight again. In minutes, they'd relieved themselves behind some bushes, used some hand wipes, and eaten a couple of meal bars. Then they were ready to go.

They really had gone farther than he'd believed. It seemed like they'd trudged forever before the scenery started to look familiar, though it was hard to tell, having only seen it in the dark. He had started to ask Angel whether she knew which way they should go when a noise reached his ears. Holding up a hand, he stopped them both and motioned her to silence.

Tonio listened. Those were definitely footsteps coming through the forest ahead, and more than one set. Had Rab gone back to get his men? Palming his gun, he grabbed Angel and pulled her back into a stand of trees. The cover wasn't perfect, but it would have to do. They crouched and waited. His pulse spiked when a body became visible. He leveled his weapon—

And sagged in relief.

"Chris," he called. "Over here."

His partner's gaze shot to their hiding place, and relief swept over his features. "Thank fuck! I thought maybe that bastard had shot you both and buried you out here where I'd never find you."

"Um." Tonio darted a pointed look at Angel. Immediately Chris realized his error.

"My apologies, Miss Silva," he said contritely. "I shouldn't have used that word to describe your brother."

"None needed, Detective. He *is* a bastard and he was shooting at us." Angel looked shaken to the core by that knowledge. Tonio wanted to kill Rab for that alone. "And call me Angel."

"Only if you call me Chris."

"Okay, Chris. Can you get us out of here?"

"With pleasure." As they started walking, Chris added, "And I have some news—not so great, I'm afraid. Rab hasn't been apprehended yet. But when he is, he'll be charged with one count each of attempted murder of a federal agent and of a police officer."

"All right. So it looks like we stick with the plan and get out of town for a while."

"That would be smart."

"And will the one charge remain attempted murder? Is Tess going to survive?"

"Looks like she might. They're a lot more hopeful now."

Angel caught up with that part of the conversation. "Wait. What? Tess is an FBI agent? What the fuck?"

After Tonio filled her in, she said, "I can't believe that. She was using you all along to get to Rab, just like you were her." She shook her head.

Tonio flushed but didn't say anything. There was no good answer that wouldn't get him in hot water, so he figured silence was golden.

Back at his car, he was glad to discover that Chris had called for a tow truck to pull it out of the ditch. They'd also changed the tire, so they were good to go.

Chris came up and clapped him on the shoulder. "Take it easy. I'll let you know when we have Silva. With any luck, it'll be soon."

"Thanks, man. I'm counting on it."

They said their good-byes and Tonio helped a clearly worn-out Angel into his car. Then he got in and started the ignition.

"Where are we going?"

"To my cousin Vincent's cabin in Texas. It's fully stocked with food, secluded, and the lake is gorgeous. We can take turns sleeping, eating, and making love for as long as we're there."

She sent him a tired but happy smile. "That sounds like the best idea I've ever heard. I'll call Andy and arrange for him to be in charge for a few days."

"Good deal."

Tonio pointed the car west and headed out of town. They had the few things they'd packed, and anything else they needed they could pick up later.

Was it wrong to look forward to days of bliss with the woman he was falling for?

Yes, he was falling hard for this woman. She'd slipped under his defenses with ease, and he found he didn't care. A few days would indeed be sheer heaven.

But they were the last days of peace either of them would know for a long while.

"How long is the drive to your cousin's cabin?" Angel studied Tonio's profile. He looked big, strong, and capable. The muscles of his forearms flexed as he drove, and his T-shirt was stretched enticingly across his chest.

"Twelve hours, give or take. There's a Walmart in town before we get to the cabin, so we'll stop there first for a few more things."

"Okay." She was silent for a moment. "Thank you for doing this for me."

He glanced at her. "I'm protecting a witness. I'd do that for anyone."

A bite of disappointment went through her initially. But then she thought about it and disagreed. "I'm not *really* a witness, since I'm not privy to Rab's dealings. And anyway, I think driving your witness to Texas is a bit above and beyond the call of duty."

A grin curved his sinful mouth, and he shrugged. "You caught me. I just wanted to get you alone in a remote cabin so I can have my way with you."

"That's much better," she said huskily, touching his shoulder. "I like the way you think."

"Then you'll like my brain even better, later."

She shivered a little, thinking of having him all to herself. Her cop. She thought about that as they rode in companionable silence for a while. Inevitably, though, her thoughts turned to how Tonio was much different than the criminal she'd believed him to be when they met. He was magnetic before. Charming, irresistible, sexy.

But now, knowing he was a man of integrity on top of all that? Surely a man such as Tonio had women everywhere in his real life as a cop, panting after him. The idea was not a pleasant one.

"So," she began. "Has there been anyone special in your life?"

For a long moment, she thought he wouldn't answer. When he did, his reply was brief and mysterious.

"There was, once."

When he didn't add more, she asked, "What happened?"

A muscle in his jaw jumped and his hands tightened on the steering wheel. "Suffice it to say it didn't work out."

"Okay." From his tone, the subject wasn't a welcome one. And it didn't sound as if there had been anyone since, if *once* was any indication. "Yeah, I haven't had much luck myself." Hopefully that was changing.

"I find that hard to believe."

"It's true. Oh, I've had a couple of serious boyfriends, but neither of them worked out. We didn't want the same things out of life. The last one wanted me to sell my bar."

He shot her a glance. "Why?"

"I think my being a business owner threatened his masculinity, to be honest. He said his job as an auto mechanic was enough to sustain us both. He wanted me at home, taking care of the house and him."

Tonio snorted. "Let me guess how that went over."

"Not so well. I broke up with him, but he was having a tough time taking *no* for an answer. At least until Rab got out of prison and scared him off. That was probably the only real favor he ever did for me."

At the mention of Rab's name, conversation lapsed for a while. Angel cursed herself for bringing his name into casual conversation, but it was hard to avoid him altogether. Like it or not, he was her brother.

The ride to Texas was long, but the day passed pleasantly enough. They talked, stopped for gas, and then found a decent restaurant and ate a late lunch. Bellies full, they set off once again.

The sun was dipping toward the horizon by the time they rolled into the small East Texas town of Sage, which was just big enough to boast a gas station, a KFC, a Taco Bell, and a Walmart. And damn little else.

At the gas station, Tonio topped off the tank and then

it was on to Walmart. They spent about half an hour adding to their collection of underwear and socks, plus more jeans, T-shirts, snacks, and a few more toiletries. When they checked out, Tonio paid for everything, flatly refusing to take any of her money.

Giving in, she followed him out to the car and helped him load their bags. Then they were off again.

"How far is the cabin from here?" she asked.

"About twenty minutes. It's been a couple of years since I was there, but I remember the directions. Vinny's got a nice place."

"So he doesn't live there full-time?"

"No. It's a getaway cabin for weekends and holidays. His family uses it. He's married, has a wife and two teenage sons."

"That's great. I always wanted a weekend place," she said wistfully. "Maybe someday."

Tonio gave her a smile. "If you want it badly enough, you can make it happen. You just have to work toward the goal every day."

"Easier said than done."

"But not impossible."

"I suppose not."

The drive got bumpy once they turned off the main road. Night had fallen as well, making the woods on either side of the car seem extra creepy. But when the trees cleared out, a big log cabin came into view, illuminated by a security light. A few lights had been left on inside, she guessed for their arrival. Beyond the cabin, a few yards behind it, a wide lake glittered in the moonlight.

"It's beautiful," she breathed.

"Isn't it? I'll admit, I'm always a little jealous when I visit. I wouldn't mind having a place like this either, though I don't think I'd build my cabin quite so big."

"It's huge!"

"Well, Vinny has a family of four, plus his and his wife's folks, and numerous friends. They love to entertain, especially in the summer. When we have family get-togethers, the place is full, trust me."

"Is he a Salvatore?"

"No. He's a Lopez, from my mother's side. Vinny is her brother's son. That's why we're safe here—nobody will be able track us down."

"That makes me feel better."

"Me, too."

Carrying everything inside took a few trips. They got the snacks settled in the kitchen and then took their personal belongings into the house. Angel followed Tonio down the hallway, and as she did it hit her to wonder where she'd sleep. She wanted to be with him but didn't want to presume that they would stay together, even after last night.

He solved her inner dilemma by pointing to the room at the end of the hall. "You take the master. It's got the biggest en suite bath and the view over the lake is stunning."

"Okay. Where will you sleep?"

He jerked his thumb at a doorway to his right. "In this bedroom. It's just as comfortable and has its own bathroom, too. I'll be close by in case you need anything."

She studied him, trying to decide whether to read anything into those words. His dark gaze seemed to smolder, but he didn't say more. She let that thread drop for the moment. "All right. You hungry? It's been a while since our late lunch."

"I could eat a bite."

She'd bet a big man like him needed constant input. "I'll see if there's some stuff for sandwiches, if that's okay?"

"Sounds great. But you're not going to do all the cooking while we're here," he stressed. "I believe in doing my fair share, even in the kitchen."

"That's great, because I wasn't planning on waiting on you hand and foot." She smiled to soften the words, and he grinned back.

"Good." Giving her a gentle kiss, he pulled back almost reluctantly. "Let's get our stuff situated, and then we can hang out for a while before bed."

After she put her things away, she padded to the kitchen and found makings for roast beef sandwiches. Ciabatta bread was a nice find, so she split the pieces and toasted them. Then she added roast beef, Swiss cheese, lettuce, tomato, and mustard and cut each sandwich in half. She'd just finished adding chips as garnish when Tonio strode in and whistled.

"Wow. I wasn't expecting deli-quality food. That looks delicious."

"Let's get comfortable in the living room while we eat. Want to see what we can get on the television?"

"He carries cable, since they use the place quite a bit. Want to find a movie?"

"Sounds good."

Tonio fiddled with the TV and soon they were cuddled together, munching on their dinner and watching *French Kiss*, one of Angel's favorite movies. She laughed out loud, especially at Kevin Kline declaring, "You people make my ass twitch!" It was funny no matter how many times she saw it.

And every time she laughed, Tonio laughed along with her, squeezing her tight. Sometimes he'd kiss her on top of her head, or on her lips. Sometimes his kisses would linger, and they'd savor each other, taking a bit to get back into the movie.

When it was over, he said, "I didn't know you had a soft spot for romantic comedies."

"I do. I guess I'm a romantic at heart."

"I had you figured as more of an action and adventure type of girl."

"Why's that?"

He brushed her arm with his fingers. "The bad-girl tat. The attitude. That outer shell of toughness you show the world."

"Hmm. Well, that's all true, and I do like the action, blood-and-guts movies. But I'm a closet softy."

"Guess what."

"What?"

"Me, too," he whispered into her lips.

Taking her hand, he pulled her off the couch and down onto the rug in front of the large stone fireplace. She felt a pang of regret that the weather wasn't cold enough to light the fire, but that was soon forgotten as he started to undress her.

Soon she was naked and spread on her back, watching as he rid himself of his clothes. As planes of muscles were revealed, she almost drooled. The man was damn near perfection. Crouched on his knees, taut skin rippling, his cock jutted proudly from between his thighs. Her sex grew moist as she imagined having him, taking what he offered.

Scooting between her legs, he touched her sex. Spread the moisture, thumbed her clit until she writhed at the attention. She loved being open to him like this, him watching. Touching, taking his fill.

At last he reached for his jeans and removed a square package from the front pocket. He ripped it open and sheathed himself quickly, then moved into position over her.

Slowly he parted her center and slid home. Wrapping her arms around him, fingers stroking his back, she marveled at how much it felt like this man was right where he should be when he was inside her. Like he was home.

He began to move, making love to her. His motions were slow and sweet, his strokes gradually building the fire inside her higher and higher. To a fever pitch. She clung to him, crying out, urging him faster, and he gladly gave her what she wanted. What they both desired.

His thrusts were fast as he held her close. He drove deep, and she began to come undone.

Her orgasm exploded and she called his name, riding the waves of bliss. He followed a few strokes afterward, shuddering against her until they were both spent and heaving gulps of air.

"Damn, lady," he said reverently. "You drive me insane."

"In a good way, I hope."

"You know it."

Giving her a quick kiss, he eased out of her and rid himself of the condom. Plucking several tissues from the box on the end table, he handed some to her and then cleaned himself, and wrapped up the used rubber. He pulled on his jeans but didn't button them or bother with any other clothing. She simply gathered hers.

He arched an eyebrow. "You going naked the rest of the night? Not that I mind."

"I'm just going to bed anyway. Why bother to dress?" She shrugged.

"So, um . . . do you really want to sleep in separate bedrooms?" He looked a little sheepish as he grinned.

"Of course not! I thought you did, so I was going to respect that."

"I was trying to respect you," he pointed out.

"Well, too much respect is overrated. Snuggling is much better."

"I agree."

So much for separate beds. A few minutes later, washed up and wrapped in Tonio's arms in the huge bed in the master bedroom, she found herself more content than she'd been in a long time.

Perhaps ever.

That was something that bore serious thought. In the morning.

Sleep claimed her in moments.

Morning brought a lazy bout of lovemaking. Then a playful shower full of soap and lots of laughter.

Afterward, they cooked breakfast together, and it hit

Angel that she could get used to this domestic heaven real fast. But was Tonio even the staying-around type? He'd alluded to a past relationship that hadn't worked out, and didn't seem inclined to talk about it. Or relationships in general.

Maybe his passing through her life, on this case, was simply that. When he was done, he'd go back to his own life and she to hers. That idea dimmed her happiness some.

"What's wrong?" he asked between bites of his pancakes.

She tried to shake off the sudden melancholy. "Nothing. Just wondering what we're going to do all day. Any ideas?"

He thought about that. "Actually I have one. Ever been fishing?"

"A few times, but not in years. Is there a boat?"

"Yep. He's got a nice one down at the slip. When we're done here we can go see what fishing supplies he's got and take her out for a while, if you want."

"Sounds fun," she said, her enthusiasm returning. "I don't know how much I'll catch, but trying should be interesting."

Once the kitchen was clean, they donned light jackets and went down to the pier on the edge of the water. Over the lake was a rather nice boathouse with a deck on top. Underneath the deck a sleek boat was raised out of the water on a hydraulic lift system.

"Keeps the hull clean, and keeps it from being damaged in bad weather," Tonio explained.

"You know how to work the lift thing?"

"I'll figure it out."

He laughed at her dubious look and went to work. It wasn't long before he did indeed have the boat lowered into the water and readied for the trip. There was plenty of fishing gear, which he took from storage in the boathouse and secured on the boat. After that, he made a trip back to the house for bottled water and snacks, fitted them both in life vests, and then they were on their way.

For a while they simply cruised around the lake, and Angel imagined that the wind rushing past was cleansing her of all her troubles. Just whisking them away, into the air, where they'd never be seen again. It was a nice thought.

About an hour later, he found a quiet cove and anchored in the middle of it. Then he fixed her rod and reel with a spinner lure and had her practice casting close to the shoreline. She got the hang of it pretty quickly.

"Looking good," he praised.

She flushed with pleasure. This was quite possibly, she realized, the very first positive male relationship she'd ever formed. She found herself extremely reluctant to give that up should the time come.

That brought her back to the conversation about his past. Steeling her nerve, she broached the subject again.

"Who hurt you so badly?" she asked in a soft voice. "Will you tell me?"

His heart gave a painful lurch. Even after all this time. "What makes you think someone hurt me?"

"It's in your eyes. I saw it when you mentioned the relationship that didn't work out. There's this sadness when you think no one's looking. But I notice people and their reactions. It's part of my job, honed from years of tending bar."

He could've lied. Or put her off. But he must've decided he was ready to talk, to confide in her.

"My fiancée left me at the altar several years ago. Ran off with my best friend. Isn't that just like a bad movie?" His expression was sad.

She couldn't imagine a more painful betrayal, and her heart went out to him. Reaching out, she grabbed his hand. "I'm so sorry. And I'd never make light of it." She paused. "Are they still together?"

"On the other side, I suppose." He wanted to throw up.

"What?" She stilled. "You mean they're dead?"

"Almost since the beginning," he said quietly.

"Can you talk about it?"

"I can now. I just don't, much." He took a deep breath. "When I found out, I went nuts for a while. Drove straight to my friend's house. Left over two hundred guests just sitting there, and went over fully intending to kill him."

"Oh no."

"Yeah. I didn't find him that day because they'd skipped out together and eloped. But several weeks later, they were coming out of a diner when I saw them. Danny and I got into a huge fight. Or rather, I screamed at them and they took it. I was so heartbroken, and angry. I yelled at them that I hoped they both rotted in hell."

She squeezed him tight, lending her quiet strength. "Then what happened?"

"Danny peeled out of the parking lot and headed out of town, driving way too fast. I heard through the grapevine they had been arguing from the start, every day. That day they were fighting after they left me at the diner, according to Rachel's sister. Rachel called her just before Danny lost control of his car and hit a tree. The police said they died on impact."

The words were choked by the end of his story. The measure of pain and guilt he still carried was etched on his face.

"You can't blame yourself for that," she said, leaning over to kiss him. "A lot of people say things they don't mean, and your words didn't cause the wreck."

"Rationally I know that. But my head and my heart tell me two different things."

"It's not your fault."

"I know. But I wish I could change what I said, how I reacted, and I can't."

It obviously still hurt him so much. It was no wonder he hadn't sustained a close relationship with another woman since. Would he ever be ready to take that step again?

Would he take it with her?

Throughout that day, and the idyllic ones that followed, it was a question that haunted her night and day.

Because she was falling hopelessly in love with Tonio Salvatore.

On their fourth day at the lake, the call came.

Tonio had been both anticipating and dreading the inevitable. Chris's name appeared on the screen of his cell phone and he sighed as he thumbed it to accept the call. "Hey. You got news."

"The best," Chris said cheerfully. "Rab Silva is in custody, charged with attempted murder of a federal agent and your attempted murder, too."

"Tess is going to make it?"

"Looks like. Rab's going away, though. And if we can pin him with Sharon Waite's murder, he'll never see the light of day again."

"Nothing back on that yet?"

"Not yet, but soon. I hope."

"I won't hold my breath."

"You heading back?"

Tonio checked the time. "It's getting late. We'll stay tonight and head back in the morning."

"Things going okay with Angel?"

"Yeah," he said, and couldn't help smiling. "Things are good."

"I'm glad. You deserve to be happy."

"Well, I don't know if it's getting that serious—"

"Shut it, man. You can't hear how you sound, but I do. Loud and clear. I know what happy sounds like, and it's you."

*"Dios."*

"Whatever. Deny it all you want, but the truth will come out."

"Hanging up now, Chris."

"See you in a couple of days. Rainey said to take a day or two before you come in to work. Make sure you're fresh."

"I'll rest a day. See you day after tomorrow."

"Later."

Hanging up, he walked out to the back deck and found

Angel sunning in a lounger. She took one look at him, phone still in hand, and was instantly on alert.

"What is it? What's happened?" she asked anxiously, sitting up.

"Rab's in custody."

She sagged, putting a hand over her face. Immediately he went to her and sat beside her on the lounger, gathering her into his arms. "You okay?"

"Yeah." She sniffed. "I'm glad he's off the street, and I'm sad, too."

"He's your brother. That's understandable."

"I wish things were different with him."

"I know, baby."

What else could he say? He'd been blessed with a wonderful family and awesome siblings. He'd never been through what Angel had suffered with her dysfunctional family from hell.

He held her close for a long time, then guided her inside and made them a simple dinner of pasta and salad. Afterward he sent her to soak in a hot bath while he cleaned the kitchen, and she didn't utter a word of protest. Testament to how upset she was.

Later he got her out of the bath and carefully dried her off, then tucked her into bed, wrapped tightly in his arms. One caress led to another and he made love to her one last time before their enforced vacation came to an end.

When they were both sated and she was asleep on his chest, he mused at how much he was going to miss being here, with Angel. How much it would hurt to leave tomorrow and go back to his life.

Suddenly he knew there was absolutely no way Angel was going back to her life without him being a part of it. He couldn't fathom that at all, and refused to even consider it.

There was no point in denying he was falling in love with Angel, and he didn't want to run.

Not this time. He'd fight with everything he had. He would die before he allowed Angel to get away. But that wouldn't be necessary.

This time, Tonio wasn't going to be the loser.

# 11

The days of lazing at the wonderful lake house and making love were just about as close to heaven as Angel had ever been.

She had left the bar in Andy's capable hands, and in the following days made the realization that she'd been working far too much and not enjoying life nearly enough. Of course it helped to actually have a significant someone to share that life with. It was easy to fall into work when that was all you had.

As much as she loved Stroker's, she loved being with Tonio even more. Sure, they'd have to go back to their jobs. She and Tonio had bills to pay. And even if the bar was self-sufficient, she had to have something to occupy her time or she'd go crazy.

After returning from Texas the day before, she'd been enjoying her day with Tonio at his house when their peace was interrupted by the sound of a car in the driveway. They looked up from their coffee and smiled at each other. Fifteen minutes sooner and their visitor would've caught them in a compromising position.

Tonio answered the knock and let in Chris. Their greeting died when they saw his grim expression.

"What is it?" Tonio demanded.

"Rab has escaped."

With those three words, her world was knocked off its foundations. Tonio's hand steadied her. "When?" she asked. "How?"

"A short time ago. He overpowered a police escort and escaped with the man's weapon. We've had a report of Rab being seen with Phil and Enrique, but that hasn't been confirmed."

Tonio let out a stream of curses, his expression murderous. "That wouldn't surprise me. For some reason, they're loyal to him. I have yet to figure out why."

"In any case, he's loose, armed, and dangerous. He may try for you and Angel again, but hopefully he doesn't know where you live."

"Shit. Thanks for letting us know."

"You bet, partner. Oh, and we'll have someone watching Angel at all times, even at the bar if she's working."

"I don't think it's a good idea for Angel to be out where he can get to her, much less at the bar."

"No. I'm not going to hide in your house or somewhere else while he runs my life off the rails," she insisted. "If you go back to work, so do I. They'll give me protection, so I'll be fine."

"Angel—"

"I don't want to argue about this."

"Listen, on second thought, maybe we should go back to Texas. Or anywhere else but here so he can't find you."

"No. Not this time. I'm not going to let him run me off again."

"You're not listening to reason," he hissed.

"You're not listening to me."

"Because you're not the cop in the room, and my orders are the ones we'll be following!"

She blinked at him. "What?"

"Don't argue with me, goddammit!"

"Oh no. You did not just—" She raised a hand. "You know what? I'm done with this conversation. I'm not going to be spoken to like that."

"I'm just trying to protect you!" he yelled.

She gave it to him right back. "Maybe I don't need you protecting me! Maybe I don't need you!"

"Whoa, guys!" Chris exclaimed, jumping in. "Let's calm down, okay?"

"You don't need me," he stated flatly. His face went stony, and his withdrawal was like an ice pick to her stomach.

Her heart sank. She'd messed up, gone over the line. "I'm sorry. I didn't mean that."

"It's fine." He shrugged like it didn't matter, but she could tell how much she'd hurt him. Turning to Chris, he said, "Can you get someone to watch her now? She'll be staying here with me for the foreseeable future, and I need to go in to work. We have to find Rab, and I've got about a million other cases lining up."

"Tonio—" she started.

"Not now."

With that, the subject was closed. Retreating upstairs,

he went to take a shower. He was out the door within ten minutes, leaving an apologetic Chris in his wake.

Angel wanted to cry, and so she did. After she excused herself, she retreated to Tonio's bedroom, where she let the tears flow.

She didn't know how to make things right, but she'd have to try.

Three days later, Tonio was no closer to finding Rab, or any semblance of peace with what Angel had yelled at him. Sure, deep down part of him knew she didn't really mean it.

But it still hurt like hell. Honestly it brought back the awful memories of Rachel deciding she didn't need him, and abandoning him. The situation was totally different, but the fear was the same—that if Angel didn't need him, she'd leave.

She had apologized again, and he'd told her it was all right. They were sleeping together, but things were tense. They hadn't made love or touched all that much, and the distance was beginning to wear on him.

"What are you still doing here, Tonio?"

Looking up, he saw his captain standing in the doorway to the office. Austin wore an expression of genuine concern on his face. "Burning some midnight oil. I got way behind while I was undercover, and I got no leads on where Rab could be holed up."

"Go home, kid. You'll be no good to anyone if you're burned out."

Kid. That was funny, considering Austin was only forty-two. Far from an old man. He was tall with dark auburn hair, and handsome if the ladies could be believed. Tonio wouldn't know. He was also stuck in a miserable marriage and used every excuse possible to work late himself.

"In a while. I've got a little more to do."

"Where's your partner?"

"Sitting outside Stroker's, watching the place and Angel. I sure could use him here, helping me."

Austin cocked his head. "I can help with that. Why don't I relieve Chris so he can swing by here and persuade you to go home? I'll escort Miss Silva back to your house when she closes."

"I can't ask you do to that," Tonio said, humbled. "You're past that kind of shit detail these days."

"Hey, maybe I want shit detail, you ever think of that?" He gave a bitter laugh. "Any excuse not to go home. What's to go home to?"

That statement struck Tonio hard. He'd never heard Austin say anything so personal in all the months since he moved to town. It was an odd moment. Sort of like bonding. Or friendship. "Hey, things will work out. I have to believe that and so do you."

"Do I?"

"Yeah. It's in the handbook somewhere."

Austin grinned and the look transformed his face. "I'll remember that. All right, I'm on my way to relieve Chris. See you later."

"Yeah, later."

He watched Austin go, then got back to work.

He couldn't wait to get home, to Angel.

* * *

Tonight, Angel couldn't wait to get the bar locked up. Things hadn't been the same between her and Tonio since their spat.

All was quiet, the music turned off. She was about to reach for the mop when a loud bang sounded from outside, causing her to jump. She wasn't the only one.

"What the fuck was that? A gunshot?" Andy almost dropped the tray of glasses he was holding before setting them on the counter. He blinked at her in concern.

"I don't know." Angel's heart pounded. "I think it came from out back."

"Isn't that where the cop is sitting, watching the place?"

"It's the captain. He's waiting for me to get off work so he can take me to Tonio's."

Jerking her cell phone from her jeans pocket, she punched in the captain's number and waited as it rang. Just as the fourth ring started, she heard someone pick up and what sounded like someone fumbling.

"Captain Rainey?"

"Miss Silva . . . call 9-1-1. Stay . . ." His voice trailed off.

"Captain? What's happened?" No answer. More fumbling noises, and a clatter. Like his phone being dropped. "Captain?"

There was nothing but silence. Standing rooted to the spot in the middle of the bar, Angel gripped her phone. Fear leeched the blood from her face.

"Andy!" Startled by her panicked yell, her bartender jumped, eyes wide. "Call the police! Tell them Captain Austin Rainey might be hurt and to send an ambulance. Hurry!"

Andy didn't hesitate to act. As she bolted, he was already jogging toward the phone they kept behind the bar, faster than she'd ever seen him move.

Angel ran down the long hallway leading to the staff exit. Her boots slid on the slick floor and she almost wiped out as she yelled the captain's name into her cell again.

"Captain Rainey? Austin?"

Nothing.

She hit the outside door at a dead run, heart slamming in her breast. Scanning the back of the lot, she spotted the dark unmarked SUV in the gloom, driver's door ajar. Passing her own car, she was almost to the vehicle when she saw him.

To her left, a man was lying on his side between two cars. Dim lamplight caught in his dark hair. Arm outstretched, a small lump next to his fingers. His cell phone.

"Austin!" Reaching him, Angel knelt at his side. The front of his shirt was saturated in blood, an inky pool widening around him. Hand trembling, she touched his shoulder, unsure how to help him. "Oh God. Captain, hang on. Help is coming."

She pressed shaking fingers to the hollow of his throat, detecting a pulse. Relief turned her insides to jelly. Alive, thank God. Even though someone, probably her brother, had done his best to ensure that he wasn't.

*To get to me.*

The thought whispered through her mind a mere instant before a small shuffle sounded behind her. She looked up, over her shoulder. Turned a fraction . . . to see a tall, menacing figure standing close, in shadow.

"Rab," she whispered. "No."

Survival instinct kicked her adrenaline into overdrive. She scrambled sideways, trying to gain her feet. As she did, her hair was seized from behind, jerking her backward. With a cry, she twisted her body in her brother's steely grasp, in time to see the glint of metal flashing downward.

Stinging pain zinged down her right arm. "Ahhh!"

On pure chance, she managed to hook one foot behind Rab's ankle and propel her body backward. The motion drove her attacker into the car behind them. Together, they bounced off the vehicle, fell to the ground.

As they hit, the knife clattered to the pavement, sliding under the car. Angel's hope that the commotion and the loss of the blade would send her brother running was short-lived.

A solid wall slammed into Angel's back, grinding gravel into her hands and knees. Unable to hold up under his much heavier weight, she collapsed onto her stomach. His knee dug into her spine, pinning her like a butterfly. One hand remained fisted in her hair while the other fumbled for something.

Suddenly her hair was released. With lightning speed, a thick cord looped around her neck. Tightened. Mercilessly crushing her windpipe.

"I could just shoot you, but I'm gonna make you suffer. Thought you could betray me and get away with it? With a fucking cop?" A low, throaty chuckle tickled her cheek. "You're gonna pay for that mistake. And so will lover boy. I'm gonna kill him, too."

*Oh, sweet Christ, he's insane. Please, somebody, help me!*

The cord cut into her neck. Twisted. Desperate for air, Angel clawed at the rope, her flesh, fighting for any sort of leverage. But she couldn't get her fingers under the cord. Couldn't buck Rab off her.

Her lungs burned. Black spots began to dance, spread across her vision. A buzzing in her ears became a roar. Blackness closed in, lapping at the fringes of consciousness. Her body went lax.

A shout sounded from far away. And emergency sirens. Or maybe rescue was only wishful thinking.

*Tonio! Oh no.* Her heart cried out for him. Wept that this monster would steal what they were building together. Their hopes for the future . . .

*Please, God, keep him safe.*

As the darkness swallowed her, Angel's last thought was of her sexy cop with the midnight eyes.

Midnight. The witching hour.

Where in the hell had that idea come from?

Tonio stared at the silent phone. Either Austin or Angel should've called by now to say they were leaving the bar, heading to his place to meet him. *Ring, dammit.* A knot of dread coiled in his stomach.

"This is ridiculous," he muttered. Quickly he gathered the files and locked them in his desk. Rising, he snatched his jacket off the back of his chair and strode to find Chris.

Tonio found his partner shutting down his computer, getting ready to leave. "I'm out of here. Angel hasn't called and neither has the captain." He shrugged, not half as calm as the gesture implied.

Chris's head snapped up. "I'll walk out with you."

Tonio waited while his friend finished straightening his desk, and then they headed for the parking garage.

"Angel must be busy."

"Yeah. But I'm dragging her butt home whether she's ready or not."

Chris halted dead in his tracks in the middle of the garage, staring at his friend. "Home? Like that, is it?"

*Well, hell.* The word had slipped out. He held Chris's dark gaze. "Yeah, it's like that. I love her."

"She feel the same?"

He couldn't stop the stupid grin spreading across his face. "Well, we haven't said the words, but. . . I think she does. God knows why."

Chris's smile crinkled the corners of his eyes. "Beats me." He clapped Tonio on the shoulder. "About time you got smart. I was starting to think some other lucky guy would have to pick up the pieces of her poor broken heart. I'm happy for you, man."

"Thanks. I appreciate it." The sense of urgency speared him again. "Come on, let's check on Rainey."

"And your girl."

Tonio hurried to his car, and they climbed in. Once inside, he checked his watch. Retrieving his cell phone from his jacket, he checked for messages and found none.

Quickly he dialed Austin's cell, anxious to hear his captain tell him everything was cool. But the call went to voice mail. Okay. No cause for alarm. Yet.

He dialed Angel's next. Nothing. *Doesn't mean Rab showed up,* he told himself. The captain would've phoned by now.

He jammed the key in the ignition, and the car roared to life. The city of Sugarland sped past in a multicolored blur of lights, and soon he left it behind. The miles to the next city and Angel's bar had never seemed more distant, and jaw clenched, he navigated the car like a stealth jet through the crazy county roads. If the car sprouted wings, it couldn't have traveled fast enough.

*They're all right. We'll laugh about this, oh, twenty years from now.*

They saw the red and blue lights from an entire block away. Dozens of them, flashing in the gloom, a macabre strobe against the brick building. A police barricade. Yellow tape.

"Oh my God," Tonio whispered.

Tonio skidded to a stop on the street, then burst from the car and ran for the barricade, heart thundering in his chest. He ducked under the tape without breaking stride. Instantly he was seized by two local uniforms.

"Whoa, buddy! Authorized access only," one burly cop barked.

Hands shaking, Tonio removed his badge from the clip on his belt. Not bothering to look at the cops, he thrust his shield outward, scanning the lot behind them. "Detective Tonio Salvatore, Sugarland PD," he croaked. "My captain, Austin Rainey, is supposed to be here, guarding a witness, Angel Silva. What happened?"

The burly cop answered, his tone flat. "Double attempted murder. Looks like we're gonna have at least one homicide out of this shit."

"Fuck," the other cop breathed. "This is Tonio Salvatore, his detective."

At that, Tonio snapped his attention to the second policeman and found himself staring into a sympathetic gaze. “Where is Captain Rainey?”

Their faces said more than words ever could. He’d seen those expressions before, countless times. Grim, quiet, empathetic. “No.”

As Chris came to stand beside him, the second cop gestured to the far corner of the lot, where two ambulances were parked. “It doesn’t look good for your captain. I’m sorry.”

“Later, I’ll want to know why the fuck we have a superior officer down and we weren’t notified,” Ford said, voice hard as granite.

“Who’s the other ambulance for?” Tonio managed.

“The bar’s owner,” the burly cop informed him. “She’s—”

Tonio left them standing there, shoving past more uniforms. A man entering the bowels of a nightmare. Again.

He reached Austin first. His captain lay on his back, face pale. His shirt had been ripped open, a compress placed in the center of his chest. Blood. God, so much of it pooled around his lifeless body.

A medic laid aside a pair of paddles. “Let’s go, for all the good it—” The man glanced up, saw they had company. Snapped his mouth shut.

Tonio’s vision grayed. He couldn’t breathe. “Is—is he going to make it?”

The medics didn’t look at him as they proceeded to load Austin’s limp form onto a stretcher. “If he has family, call them and tell them to hurry,” the second one said. “We’re taking him to County General. It’s the closest.”

Carefully they slid the stretcher into the waiting vehicle. "Someone should ride with him," Tonio heard himself say. "In case."

"He's in good hands," Chris said gently. "He won't know the difference right now. I'll call his wife on the way, okay? Let's find Angel."

Three more uniforms stood hovering in a group just a few feet from where Austin's body had lain. Two more medics crouched over a still figure.

Tonio wasn't sure how he covered the short distance. Only that the cops turned, as though in slow motion. Underwater. Recognition bloomed on one man's face. The cop lunged for him—*Jesus Christ, stop him*—then they were shouting words he couldn't hear. Shaking their heads. Hands, grabbing his jacket, trying to hold him back. To keep him from seeing—what? What?

Terror snapped his reason and he fought. Broke past the press of towering cops. And saw Angel lying as still and pale as Austin had been.

Blood coating the torn sleeve of her jacket.

A garrote looped around her scratched and bruised neck.

Horror slammed him. Anguish ripped out his heart. Finished him. He'd never survive this again. Didn't want to.

Gone in a blink.

Like Rachel. Like Danny. He'd argued with them, too.

Then they were dead.

More hands were pulling him backward. Arms wrapped around his chest, wrestling him to the ground.

Who was screaming?

The awful sound ripped through the night, like an animal being skewered by a large predator. An animal that needed to die. But it couldn't, just kept screaming—

A weight straddled his chest. "Get me some fucking help over here!" Chris bellowed. He squashed Tonio's face in his hands. "Stop, goddammit! She's alive, do you hear me? She alive!"

Alive.

The word penetrated the madness. Seeped into his whirling brain. Slowly his friend came into focus. Disheveled brown hair, damp with sweat, clung to Chris's worried brow. The screaming stopped, the stillness punctuated by his own gasping breaths.

"This isn't the same as before," Chris said, holding his gaze. "You understand? She's not Rachel. Angel is alive, and you didn't cause this."

"I should've been here."

"No. Austin volunteered to watch her so we could find the answers we need. Get hold of yourself so you can help Angel."

A circle of cops, equally concerned, frowned down at him. A young paramedic appeared, holding up a syringe.

"Dude, you're not helping your girl like this. Get a grip or I'm gonna send you to la-la land to dance with the fairies. Got it?"

Alive! Angel was going to be okay. Wasn't she? He nodded. "Is she awake?"

"She hasn't regained consciousness. She caught a stab wound in the muscle of her arm and sustained deep bruising from the ligature applied to her neck, but her vitals are rockin'," the medic replied. "Don't worry. She's tough. Dealing with you takes my attention from your lady. She needs us both, understand?"

Tonio nodded again, and the young man disappeared. Angel. He needed to be with her. Fear for her clawed at his sanity. But with a monumental effort, he reined it under control. For Angel.

"You can get off me," he said to Chris.

"You sure?"

"Yes."

The second his friend moved off him, Tonio pushed to his feet and went to Angel. This time, he curbed the madness threatening to overwhelm reason. Didn't dare give them cause to separate him from her again.

They'd already placed her on a stretcher and were loading it into the ambulance. "May I ride with her?"

The young medic motioned for him to get in. His buddy climbed in opposite Tonio to dress Angel's arm, and the doors slammed shut behind them.

Tonio winced, trying not to think of how much the suffocating box of the interior reminded him of a coffin.

As the vehicle began to move, he took one of her abraded hands in his. Studied her white face. One cheek was scratched and bloodied much like her hands and knees. From being held down, crushed into the pavement as she fought for her life? As she'd torn at her throat, desperate to breathe?

He began to tremble. Brought her hand to his lips, kissed her slender fingers again and again.

"I'm here, baby. You're going to be all right." Tears filled his eyes. "I'm sorry, so sorry."

Tonio bowed his head and closed his eyes, letting the

tears flow. Not giving a damn about the medic silently watching.

He'd been lonely for so long, after Rachel. He'd wanted Angel and in spite of the danger to her, he'd taken what he wanted. Stupid. Selfish.

Angel had nearly died because of him. No, because of Rab. And Austin still could. He might be dead already.

*Yes, Rab did this. Rab, who's twisted and evil. But I should have made you go back into hiding when he escaped.*

*You almost paid the ultimate price for my mistake. Please forgive me.*

*And please forgive me when I kill your brother for doing this to you.*

# 12

Angel dreamed of Tonio. Curling into his big naked body, his heat. Bringing him inside to fill her completely. Loving him, needing to crawl under his skin.

But the wonderful interlude began to fade. She whimpered, reaching to hang on to her love. He disappeared into mist; his comforting warmth, his strength gone. She grieved his loss, searching for him. *Please don't leave me.*

Quiet weeping. Whose? Hers?

No. Someone else, nearby. Sad and hurting. She sought the source, and realized this was not part of a dream. Awareness sharpened, and the soft, muffled noise did not go away.

Light speared her eyelids, prodding her into wakefulness. And with the return of her senses came the aches in her battered body. Pain, everywhere. Especially in her right arm and throat. She swallowed, and winced at the burn. Someone had poured acid down her windpipe. Stuffed her mouth full of cotton balls.

Opening her eyes, she blinked against the sunlight.

The terror of the night before—if it had been last night—returned in a dizzying rush.

Sweet Jesus, she'd survived!

But, oh God, what about the captain?

Angel turned her head, the slight movement causing the room to swim. When the pitching ceased, she saw Tonio. Her heart constricted at the sight of him hunched in a chair by her hospital bed. He was bent over, elbows on his knees, face buried in his hands.

Crying. Her big, tough-as-nails cop. Sobbing as though his world had ended, broad shoulders jerking from the strain of struggling to hold back. And failing. *Please, no. Don't let it be Austin.*

"Tonio?" He didn't hear her pathetic croak. She licked her lips and tried again. Louder, but not by much. "Hey, my sexy cop."

His head snapped up, and his dark eyes were red, swollen. Relief flooded his haggard features, and his face crumpled. "*Dulce.* Ah, *Dios mio*."

"Jeez, don't bury me just yet." The lame attempt at humor was lost on her man. He leaned close, wrapped his long fingers gently around her hand. Bowed his head as if in prayer, fat tears dripping off his chin, plopping onto the sheets. "Austin?"

Tonio raised his gaze to hers. Wide, guilt-ridden. "He made it through the night, but the doctors don't think he'll survive." He shook his head, sucked in a deep breath. "Nobody's been able to see him except his estranged wife and his parents. Did you know he's their only son? Their only family?" His voice cracked on the last.

"No, but—"

"All of this is my fault. Mine."

"Oh, Tonio, no."

His laugh was ugly. Angry. "I insisted on working late, trying to find a lead on where Rab might be, and I told Austin I wanted Chris with me. There wasn't anyone else available, so Austin took the watch himself."

"That's not true," she said hoarsely, wincing at the pain in her throat. "Austin chose not to assign another officer because he didn't want to go home to another fight with his wife."

Tonio's head snapped up at that. "He told me that, too."

"It's true. There were plenty of men he could've chosen, but the truth is, he just didn't want to go home, Tonio. He told me he's been feeling more and more useless lately, too, and thought maybe getting out in the field again a bit more would help."

Ignoring the IV in her hand and the pain from the stab wound, she opened her arms to her lover. Enfolded him, cuddled his head against her breast like a mother comforting an anguished boy. Stroked his silky hair as he grieved. This went much deeper than the attack on Austin.

It had to do with the deaths of his ex-fiancée and best friend.

"Shh, sweetie," she crooned, pressing tender kisses to the top of his head. She wanted to tell him everything would be all right but couldn't force out the lie. "Honey, you're going to make yourself sick."

He probably already had. Belatedly she noticed he

was wearing the same clothes he'd had on when she last saw him, and needed a shave. He'd been awake all night, terrified. His nerves were shot. The attempt on her and Austin had leveled him.

His shaking finally subsided and he quieted, so still Angel thought he might've fallen asleep in her arms. Breathing wasn't easy with more than two hundred pounds of limp man on her chest, and she shifted, trying to reposition him.

"I'm sorry." He sat up, wiping his face. Exhaustion lined grooves around his mouth and crow's-feet at the corners of his eyes. "I should be comforting you."

"Stop apologizing or I'm going to smack you." There. The hint of a fleeting smile. But the sorrow remained.

"How are you, sweetheart, really?" He clasped her hand.

"Numb. Like it happened to someone else. Hasn't hit me yet."

"It will. When it does, I'll be here."

"I know. I love you, Tonio." It was out before she could stop it, and so natural. It was the truth, and he smiled.

He pressed her hand to his roughened cheek. "I love you more. Are you in much pain?"

"Not really," she fibbed. At his look of reproach, she amended the little white lie before he launched into an inquisition. "Okay, some. My throat is sore and my arm is throbbing."

Without hesitating, Tonio grabbed the white control box attached to her bed and punched a button. "I'll have the nurse bring you something."

"But—"

"No arguments. You need to rest and you can't do that if you're in pain."

"Bossy." No smile. Only haunted shadows, and something else she'd never seen in his eyes before. A sudden, eerie calm. Gooseflesh pricked her arms. "What's going through your head?"

"You don't want to know," he murmured, promptly changing the subject. "Baby, I need you to tell me what you remember about the attack. Was it Rab?"

A nasty jolt electrified her nerve endings. He had to ask. She should've been prepared, but her bravery had caught a serious black eye.

"Yes." Angel licked her lips and cleared her scratchy throat. "Andy and I were cleaning up the bar when we heard what we thought was a gunshot out back."

Tonio nodded wearily. "They figured out he and Rab had a fight. Sometime during the struggle, Austin's gun went off. The gun was knocked away, and Rab stabbed him."

"God, that's horrible." She took a deep breath. "I used my cell phone to call Austin and see what was going on. At first I thought we had a bad connection. Then I realized he could hardly talk. He told me to call the police. Then he said 'Stay.'" Tonio's face darkened and she hurried on.

"I was too concerned about Austin to understand at the time that he meant for me to stay inside. I found him sprawled on the ground." She faltered. The horror of discovering his prone, limp body awash in blood struck her anew. "I felt so helpless."

He gave her hand a reassuring squeeze. "What happened next? You got a good look and you're sure the attacker was Rab?"

"Just a glimpse. He jumped me from behind while I was bending over Austin. I fought, but I couldn't shake him after that or even get turned around to see who had me. There was no mistaking his voice, though, and he was crazed about me betraying him by being with a cop."

"What did he say, specifically?"

Angel considered lying. She didn't want to see him hurt any more, but she looked into his face and couldn't lie. "He said I was going to pay, and that he was going to kill you, too."

Tonio sucked in a breath as though she'd socked him in the stomach. "He's wrong. That bastard's not taking anything else from me."

A plump, aging nurse bustled in carrying a tiny paper cup containing two capsules. The sweet-faced woman made a fuss, checking her vital signs and dispensing advice to take it easy for the next few days. Last, she handed Angel the capsules and a glass of water, declaring that these were stronger than Tylenol and would help her rest. After she downed them, the nurse hurried out with the promise to return later.

Angel studied Tonio, thinking on his cryptic statement before. The cold determination frightened her, for his sake. "What are you going to do?"

"First, I'm taking you out of the picture. You and Austin are under the FBI's protection until this is over. When you're released tomorrow or the next day, you'll stay at your house or a hotel with an agent."

"What about you?" She knew before he spoke that she wasn't going to like this.

"Your brother's ready to make another move on me. I'm pulling everyone back so he can maneuver."

"What? No!" she cried. "He nearly killed you before we left town, or have you forgotten?"

"No, I haven't forgotten. But I'm still wearing a hidden tracking device, just like I have been, and we're putting one on you and your vehicle, too. Chris has a team ready to move in the second either of us strays off course. Don't worry, sweetheart."

"No, there has to be another—"

A knock at the door interrupted. She and Tonio turned their heads to see a large older man in a suit, one she hadn't met before.

"I'm Tess's boss, Special Agent Harold Worth." His features were schooled into a tight, polite smile. But it was the woman standing behind him, clutching a vase of flowers, that stunned Angel into near shock.

"This lady says she's Miss Silva's mother. Just checking," the agent said to Tonio. The agent glanced at her, then back to Tonio for the affirmative. "Detective?"

"Actually we've never met," Tonio said, standing. Turning slightly, he positioned himself protectively between her and the slender woman glancing nervously around the room.

"Yes, that's my mom," Angel confirmed, finding her voice. "She's fine."

"All right. I'll be just outside."

After the man spun on his heel and walked out, her

mother walked over and set the flowers on the bedside table.

"They're beautiful." Angel smiled.

Her mother straightened, brushing a few stray petals off her blouse and khaki pants. She moved cautiously forward, staring at Angel as though she half expected to be thrown out any second. Finally she took the seat Tonio had vacated.

"They're from everyone in my book club. We all chipped in. Myra and some others said they'd come by later if you're up to visitors."

Her heart sank, and she worked to hide her anxiety. The last thing she wanted was a horde of her mother's friends descending on her, exclaiming over the attack and asking a bunch of questions. And the only visitor she needed was the man she loved. "That would be nice. And tell them I love the flowers." At least the second part was the truth.

"I'll do that. Angel . . . When the police came to the house and told me what Rab did to you, I had to come. To see my baby girl. How are you? I mean, really?" Her mother's voice was soft, her eyes worried. They also filled with tears, and something else—raw, pure rage.

That was another shock in a day full of them. She swallowed hard. "I'm okay, Mom. The FBI's going to keep an eye on us. Probably you, too, just in case."

Her mother snorted. "They probably think I'll give him a place to hide, but that's the last damn thing I'd ever do now. Over my dead body would that ever happen. He's always been a difficult son, taking after his daddy with all the stealing. But to murder that other girl in cold blood, just because he could? And now to hurt his own sister? That animal is no son of mine."

Angel blinked. "I must be dreaming."

"No." Her mother took her hand, and Angel noted how it was slightly chilled and trembling. "We haven't had it easy, and I've been weak. Too afraid to stand up, first to your father and then to Rab. To anyone else who wanted to run right over me. But I'm turning over a new leaf. Getting some counseling set up."

A tear escaped to roll down Angel's face. "Oh, Mom. That's great."

"I think it'll be a good thing. Who knows?"

"Maybe I'll come with you at some point," she offered, remembering her conversation with Tonio not so long ago.

Her mom smiled. A real smile that lit her face and reminded Angel that her mother was still relatively young and a very attractive woman. Once she got herself straightened out, she would blossom like a rose. Do anything she wanted.

"I'd love that," Angel said.

"Me, too."

"Well, I can't stay. I just wanted to bring the flowers and see for myself that you're okay. Tell you I love you." Her mother's heart was in her eyes.

"I love you, too, Mom."

Her mother stood, nodded at Tonio. "Take care of my baby, Detective."

"I plan on it, Mrs. Silva."

She smiled. "Frances."

He returned it. "I'm Tonio, Frances. I'm sure we'll meet again soon, once all this is settled."

Once Rab was behind bars again, where he belonged. But he was too polite to say so in front of her mother, even with the woman's newfound resolve.

"I'm sure we will." Her mother bent and kissed her cheek. "Bye for now, baby."

"For now," she said softly.

After her mom left, Angel relaxed into the pillows, not surprised to find she'd been rigid as a two-by-four for the short duration of her visit.

Tonio settled back into his chair, taking her hand. "How are you after that visit?"

"I'm really good," she said. It was true. "There's hope."

"Always. Your mother loves you, that's obvious. Sometimes it takes something really terrible to wake people up from the dream state they're living in, and almost losing you must've done that."

Angel reached for his hand. "First you need to go home and try to get some rest, or you won't be alert enough to recite your own name."

He enfolded her hand in his big palm. "You're the one who needs to sleep. You're banged up and you've got twenty-four stitches in your arm."

"Don't change the subject. I'm serious, Tonio."

"I've got some leads to run down. Then I'll go home and rest. I promise." He let out a weary sigh. "I have to leave for a while, but I'll come by before I go home tonight."

She shook her head. "You don't have to. You're wiped out."

"Doesn't matter. I won't be able to sleep until I check on you and Austin."

No use arguing with the stubborn man. "Just be careful, okay?"

"Always." He leaned over and pressed a soft kiss to her lips. "I love you, *dulce*. So damn much. Hope you don't get tired of hearing it."

She buried her fingers in his hair, inhaling his masculine scent. "Not a chance. I'm the luckiest woman on earth to have you."

Tonio tried for a smile, but it came out lopsided. A little sad. "That remains to be seen." Another quick kiss; then he pushed to his feet. "See you, baby."

"Bye."

As he disappeared through the doorway, Angel tamped down a wild, almost desperate urge to call him back. To feel his strong arms around her again, his sweet kisses.

A profound sense of loss chilled the marrow of her bones.

"He'll be all right," she whispered.

But Angel couldn't shake the awful feeling that she should've told Tonio, just once more, how much she loved him.

Tonio scrubbed at his bleary eyeballs, grinding them with the heel of his hand. He and Chris had worked all day following tips as to Rab's possible whereabouts that had led to nothing but dead ends. Time after time, the same story.

Nobody had seen Rab, or heard from him. At least

one or two of them had been lying, the detectives were certain. But they were more afraid of the gang leader than the cops.

Christ, he was so tired. Emotionally drained and running on empty. He had one more lead to follow tonight before he wound up falling asleep at the wheel. Checking his watch, he opted to swing by the hospital first. Visiting hours would be over soon.

First stop, intensive care. Austin's parents and estranged wife hadn't budged. Tonio hadn't noticed before what an attractive couple the older Raineys made. Austin got his all-American good looks from his father, a tall, lean man with auburn hair gone mostly gray. His mother was a slender brunette with short hair, almost tomboyish.

Working-class people, Tonio noted. Jeans and T-shirts. Jim Rainey's hard jaw and rough hands testified to years of toil. The proud tilt of his head let everyone know he'd make the same choices again.

At his approach, Marsha Rainey looked up from her seat and shot Tonio a quick, tremulous smile.

"Mrs. Rainey." He nodded respectfully, reaching down to take the woman's hand. He took the vacant seat next to her. "How's Austin?"

"He's had a rough day. Once, his h-heart stopped and the d-doctors h-had to—" Unable to finish, she let go of Tonio's hand, covering her mouth with trembling fingers. Her husband gathered her into his arms, laying her head on his chest.

Across from her, Austin's wife made a broken sound. Tears were rolling down her pretty face.

The awful guilt riding Tonio nearly drowned him. Only the fact that these wonderful people made it clear they didn't blame him was keeping him sane.

"Hush, darlin'," Jim said gruffly. "Don't cry any more. Remember how stubborn our boy is. He'll make it." He raised his gaze to Tonio's. So full of remorse.

"He's fighting hard. They're letting people see him for a few minutes now, one at a time. Some of the guys from the station were here earlier. Don't know 'em all. But Austin thinks you walk on water, boy. I know he'd appreciate your being there. Might help."

*Jesus, I can't do this.* "Okay," Tonio managed. "I'll sit with him for a while."

"One more thing. Don't you go blamin' yourself no more for what a monster did. Trials happen to a family for a reason."

"Mr. Rainey—"

"Listen. Me and Austin don't always see eye to eye, but I understand my boy better than he knows. He's a police officer. He puts away criminals, makes people safe. No one in our family ever did anything that important. Before this, he didn't know how goddamn proud I am of him, 'cause I never told him. Now I will. Remember that, son."

"I'll try, sir."

Remarkably the man's unwavering faith helped steady Tonio as he covered the short distance to Austin's room. Was it possible this would cause Austin and his father to mend a few fences? Lemonade from lemons. But Austin had to pull through first. Tonio nodded at the agent guarding his captain's door.

Inside, Tonio's resolve sustained a blow.

*He looks dead.*

Most likely would be, except for the breathing tube down his throat. And about a dozen others poked into every available place. His arms, hands, and a large one in his chest. All connected to blinking machines, so many of them bristling around his bed that the area resembled the cockpit of a jet. All working to keep his boss—and yes, his friend—alive.

He seated himself in the chair by Austin's side. His friend's face was so pale, his body so unearthly still he appeared to be made of wax. Tonio laid a hand on his arm, startled that the burnished hair fanned around Austin's head looked like spilled blood.

"Austin? Hey, Cap, it's Tonio. I met your parents and I have to say, they're pretty terrific. Even the wife doesn't seem so bad, though I know you two have had it rough lately. They're outside, waiting for you to wake up."

*God, help him make it back.*

"We're all here for you. Don't give up, big guy. Stay with us, okay?"

Was that a flicker behind his eyelids? Probably wishful thinking. But he kept talking, just in case. Told Austin a funny story about how he and some other cops had gotten drunk down on the River Walk in San Antonio one time, off duty, of course. One of the assholes had shoved at Tonio and he'd stumbled—and had gone right into the dirty river.

"I'm surprised I didn't end up with a flesh-eating bacteria from landing in that shit. Mama yelled at me for days."

"Sir?" A young nurse hovered in the doorway, voice soft with gentle apology. "I'm sorry, but you'll have to come back tomorrow. Mr. Rainey needs his rest."

Rest. What if he rested forever? "I understand."

She slipped out, affording him the privacy to say good-bye. But good-bye seemed like a bad omen somehow, so he opted for a more positive departure, for Austin's sake.

"Well, looks like I'm getting the boot. But don't think you're off the hook, okay? I've got a thousand stories like that one, and unfortunately you're going to listen to them all. Hang tough, my friend, and I'll see you tomorrow."

Giving Austin's arm a squeeze, he turned and walked out before he got sloppy again. Enough crying like a fucking baby. Time to man up and find Rab, that fucker, before he hurt anyone else.

He said good night to Austin's folks, then rode the elevator up to Angel's floor. Visiting hours were over, but no one stopped him as he greeted the agent who'd pulled the night shift at her door and went inside.

The lights were dimmed, her lean form huddled under the blankets, lying on her left side facing away from him. Her bandaged right arm lay on top of the covers, moving up and down slightly with her deep, even breathing.

Worried that she might've tangled her IV line, he walked around to the other side of the bed to check. He found it secure in her left hand, the line straight, and breathed a sigh of relief.

For a few minutes he stood simply looking down at Angel, sleeping peacefully as a child. He loved watching her, adored the pink bow of her lips when she slept, the delicate curve of her jaw. Gazing at her, the portrait of sweet innocence housing a woman with immeasurable courage, he could hang on to the hope that this time, he would win. He'd make a life with the woman he loved. If he didn't have that dream, he had nothing.

Several more batches of flowers had arrived, including the two dozen roses he'd sent. Someone had placed his arrangement by her bed and moved the one from her coworkers to the floor against the wall. He was ridiculously pleased that she'd placed his the closest, and wished he'd been there to see her reaction.

More spring bouquets were parked on the rolling tray. Curious, he plucked the cards out and read them one by one. The first was from her mother, the next from her bartender, Andy. A couple were from friends he didn't recognize. But the largest of them—

It was from Rab.

"Goddamn," he hissed. "That ballsy motherfucker."

Careful not to wake Angel, he stalked to the door with the card and arrangement and waved to the agent on duty. "Did you see who delivered this?"

"Hospital staff, same as the others," the agent said, eyeing it warily. "Why?"

"It's from her brother," he snapped, shoving the flowers at the man and hitting him in the chest. "You haven't been screening these?"

The agent flushed in anger and embarrassment. "No, I didn't think to check the flowers. They seemed harmless."

"Well, these aren't, because they're from the murdering son of a bitch who put her in that hospital bed. Get someone up here to get these and see if they can find out where the order originated."

"Sure thing."

Ignoring the curl of the man's lip, he turned back into Angel's room and took up his spot by her side of the bed. They probably wouldn't find much. Rab was too smart for that. No, this was a clear taunt. Thank God the flowers had been delivered while she was asleep—they must have been or she wouldn't be calmly sleeping with them sitting there. No way was he going to mention them.

Replacing the other cards in the flower arrangements, he turned his attention back to Angel. He touched the top of her head and leaned over, pressing a kiss into her hair. Breathed her warm, sweet scent. Careful not to wake her, he whispered, "Gotta go. I'll see you tomorrow morning, first thing. I love you, baby." She didn't stir.

He hated to leave her. Hated it. But if he didn't get some rest, he wouldn't be any good to her or anyone else. Sleep first; then he'd find Rab.

There was nowhere the son of a bitch could hide.

Nowhere.

# 13

By the time Tonio pulled into his driveway, he had trouble staying awake. He ignored the van he knew contained two agents, just hoping Rab would show. Then he pulled into the garage and parked, hitting the button on his key chain to close the automatic door. Dead exhausted, he trudged inside, then remembered he hadn't checked the mailbox at the end of the drive in two days. Screw it, he'd walk out there tomorrow.

Barely able to put one foot in front of the other, he dumped his keys, wallet, and gun on the kitchen bar. The blinking light on the answering machine caught his attention, and he leaned close. Damn, ten frigging messages.

He debated whether to let them go until morning, but a sudden bolt of fear galvanized him into hitting the PLAY button. What if something had happened to Austin?

"No, God, please."

The first was from his sister, saying she and Mama were worried. The next five were hang-ups, and his skin crawled. On the seventh, a low, bass voice floated through the kitchen, vibrating with malice.

"I'm gonna fucking kill you, Salvatore. You listening?"

He snarled. "Yeah, you'll try, you piece of shit. I'm gonna catch you and they'll cart your ass back to prison." Careful not to delete that one, he listened to the rest. Angel's sweet voice drifted from the machine, curled around his heart.

"I couldn't go to sleep without telling you how much I love you. Hope you didn't stay out too late. Get some rest and I'll see you tomorrow. Bye, my sexy cop."

His smile withered as the next message kicked in.

"Salvatore, this is Tyler, from the lab. I have some good news for you. I've got the DNA results on that tequila bottle. Call me ASAP." Breathless, he left the number to the lab and hung up.

Good news? Sounded better than good. How amazing did the news have to be to send Tyler to the moon? Oh yeah. This was it. He tensed, listening to the final message.

"Salvatore, Tyler again. Where the hell are you? Listen, I'm ready to head out for the day, so call me at home. No matter what time you get this, just call." This time, he recited his home number.

Anticipation hummed in his veins, along with a healthy dose of bone-numbing relief that none of the calls had been bad news about Austin. Restless, he snatched the cordless phone and walked into the living room. He punched in Tyler's home number, and the guy answered on the second ring.

"Talk to me, Ty. I could use some good news right about now."

"Jesus H. Christ, took you long enough. I've left messages all over frigging town for you. Been wired for hours waiting for your call, and with your captain out of commission the chain of command is little slow."

"Yeah. What do you have?"

"Listen, I sent the lab results over this afternoon, but given what's been going on with you, I wasn't sure you'd made it by the office to see them."

His grip on the phone tightened. "No, I haven't, and neither has Chris. We're stretched thin on manpower. What have you fucking got?"

"DNA, from saliva on the tequila bottle at the Sharon Waite murder scene. It matches not only our victim, but Rab Silva. Guess they were taking turns drinking from it at one point."

"You're sure about that?"

"Yes. It'll hold in court."

*Thank Christ*. "Anything else?"

"Actually yes. I got a hit on some DNA from a murder that took place shortly after Rab was released from prison, near Nashville. A trace amount of semen was left on a woman's body in a motel room, on her abdomen. The killer had cleaned it up, but DNA is a lot harder to get rid of than people think."

"It matches Rab's semen?"

"To a tee. So that's two murders for sure. Who knows how many others?"

"Hopefully not any," Tonio said. "Those, plus the two attempted murders on law enforcement officers, will hang him."

"Yeah. Well, I'll let you go. Just wanted to let you know as soon as I could."

"I appreciate it, Ty. Thanks."

"No problem."

He dialed Chris's cell phone and got his voice mail. "It's me. We got the DNA results back from the lab today. You're not going to freaking believe it. He's going down for two murders. Call me."

He started to dial Shane, another detective in his office, then froze.

He never knew what alerted him.

A shuffle.

A shift in the air.

A warm sigh against his neck.

Heart in his throat, he spun.

And found himself looking into dark eyes. Hollow eyes, he thought. A walking corpse with no soul.

"Rab," he said. Shock held him immobile. The unreality of finding the man standing before him, in his own house. "How did you get in here?"

In truth, deep down, he knew the agents outside were probably dead.

The gang leader hadn't suffered any from being on the run. He wore jeans and a snug dark T-shirt defining his chest. His biceps were firmly delineated with muscle, and Tonio knew he was as fucking strong as he appeared.

A long butcher knife gleamed in his hand. Tonio squashed a wave of fear as Rab glared at him, his gaze feverish with anger. More than a bit crazed. Coupled with the odd, dead smile, the effect was frightening. His heart sank even more when he saw Phil and Enrique armed and waiting nearby. Ready to jump in if needed.

"You ready to die, Tonio?"

He held up his hands. "Even if you kill me, you're not

going to escape. You realize that, right? The whole county, and the state, is looking for you."

His angular face twisted into an ugly snarl. "They may find me, but I'll be rid of one less cop first," he hissed, jabbing at Tonio's middle with the knife to punctuate each word, backing him against the mantle. "A lying cop who made me think he was my friend."

*God, think.* His weapon was lying on the kitchen counter with the car keys. But Rab was armed only with a knife, so Tonio could take him. Or prayed he could. First, he had to try to calm him.

"I had a job to do, same as you. Let's talk this out—"

"Shut up!"

Shit. He tensed, but before he could lunge, Rab launched himself at him, his momentum slamming his shoulders into the mantel and sending framed pictures flying. His solid weight and their awkward position unbalanced him, and they crashed to the floor together.

Tonio rolled, trying to pin his attacker and grab his wrist to keep the slashing blade from slicing him. He was barely aware of the other men's jeers as they collided with an end table by the sofa, upsetting a lamp, which shattered on the hardwood flooring. Rab managed to land on top of him, straddling his rib cage. Tonio was wedged next to the table, hardly able to maneuver.

He made another grab. Missed. The knife flashed in a downward arc, the blade driving deep into his right shoulder, just below the collarbone.

Agony took him in waves, and he threw back his head with a sharp cry. Rab yanked out the blade and drew his arm back again. Tonio bucked, throwing him into the coffee table, scattering items everywhere. The knife was knocked free, out of reach, but in the end it didn't matter.

Panting, he used the sofa to push up on his knees, searching for the phone he'd dropped. Where? God, the pain. He glanced down, saw blood everywhere. His shirt, the floor, on the cushions. Sickness rose, drowning him. *Get away, outside.*

He stumbled, hoping to reach the kitchen. But this time all three of them were on him again, tackling him to the floor. Phil and Enrique held him down firmly while Rab went to work. Though he fought hard to get loose, he couldn't break their hold.

The blows rained down. Punches and kicks, to his head, ribs, chest. So many, fast and furious, he knew Rab was going to kill him. Just as he'd promised. The knowledge filled him with helpless rage, and yet he could do nothing.

Blood flowed. Time seemed to slow, his vision growing dim. Twisting his body, he made one last-ditch effort at survival. Tried to break away—

Just in time to see Rab's meaty fist coming at his head.

His temple exploded, the brute force of the blow snapping his head sideways. Detonating his world into a million shards. His body went limp, the jagged fragments of his consciousness struggling to regain purchase.

His head hit the floor with a *thunk*. He blinked, his vision clearing only to a blur. Wetness trickled down the side of his face, into his mouth. Above him, Rab laughed, the sound distorted and far away.

"Did you really think I was gonna let you off easy?

You betrayed me, cop. But you did save my life once, so I'm gonna give you a chance. If you live, then you live. Doubt anybody will find you where we're taking you, but it's a shot."

"No."

His body was lifted, then rolled into one of his own quilts. His vision went dark, and he thought of how they'd disposed of Stan the same way. Now he was about to end up like that poor bastard. The horror of it all was almost beyond comprehension.

Dios, *give me courage. Keep Angel safe, please.*

Then the black water closed over his head, and he knew nothing more.

Angel's worried call stopped Chris's heart.

Tonio hadn't shown up to visit her or Austin this morning. Wasn't answering his home or cell phones. No one had heard from him since the urgent message he'd left on Chris's cell after midnight. Something about the DNA results, but in light of his friend's disappearance, Chris decided to call Ty later.

"Goddamn."

Chris pushed his car toward Tonio's place as fast as he dared and still get there in one piece. The tiny tracking device they'd hidden in Tonio's shirt pocket showed he was at home.

"Could be a lot of reasons," he muttered, willing down panic. "He could be sick in bed. Maybe he was outside, in the garage."

But he was lying to himself. Tonio would never go silent at a time like this and leave everyone frantic with worry.

The second Chris pulled into the drive, even before he saw the silent SUV, he knew.

Call it intuition, his years as a detective, whatever. He'd felt this before, on countless occasions. That ominous chill of stepping into the presence of evil slugged him in the chest as he got out of the car. Checked the SUV and found the bodies inside. He called in for backup, then walked the dreaded steps to the front door. Tonio wouldn't answer. He knew this without question.

He rang the doorbell anyway, and waited.

Rang again.

"Fuck it." Bracing himself, he slammed his foot into the wood, kicking in the door on the third try. If he was wrong, he'd apologize to Tonio later for the mess. He'd pay for the damage and—

In the foyer, he halted, staring into the living room. Cold terror bloomed in his chest. Seized his lungs.

Hardly aware of his feet moving, he walked to the end of the sofa, scanning the room. The place was in shambles. A smashed lamp, scattered debris of books, broken picture frames. A cordless phone near the fireplace.

Blood, everywhere. Smeared down the front of the sofa, pooled on the floor.

"Oh no." He put his face in his hands. "Sweet Jesus, no."

The bastard finally got him. By now, Tonio was probably dead.

His shoulders began to shake, but he couldn't lose it. A slim thread of hope existed that maybe—just maybe—

the gang leader would keep him alive for a day or two. For Tonio, he had to hold it together. Call in the team so they could start searching.

Then the toughest task of all.

Somehow he had to tell Angel.

# 14

Angel's tummy did a somersault every time a male voice echoed in the hallway. None of them were Tonio, and with each passing hour, worry slid deeper into fear.

What could be keeping him? Why hadn't he called?

The black-and-white image of Ricky yelling at Lucy flickered on the wall-mounted television facing her bed, but not even her favorite classic comedy could loosen the hard knot in her chest.

Angel glanced around, thinking it oddly surreal, the sunny hospital room brimming with colorful flowers, canned laughter bursting from the television, the agent outside her door and the reason for his presence. She jabbed the remote, and the TV blinked off. Nothing but the empty eye of the screen staring at back her.

And the ominous hush. No ringing phone, no Tonio striding through the door wearing a supersexy grin, apologizing for scaring her to death. No word from Chris, either.

Something was very wrong.

"Agent Worth!" she yelled.

For such a big man, Harold Worth moved like a ghost. He topped Tonio by an inch and at least fifty pounds of not-so-ripped muscle. Or so she supposed from the way his shoulders and arms strained in his dark suit.

He stood about five feet inside the room as if careful to keep plenty of distance between them. In spite of her shout that had brought him so swiftly, the expression in his eyes remained inscrutable.

"Yes, Miss Silva?"

"Have you heard any word from Chris? I haven't spoken with him in over three hours."

The agent hesitated, the barrier lifting for a split second. A flash of remorse?

"The detective will be here as soon as he can."

Angel gripped the sheets so hard her knuckles turned white. "Which means what, exactly? Where in the hell is Tonio? Details, Agent Worth."

His jaw clenched, the cool facade cracking wider. "I'm sorry, Miss Silva. He'll brief you when he arrives."

"Brief me?" She stared at him, dread choking her. "Something bad has happened to Tonio."

The agent didn't bother to deny it. He shifted, looked down at his shoes. When he raised his troubled gaze to hers, the unruffled exterior had vanished, replaced by warmth. Sympathy.

She clapped a trembling hand over her mouth. "My God. He's dead, isn't he?"

He shook his head. "We don't have any proof of that. Please, wait for—"

"You mean Tonio's missing?" she whispered. "He was wearing a tracking device. How could this happen?"

"Miss Silva, until the detective gets here, I'm afraid—"

"I'm here." Chris walked in, halted next to Agent Worth. The glance they exchanged spoke volumes. "Agent, could you . . ."

Chris's voice wavered, trailed off as though finishing the request was too much of an effort.

Worth laid a hand on his shoulder and squeezed. "I'll be right outside, son."

Angel was hardly aware of the agent's departure. "Tell me," she croaked.

Chris avoided meeting her eyes, focusing his attention on the rolling cart of flowers parked at the foot of her bed. His tie had gone missing, his starched white shirt unbuttoned at the throat. He stood as if carved from stone, face pale. A man living a nightmare.

A sob welled in her throat. This couldn't be real. "For God's sake, what happened?"

His lips moved, but it took him several attempts to speak. "I went out to Tonio's place. He didn't answer, so I kicked in the door. The living room was a wreck, stuff smashed everywhere. His tracking device was discarded on the floor. The other device is on his car, but they didn't take it." Chris shook his head, shock and disbelief battling each other. "Angel, he's gone."

She sucked in a breath, those two words like lethal bullets pumped into her heart. Somehow she forced herself to ask. "Dead?"

"We don't know that. All we've got is Tonio's been kidnapped and we don't know where Rab might've taken him." Chris moved to her bedside and lowered himself into the chair, raking a hand through his streaked brown hair.

"I've pulled every possible cop from every fucking unit. I've notified anyone and everyone who wears a gun. The local and state police, the Texas Rangers, you name it. Tonio's out there somewhere, and by God, we'll find him."

Find his body was what Chris really meant, and they both knew it. None of the killer's previous victims had lived to see the next sunrise. Tonio had been missing for hours, long past dawn.

"Rab might keep him for a while," Angel heard herself say.

Chris nodded. "It's possible. He's been nurturing his hatred and his need to make Tonio pay. It's our best shot at finding him alive."

The horror of that scenario struck her. "My God, if that's true, my brother could be torturing him."

*Oh, Tonio. Is it cruel to hope you're hanging on, waiting endless hours for rescue while he tortures you to death?*

"Yeah, either way it's bad. Even if he's alive, we don't have much time. Apparently he was injured during the struggle and has lost a lot of blood."

*No, no.* "You don't know whether it was his."

Chris took her hand, unshed tears swimming in his eyes. "If the blood was Rab's, Tonio would be here and we'd be having a different conversation," he said softly.

She digested the awful truth of that. A low moan escaped, but she held the sobs at bay.

"Go ahead and cry. I'm here." Chris's fingers tightened around hers.

"No," she said, low and fierce. "Crying means I've already given up, and Tonio doesn't deserve that. I'm not going to fall apart while he's out there somewhere, fighting to survive."

"That's the spirit. Tonio's a lucky man." Chris's mouth hitched up in a sad smile.

*Chris believes he's dead.* Suddenly she was angrier than she'd ever been. Resolve stiffened her backbone, and she threw off the covers, swinging her legs over the side of the bed.

"What are you doing?" Chris sputtered.

She slid off the mattress and stood, testing her strength. So far, so good. "Getting dressed and getting the hell out of this place."

"Angel, wait—"

She narrowed her eyes and poked him in the chest with her index finger. "I'm going home and changing clothes. After that, I'm going to find Tonio. You can humor me or you can help me. But you will not fucking stop me."

Startled, Chris stared at her a long moment. A flush crept up her neck. She'd never spoken so harshly to a cop in her life. Then again, the stakes had never been higher. Thankfully her new friend understood her need to be a part of the search. To do something, anything to help.

"All right. I'll go see about having your release papers drawn up while you change."

Chris pulled her into a gentle hug, careful not to hurt

her injured arm. After a moment, he pressed a quick kiss to the top of her head, let her go, and headed for the door.

"Chris?"

He stopped and turned. "Yeah?"

"Thanks. Tonio's lucky to have a wonderful friend like you."

A bitter laugh erupted from his chest. "I'm so fucking wonderful I couldn't protect my partner or the woman he loves from a killer."

Chris spun on his heel and left, his misery hanging in the air like smog.

So much guilt, when the blame lay solely at one person's feet.

Angel's hands fisted.

"When I find you, you crazy-ass bastard, I'm going to rip out your shriveled heart. That's a promise."

The stench reached his consciousness first.

Then the pain. All-over, racking agony that proved he wasn't dead yet, though he didn't have a clue how that could be.

Awareness of being trapped came next. Buried. But not in the dirt. As he tried to move, various items surrounding him shifted and rolled away. With his fingertips he felt . . . cans. Paper. Slime. Old food? Cold knowledge gripped him, turned his blood to ice.

*After the bastards finished with me, they threw me in the garbage. Literally.*

*Move, Salvatore. Move or you're dead.*

Using his hand, he sought the air. Pushed and clawed,

twisting his body in the stinking refuse. The weight on top of him was heavy but not crushing. They'd meant to hide his body, completely confident he wouldn't wake, or make it out even if he did. He tried not to think they might be right.

At last, fresh air. But as he broke through the pile, the heap sloped downward sharply and he was tumbling sideways. For several feet he fell, jabbed and poked by sharp edges until he landed in the dirt at the bottom, the wind knocked out of him. Breathing was almost impossible, his lungs burning. He was hurt inside, and out.

His eyes opened to slits, and he tried to peer into the darkness. All he could make out was a sea of garbage. No moon or stars. Worse, little hope.

They'd thrown him into the dump miles outside the city, where nobody in their right mind would venture.

*Don't give up.*

Drawing his legs under him, he pushed upward. His legs were like rubber, his strength almost nonexistent. He made it halfway to a standing position before crashing back to the ground with a hoarse cry. God, the pain. His entire body felt hot and cold by turns, and swollen like a balloon. Any second, he would split and spill onto the ground like the plastic bags all around him vomiting their guts. His skin and clothing were wet, too, from head to toe.

He knew it wasn't all from the slime of the trash.

Shaking, Tonio crawled forward on his belly, inch by inch. Time lost meaning. An hour or three might have passed, though he didn't think it had been so long—he would already be dead.

Wetness ran down his forehead, down the bridge of

his nose. Gradually he grew cold. So cold he knew he'd never get warm again. What was he doing? Why had he been abandoned in this godforsaken place? Too much blood loss. Confusion. He tried to remember, couldn't.

Knew that was the beginning of the end.

*Anthony. I'm Anthony Salvatore, and I'm a cop. Have to get out of here, get help. Let them know—what?*

Her name whispered through his mind like a promise. Or a nightmare. He didn't know which, and now he might never.

*Angel.*

*Have to let Chris, somebody, know about Angel. Because if I fail . . .*

Brother or not, Rab would kill her. He would show her no mercy, and she would end up here, in a grave next to Tonio. He couldn't let that happen.

"Angel."

Her name was on his lips, her beautiful face in his mind and the memory of her warm, supple body close to his heart when his strength finally deserted him.

He'd wanted years to learn her secrets, her joys, and had been granted only weeks. It would have to be enough.

"Be smart, baby," he rasped. "Stay safe."

Against his will, his eyes drifted shut.

And Tonio surrendered to the darkness.

A noise speared his consciousness. Coming closer.

Found? He was rescued?

Tonio tried to raise his head but couldn't. He waited for the familiar, welcome sound of his partner's voice. What he heard instead was a nightmare.

"You're still fucking alive?" Rab yelled. "I come back to move your body and you're crawling across the ground like a damn bug. How are you still breathing, you maggot cop?"

"No." *No more. Please.*

"Yeah, I'm gonna fix you now. Fix you real good."

Rough hands lifted him, carried him away again.

Back into the nightmare.

Pain.

Pain and the musty odor of damp earth, rotted wood.

Not dead. The dead couldn't feel agony or smell the stench of their own fear.

Buried alive?

Tonio concentrated on opening his eyes. After several tries, he succeeded. Or had he?

He blinked, strained. Nothing but darkness. Where was he?

Turning his head, he shifted his upper body. A burst of fire speared his shoulder and he moaned, riding the pain and sickness. He fought the bile, desperate not to be reduced to lying in his own filth.

The waves passed, a momentary respite. Testing his fingers and toes, he was able to wiggle them and would've wept with relief if he'd had the strength. Thank God. Alive and whole. For now.

The effort, not to mention the battle to avoid throwing up, left him weak. His limbs might as well have been made of lead. He couldn't move his arms and legs, which seemed strangely detached from his relaxed body.

Drugs. Rab had shot him up with something?

That might explain his confusion earlier. He had a concussion, for sure. How long had he been here? Had he been missed yet? Hours and minutes meant nothing in inky blackness.

What would his captor do to him when he returned?

But he knew. Oh God, he knew.

Rab would butcher him like an animal. His life doomed to end like a stinking, gutted corpse rotting on the side of the road.

Maggot food.

"Oh God."

Tonio's stomach rolled, and he turned his head to the side, retching. Dry heaves shook him, wrenching an empty stomach. One small thing to be grateful for in a sea of misery.

When the spasms passed, a new awareness crept in. His arms and legs were bound, his body spread and lying on a bare mattress. They'd taken his clothes, no doubt to humiliate him.

A chill caressed his skin and he began to tremble as though it were the dead of winter. Spring couldn't touch this evil place.

The prison where he would die. Food for the maggots.

"Stop," he choked.

Footfalls sounded from above, slow and steady. Squeaking across old boards, some demon gunslinger entering the You're Fucked Saloon to descend and escort him into the bowels of hell.

Light spilled into his hole. A tall, muscled form descended rickety steps, knife glinting in one hand.

Hysteria seized him and he had the wildest urge to

laugh. But terror froze the cacophony into a million icy crystals in his brain, preventing him from making a sound. Locking the chaos deep inside. He wouldn't give Rab the satisfaction of breaking.

Not ever.

"Well, you're finally awake. I trust you had sweet dreams?"

The smile in the low, masculine voice slid over his skin like a snake. Blinking against the light, he clamped his lips together, not trusting himself to speak. He could barely form a coherent thought, much less negotiate the twisted path of the man's mind.

From now on, every word he uttered would be the wrong one. There was nothing he could say to the crazy fucker bent on destroying him.

"Speechless, cop? You want to know what hell is?"

While he struggled with a response, Rab walked to his side and stood over him. Even with his face in shadow, Tonio saw that the other man's expression wasn't a smile at all, but a snarl. Rage contorted his features into an ugly mask as he waited.

"Where am I?"

"Is that all you have to say for yourself?"

Cold, like a parent scolding a problem child. Tonio fought to suppress his shakes.

*This is a nightmare, and I'll wake up. Please . . .*

"What do you want me to say?" he slurred. Jesus, he was weak. How much blood had he lost? Speaking was more difficult than he'd imagined. "Thanks for fucking up my day?"

"Smart-ass pig," Rab hissed. Kneeling beside him, he

leaned over and jammed the heel of his palm into Tonio's wounded shoulder.

A harsh cry ripped from his throat. Shock waves of agony radiated through his body and he thrashed, yanking uselessly on the bonds. Merciless, Rab ground hard, reopening the wound. Tonio groaned, sweat beading on his forehead, trickling down his face.

By God, he wouldn't beg.

"Go ahead and kill me," he rasped. "Get it over with. It's not like I can stop you."

He suspected—no, prayed like hell—that killing him outright wasn't on Rab's agenda. But he'd take the gamble, anything to distract the man from hurting his inflamed shoulder.

The ruse must've worked, because Rab removed his hand. Then he wiped it on Tonio's chest, smearing him with his own blood. He panted, close to passing out from the pain, and knew oblivion would be preferable to whatever Rab had planned.

"I'm gonna keep you here for a really long time. Just keep you alive so you can entertain us with your suffering. To atone for your sins."

Us? All three of them. *Christ, somebody help me.*

He stalled, the mercurial switch in Rab's mood playing havoc with his pathetic attempt to form a strategy. "What sins? What have I done to you? I didn't do anything but my job. You break the law, you go to jail."

"Shut up. I told you what happens to those who betray me. You're going to find out firsthand."

Light flashed off the blade as Rab brought the knife to the left side of his face, skimming his cheek with the flat surface. Terrified, he fought to suppress the shudders racking his body, but it was no use. The thug didn't seem to notice, or care.

"I'm going to slice open this pretty face of yours. Maybe I'll cut both of your eyes out, then your tongue. Your dick and balls should be next, I think. As a special bonus I'll shove the knife in here." He placed the sharp tip just below the soft flesh of Tonio's navel. "Then I'll plunge it in and rip upward. You know what happens with a cut like that?"

"Yeah," Tonio rasped. "I know."

"Good. That's what I'll do. And when you're dead, I'll dump you on my sister's doorstep so she can see what her pretty boy looks like all filleted like a steak."

"You'd hurt her like that? When all she's tried to do is help you?"

"You know nothing about Angel and me," Rab hissed.

"I know she's the only one who gave you a chance when you came back." There. A small chink in the other man's rage.

"She hooked up with a cop."

"She didn't know, man. I swear, she didn't know." He blinked, trying to concentrate. Not to pass out.

For a long while, Rab just stared at him. Then he said, "I'll think about what you said about Angel. But you? You're going to suffer, cop. Just like I said."

Turning, he stalked back up the steps, leaving Tonio to contemplate all the tortures he'd described.

And for the first time, Tonio began to have a clue about what drove the strongest of men to pray for death.

* * *

Angel stood alone on the balcony of the hotel where she'd been hidden away, gazing at the people in the nearby park below. So many out at sunset, enjoying the last breath of a beautiful spring day. Joggers, children, dogs. Lovers.

Sadness squeezed her heart, and her hands tightened around the mug of hot coffee. She'd brewed a pot for Agent Worth, and poured some for herself as well. She wouldn't sleep without Tonio curled around her, safe and warm. The shadows were lengthening into evening, fast closing in on twenty-four hours since he'd been taken.

"Baby, where are you?" Her throat ached from holding the grief at bay for hours and hours, as much as from the attack.

Tonio was out there somewhere, waiting for rescue. Badly hurt, maybe dying.

He might already be dead.

The mug slipped from her hands and plummeted to the sidewalk four stories below, shattering. The dark stain that splattered across the concrete might've been blood. Tonio's blood, spilling from his broken body—

A large hand on her good arm caused her to jump.

"Miss Silva, are you all right?"

"Agent Worth, you startled me." Splaying a hand on her chest, she attempted a smile and failed miserably.

His amber eyes softened. "Harold, please."

"Harold." She nodded. The name suited this quiet, gentle man. Or at least he was with her.

The corner of his mouth lifted. "Why don't you come back inside? I've got a George Washington that says you can't beat me at Go Fish."

She shook her head. "Harold, I appreciate what you're trying to do, but I'd rather be alone for a while."

"Nah, being alone sucks. I need some company. Come on." Worth jerked his head, indicating for her to follow before disappearing through the sliding door.

Hesitating only a second, Angel trailed the agent inside. *So strange to be here,* she thought. *A few days with Tonio and even going back to my house won't feel like home anymore. More like a prison without bars.* How could she call anywhere home again, without him?

If he never came home.

If he was dead.

Her hands shook, lungs burned.

"I dropped my mug. I'd better go down and clean up the mess before someone steps on a broken shard," she said to no one in particular.

Worth turned to face her, saying something.

She blinked at him. She'd forgotten he was there. "I'm sorry. What?"

"I'll call downstairs. Sit down while I take care of it."

Lowering herself to the sofa, she listened as his deep voice drifted from the kitchen. Idly, she studied the lovely peach petals in the hotel's flower arrangement. *We have to find Tonio before the roses die.* An irrational tangent, but she couldn't help thinking that if the flowers died before Tonio was found, he was gone forever.

A couple of minutes later, Worth returned with a fresh mug and offered it to her. "They're going to send someone to sweep up the mess."

She accepted the mug, grateful to wrap her hands

around the warmth, even if she didn't really have the stomach to drink it. "Thank you."

"No problem." He seated himself in a plump upholstered chair across from her and retrieved his own mug from the coffee table. He took a sip of the brew, then set it down again.

A deck of cards he'd produced, probably from the kitchenette's drawer, rested on the table next to the rose vase. He made no move to retrieve them.

"You don't really want to play Go Fish, do you?" she observed wryly.

"Nope. That was a shameless ploy to get you to stop brooding out there by yourself." His eyebrows drew together, his handsome face growing serious. Thoughtful. "I know this is none of my business, but I need to ask whether you have a support system. Plenty of family, friends. Because you're going to need them to help you through if—"

"No. Tonio is not dead," she choked, holding up a palm. "I'd know."

"I'm not saying he is, but . . ." He rested his elbows on his spread knees and clasped his large hands. Letting out a deep breath, he lowered his head, apparently struggling with the right words. Finally he lifted his gaze, the haunted shadows in their golden depths stealing her breath. "Nobody wants to believe they'll get the worst news, but you and I both know the reality of this type of situation. No one should go through hell alone."

Yes, she knew the terrible odds Tonio faced. And she refused to accept it. "I have my mother, and a few friends."

Indeed, she'd had to do some fast talking to convince the gang from Stroker's not to drive up and storm the hospital after the attack.

Worth nodded, some of the tension easing from his broad shoulders. "Good."

This wasn't the aloof man she'd been introduced to at the hospital. He'd made a valiant attempt to distance himself from Tonio's kidnapping and her pain. The compassionate side of his nature had won out, and Angel wondered why he'd tried so hard to bury it in the first place.

The plain gold band on his left hand caught her attention. Some woman had snagged herself quite a nice and sensitive man. She gave him a tentative smile.

"You're a lucky man to have your wife to discuss things with during the bad times. I hope I know that sort of closeness one day." When Tonio is found safe.

Worth's face paled and he flinched. "Lisa and I used to share everything. She was an extraordinary lady."

*Oh no.* Angel set her mug on the table. "If you don't mind my asking, what happened to her?"

"Lisa and our five-year-old daughter died on September eleventh," he whispered, gazing into his coffee. "They were on American Flight 11 that hit the north tower."

"Oh, I'm so sorry." She shook her head, the horror of those events slamming her all over again. "I don't know what to say."

He looked up, the portrait of bone-deep sorrow. "You can promise not to shut yourself off from your loved ones, should we get bad news about Tonio. I forgot everything Lisa and I believed in, lost the man in myself that I stood for. In the end, my grief nearly killed me. Don't make the same mistakes I did."

The burning in her throat became unbearable. "I have no intention of sitting around here much longer waiting for someone to tell me whether he's alive. But if the worst comes, I swear I'll do my best." Given the tragedy this man had survived, how could she do any less?

"Make sure you do."

Subject closed. Harold didn't offer an account of his fall, or how he'd survived the aftermath of his family's murder. Relieved and a little guilty, she took the hint and let the matter drop.

A knock on the door interrupted their conversation. Otherwise they might've been reduced to Go Fish after all.

The agent stood, reaching into his coat to palm his gun. "I'll see who it is." He crept to the door and peered out the peephole. "Salvatore's partner."

His stance relaxed and he reholstered the weapon before opening the door. Chris walked in, grim-faced and haggard. His normally pressed shirt was rumpled, shirttail hanging out.

She stood, heart thumping, as Worth locked the door behind him. "What's wrong? Do you have news about Tonio?"

"I wish I did," Chris sighed, miserable and exhausted. "We've had a break, though."

"But that's a good thing, right?" she pressed.

Chris and Harold exchanged a somber glance.

"Why don't we sit down?" Chris suggested, avoiding her question.

Knees shaking, she complied, biting back a sharp retort. None of this was his fault, and blasting him the minute he arrived wouldn't help anyone. Harold resumed his seat in the chair while Chris took a place beside her on the sofa.

"First," Chris began, "I just came from the hospital. Austin has finally stabilized and is showing signs of waking up."

"Thank God!" she gasped. "That's wonderful!"

Harold smiled. "Best news I've heard all day."

"He's breathing on his own now, and the doctors think he'll come around by tomorrow. He's not out of the woods by a long shot and recovery will take a few months, but the guy's tough."

Chris stripped off his tie and undid the first couple of buttons on his shirt. He gave Angel a pointed look. "As for the break, what I'm about to say doesn't leave this room."

She stared at him, stung. "Tonio's life is at stake. I would never repeat something that might jeopardize his rescue and you damn well know it."

"Just doing my job and *you* damn well know it," he snapped.

Yes, he was. Chris was under heavy fire, dealing with an awful situation. "Fine, we're clear. The break?"

"Tonio tried to reach me on my cell phone right before he was kidnapped, apparently to tell me that the DNA reports on two murder victims came back from the lab yesterday. I didn't mention this to you earlier because I wanted to go through the paperwork, see for myself what Tonio had learned."

She stilled. "Which is?"

Chris raked a hand through his hair, unable to keep the residual shock and dread off his face. "I'm really sorry to have to tell you this." He hesitated, closed his eyes. Then opened them and met her gaze.

"There was a homicide a while ago, a woman strangled. She'd been partying in a motel room with an unknown man, but DNA was found on the tequila bottle in the room. I'm sorry, but the DNA match came back to Rab."

She stared at Chris, stunned. "My brother killed a woman? In cold blood?"

"She's not the only one, I'm afraid. He matched the DNA found on a previous victim who was killed right after he was released from prison." Chris's look was full of sympathy.

"He's a monster," she whispered. "I harbored a killer and I didn't know it."

"In my career, I've never run across a felon like this Rab."

God, it was going to take more than great, old-fashioned sleuthing to find Tonio alive. It was going to take a miracle.

# 15

"How are the murders a break in finding Tonio?" Angel asked in confusion.

Chris hesitated. "Missing from both victims' possessions were their driver's licenses and their keys. We know Rab is a thief. Taking things is what he does."

"I still don't understand how that helps."

"The key to finding Tonio is understanding your brother," Chris said. "The main thing that made Rab so hard to apprehend before his first prison stay is that he's proficient at finding a bolt-hole. I don't mean a place to stay, like when he's at your house. I mean a hiding place when the heat is on."

"And?"

"He's disappeared this time, too, which means he's employing his old methods. Or at least I'd be willing to bet that's what he's done." Chris leaned forward. "Before, he simply found a vacant house, falsified some ID, and moved right in under his assumed name. Took the authorities a while to catch on. Con artists do it all the time. It's shockingly easy to steal a house, and can be tough to get the fraudulent homeowner legally vacated."

"Is that what you think Rab has done?" She frowned. "You think he's stolen a house to use."

"In a manner of speaking, only he's not quite organized enough to file the paperwork. No, he just needs the place temporarily, and would use one that's vacant and out of the way."

The pieces began to come together. "So you believe he's using a home belonging to one of his recent victims?"

"I'd say it's a good place to start. We already checked out the two women's residences, and there's no sign of anyone. But we found several addresses between them belonging to family members. Assuming Rab used their keys and snooped through their homes before their bodies were discovered, he had a trove of information at his disposal, including possible bolt-holes to use."

"That could be the answer," she cried, shooting to her feet. "Why are you just sitting here when you should be out looking for him?"

"We are, trust me," he reassured her. "We're going through every possible home in this part of the country. I don't feel he got far, personally. We'll find him."

That would take time Tonio didn't have. But what choice was there?

"Can I do anything to help?"

That was a heartbreaking question her friend couldn't answer, because there was nothing. Shoulders slumped, he left, shutting the door quietly behind him.

* * *

Fire.

Tonio's shoulder, his entire arm, throbbed. Burned.

He vaguely remembered being starved for something, anything, to eat. But hunger had long passed to nausea. The thirst, though, was unbearable. His mouth was dry, his tongue swollen. Even through his haze, he knew if Rab didn't give him water and antibiotics soon, he'd die.

Rab had left him alone some time ago. How long? Hours, days? Didn't matter, so long as he stayed the fuck away.

*Please, God, let them find me. Even if I die, don't let me rest in this evil place forever. I want to go home.*

*Too morbid. Focus on the positive.*

*I'm breathing.*

Yeah, that was all he had. It would do.

He lay on his back, wrists and ankles still spread and bound, and concentrated on taking stock of his condition. Sweat rolled in rivulets off his face. Not dehydrated yet, but very ill. His body burned like the fires of Hades, scorching him from the inside out. His stomach pitched. With every breath, his lungs wheezed.

"Oh *madre de Dios*." Infection had set in. Without water and medical attention, death hovered near. The beginning of the end.

Heavy footsteps moved toward his hole. His heart constricted, morose thoughts scattered. Deliberately he blanked his mind, attempting to rise above the fear. The urge to beg for his life nearly overwhelmed him. But his professional experience and his intelligence were the only weapons he had left to fight with. If he lost those, he had nothing.

All too soon, Rab descended into his private hell. Hesitating at the bottom of the steps, he pulled a string to click on a single lightbulb dangling from overhead. Expression closed, he walked to Tonio's bedside and stood over him.

He squinted against the sudden brightness, letting his vision adjust, and got his first clear view of his captor and the surroundings. Like before, Rab gripped the ever-present knife in his hand. A fresh syringe poked up from the front pocket of his shirt.

Best to take advantage of his somewhat clear head, before the asshole drugged him again. Swallowing hard, he tried to lick his dry lips. Taking a deep breath, he injected as much venom into his tone as possible. "What took you so long, you fucker?" Damn, his voice was rusty.

Surprise flickered across Rab's face. Then anger. He sat on the mattress next to Tonio and fingered the tip of the knife. "I'm here now, cop."

"I'm glad." Christ, he wanted to vomit. "Why don't you just kill me?"

"Maybe I will."

"Where am I?"

"You're in the storage cellar of the barn on some property I'm borrowing from the grandfather of an old friend. Sharon Waite. Sound familiar?"

Sharon Waite . . . She was a murder victim. Rab had somehow gotten his hands on her grandfather's property? That was evil. *Keep him talking.*

"You killed her."

"The place is nice. Probably more than she deserved anyhow."

The monster had no remorse. Tonio shivered.

"How long have I been here?" he slurred. He felt himself sinking, tiring fast.

"This is day two, but what difference does it make?" Rab paused, smiled a little. "You'll be gone soon anyway."

"Wow. Time flies, huh? Say, since you're going to kill me anyway . . . I'm pretty thirsty and my shoulder hurts. I was wondering—"

"Wondering what?" he snarled, jabbing the open shoulder wound with the handle of the knife. "I don't give a fuck if you're in pain or thirsty, lying cop!"

*Shit!* The white-hot agony shooting down his arm made his head spin. "Wait, please. I just need a little water—"

The hand with the knife pressed the tip into his chest, just under his left nipple. Blood welled and ran down his side.

"Rab, please." His voice broke. "Forgive me for betraying you."

"Why should I?"

"I saved your life," he rasped. "That has to be worth something."

*Don't let me die this way!*

Heart in his throat, he panted, staring at the gang leader, anticipating the deadly stroke. His words seemed to penetrate, and the other man's anger slowly drained. Rab lifted the blade from his chest.

"Sure. Some fucking water. I'll bring some next time."

There wouldn't be a next time. He didn't believe Rab would make good on bringing a damn thing and his throat, his whole body, burned with the need for water.

The all-too-familiar sting pricked his arm and his captor retreated, leaving him blessedly alone.

Only when his footsteps had faded did he give in to his sorrow. The truth hit him hard. He wasn't going to leave here alive. Who'd tell his mama and Maria? He would never see Angel again, never make love to her. The laughter of children would never fill their home, but in time, she'd heal and move on. Have babies that weren't his.

*"Dios."*

Grief left him spent. Hollow. The drug rushing in his veins beckoned him into the darkness, a gentle lover soothing the pain. The terror. He welcomed the caress.

*Yes, sleep.* Forget, just for a while, that when Rab returned, so would his waking nightmare. *Don't think of the depraved, horrible torture he intended. None of it mattered anymore.*

Because when Rab crept into his dark, miserable hole again, the monster would kill him.

In the hotel bedroom, Angel surfed the Internet, searching for an article she'd read before. The one covering the murder of Sharon Waite. What she hoped to gain by finding it, she didn't know, but it beat going insane from waiting on word from Chris.

He'd called once earlier in the day, only to say his colleague Shane had pulled two detectives from another case to assist in poring over Rab's victims' files. As promised, he was closing in on her brother's criminal past. Seemed her brother had stolen from people in several states, and appropriated homes in many of them for his own use.

He hoped to have a list by this afternoon of the most likely places Rab and his men could be hiding.

That had been hours ago. What if the lead turned out to be nothing?

With grim resolve, she shoved the unacceptable thought out of her mind and concentrated on the screen. There. Sharon had loved visiting her late grandparents' home outside Nashville, where she spent long summers canning peaches with her nana. As an interesting side note, Sharon's grandfather, Ralph Waite, was a former City of Sugarland employee.

What did that prove? Just that Sharon and the grandparents were all deceased now. The article didn't say whether the home was vacant, or exactly where it was located.

As she printed the article to show Chris later, the soft noise of the television drifting from the living room reminded her of Harold's presence. The poor man had been stuck to her side for forty-eight hours. When she'd apologized and asked whether anyone could relieve him, the agent merely grinned and declared he didn't have a problem watching over pretty damsels in distress. And he liked the overtime even more. Angel suspected he was really a workaholic who avoided going home to an empty house and painful memories of his lost family.

Article in hand, she padded into the living room and smiled. Worth's big body was stretched out in a recliner, TV remote in hand, flipping channels. Must be branded into the male genetic code. When in the vicinity of a television, her father and brother used to assume the same position.

She prayed she'd have the chance to see Tonio resting comfortably in his favorite chair, channel surfing. Every day, for the rest of their lives.

"Can I get you something to drink from room service? Coffee or soda?" Her voice came out strained, husky.

Harold turned his head and grimaced. "I'd sell my soul for a cold beer right now, but I'm on the clock. Coffee, I suppose. But don't let me stop you from getting something to ease the nerves."

She shook her head. "Coffee's good for me, too. I don't need a downer on top of being terrified for Tonio."

"I know exactly what you mean."

Oh, she couldn't handle the sadness in his voice. The empathy. Retreating to the kitchenette, she laid the article on the counter and busied herself with the mindless chore of putting on the coffee.

Glancing into the other room, she noted the roses. The blooms had fully opened. Some drooped. Balanced upon the threshold of life and death. Tomorrow, they would begin to fade.

She fumbled, switching on the coffeepot. A knock came at the door.

For such a big man, Harold moved like a graceful cat. He palmed his weapon, checked to identify their visitor, and stepped back to admit Chris.

Coffee forgotten, Angel rushed to meet him. Her friend looked worn, at the end of his rope. Not good news.

"Waite's parents are deceased as well," he said without preamble. "They lived in Clarksville. I had a couple of Clarksville detectives visit the parents' old house. According to a neighbor, Sharon sold the house after they died, and there's nothing suspicious about the new owner."

Worth swore. "Now what?"

Chris sighed before continuing. "I need just one goddamn shred connecting Rab to any one of these residences and I'll be all over that bastard. I won't need a search warrant, either."

"Literally?" Angel glanced between the two men.

"Yes. Because a law enforcement officer's life is in danger," Worth explained. "Under the law, that's an emergency not requiring us to obtain a warrant to search private property, or anywhere else."

Chris nodded, face grim. "Yeah, but we must have strong probable cause first. If we barge in there and Tonio's nowhere to be found, and we don't turn up compelling evidence related to the case or that he'd been held there, the chief will roast me over an open fire."

In English, they had zilch. At least until one of the leads panned out. The wait was maddening.

Chris made a poor attempt to distract her by changing the subject. He gestured to her bandages. "How's your arm? Are you taking your medication?"

"Throbbing just enough to make sure I don't forget about it, but healing. And yes, I'm drugged to the eyeballs," she lied. Okay, just a tiny half lie. The antibiotics were fine; she shied away from the painkillers. She didn't want anything impairing her thinking, especially now. "How's Austin today? Have you been to see him?"

"Yeah. Good news, finally. He woke up this afternoon."

"Thank God! When?"

"Around four. He's heavily medicated and can't hold a conversation yet, but he's on his way back."

"Man, that's great." Worth nodded.

"I intend to visit him tomorrow, whether you like it or

not," she informed Chris. "I won't stay holed up here indefinitely."

"You will if you're a witness under my protection." At her fierce scowl, he relented. "But if Worth doesn't mind driving you over, I guess that's all right."

"I don't mind," Harold put in. "I'd like to see him myself."

That settled, she retrieved the article from the kitchen counter and handed it to Chris. "Take a look at this."

He murmured the title aloud, then read the article to himself. When he finished, his eyebrows drew together. "Your point is?"

"It's another possible place to check out."

He swore. Harold came to stand next to Chris, peering down at the paper.

"I found the article on the Internet this afternoon. It says she used to spend the summer at her grandparents' place. I thought it was worth a look."

Chris skimmed the piece again. "Good thinking. I'll put this on the list."

On the list. She wanted someone out there, at every possible place, now! But he'd explained the need for caution. More hours to wait, precious time wasted. Frustration and anger swelled, a hot bubble in her breast. Soon she would either suffocate or explode.

*Unless I take action.*

Chris put an arm around her shoulders and drew her into a hug. "Don't worry, sweetheart. We're gonna find him."

She clung to him for a few moments, taking the comfort her friend offered. Resting her head against his broad chest, she let his strength blanket her, inhaled his dark, musky scent. Pretended these strong arms belonged to a laughing, Latino cop with onyx eyes . . .

The dam broke at last. There was no stopping the flood.

"Go ahead," he whispered, tucking the top of her head under his chin. "You've been so brave. Let it out."

Her body jerked with the force of her sobs. The black abyss she'd been staving off engulfed her, turned her inside out, exposed her worst fears to the light. She cried until the sobs tapered to hiccups and even then, couldn't stop shaking.

Awareness returned. She sensed Harold hovering, unsure what to do. And she felt Chris's hitching breaths, realized he was trying to hold back. She tilted her face up to look at him.

His disheveled, brown-gold hair shone under the bright kitchen lights. His sad whiskey eyes were glossy.

"We're doing everything we can to nail Rab and find Tonio," he choked. "But I'm not going to lie to you about what we're facing. Angel, he's been missing too long."

"You believe he's dead." Hands trembling badly, she wiped her face.

"With all my heart, I hope I'm wrong." Gently he touched her face. "I'd give my life to bring him home to you. To everyone."

She took his big hand and pressed a kiss to his knuckles. "I know. Thank you."

He pulled her into a last, brief hug and let go. "Better shove off and see if the boys combing over the files have hit on anything. They're tag-teaming, working around the clock on leads until we find him." He glanced at Harold. "Agent Worth, take good care of her."

Harold cleared his throat. "You bet."

She didn't miss the regret etched on Chris's face as he left, article in hand.

After he'd gone, she poured the coffee neither of them now wanted. They sat in the living room making small talk, whiling away the bleak hours long past midnight, sipping the brew. She drank a second cup, knowing she had to stay awake for what she was going to do. Nothing would stop her.

Yawning, Angel finally excused herself for the night, leaving Harold to stretch out on the sofa. Ensconced in her bedroom, she paced, waiting for him to fall asleep.

Chris had to follow restrictive, by-the-book, time-consuming procedure, but she damn well didn't. The problem was, she needed help to carry out her plan. How in the hell did one go about finding an address for Ralph Waite, a former city employee? Who possessed the knowledge and authority to do such a thing, and wouldn't mind risking Austin's wrath if caught?

She didn't know. Who—oh! She had it.

Andy's older sister, Honey Webster. The woman worked in records at the Sugarland PD and missed nothing that went on at the station. If anyone knew how to get a simple address, Honey did. Would she be willing to help?

Pulling out her iPhone, she texted Andy and asked for his sister's number. True to form, the young bartender was never without his phone on him at all times. In seconds she had the number. Taking a deep breath, she punched it in. Honey answered on the third ring, voice muffled with sleep.

"Hello?"

"Honey," she whispered urgently. "It's Angel. Andy's boss at Stroker's."

"What? Who?"

"It's me, Angel."

"Oh! Angel?" A rustle, like she was sitting up, ended on a gasp. "My Lord, have they found Tonio? Andy's been keeping me posted, and of course it's all over the station, what with a detective being kidnapped."

"No, and that's why I'm calling. Honey, I need your help. What I'm asking could get us both into a lot of trouble with a lot of cops, but I don't know where else to turn."

Fully awake now, Honey gave a rueful laugh. "Sugar, I divorced the world's biggest asshole. There's trouble, and then there's trouble. What's cookin'?"

Relief made her dizzy, and she closed her eyes briefly, outlining her plan.

"That's all? Not a problem. I normally man the front desk, but I've had to sub for Glenda in personnel plenty where they have access to more records. I can probably retrieve the information and be out in a jiff."

"Are you absolutely sure you want to do this?" She squeezed the phone in a death grip.

"Positive. What time do you want to meet?"

"Four thirty?"

"Okay. By the front entrance. You wait outside all nice and casual until I come out."

"Will do. And, Honey, thanks. I owe you."

"Make that a long cocktail lunch, and I'll collect."

"You got it."

Hanging up, she stood, readying to leave, and tucked her iPhone in her pocket. If all went well, she'd need it handy. Then she turned off the bedroom light and opened the door slowly. Listening. The rumble of Harold's soft snoring drifted into the hallway. Gritting her teeth, she crept down the short passage, past the kitchen to the dining table where her purse and keys rested.

The keys! Damn, she should've put them in her purse before the agent went to sleep. Throwing a nervous glance at Harold, she saw him lying on his side facing her, breathing evenly. Deep in dreamland. A stab of regret pricked her conscience. She hoped he wouldn't be in too much hot water with his bosses over this. Or with Chris, even though they worked for different law enforcement entities.

*Sorry, big guy. You won't help me leave and you'd only be in my way.*

She eased the strap of her purse over one shoulder, then closed her hand tightly around the ring of keys before lifting them off the table. Done. The only remaining barrier was getting out the door without waking him.

She tiptoed to the entry, turned the dead bolt by slow degrees. The sound of it releasing cracked like a gunshot and she looked fearfully to Worth. The agent didn't stir.

Before slipping to freedom, Angel gazed at the roses. In a patch of moonlight, the blooms drooped, forlorn.

Several petals lay scattered around the vase like silvery tears.

# 16

Honey had no trouble pulling Sharon Waite's grandparents' address from employee records. The station was running with a skeleton crew at that early hour, none but a few early birds about.

Sure, she could've just asked Chris. After all, he'd already checked and knew where the house was located. But her friend would've known what was in her head the instant she broached the subject, and nipped her covert op in the bud.

Driving north, she hoped the station had the correct address in their files. It was located a mere eleven miles from Tonio's home. Perfect for the abduction.

It occurred to her that the FBI and Sugarland PD already knew this as well. Chris must have the house under surveillance, awaiting the tangible evidence that would allow his men to move in rapidly. He hadn't let on, but she didn't have a single doubt that was what he'd done.

She'd have to be careful to keep out of sight until she'd had a chance to search the premises. That way, no one could question her status as a private citizen who'd acted on her own, and the joint FBI/police case remained clean. One way or another, she'd soon learn whether Tonio was there.

Exiting the highway, she took the road west to a town called Blue Ridge. Within minutes, her headlights illuminated the small green sign of the county road she'd been looking for. She made a left, grateful for the concealment of the heavily treed landscape. Damn creepy in the dark, but better than being completely exposed on approach.

A mile or so down the road to her right, the foliage parted to reveal a gravel driveway. Beyond that, a small white one-story frame house crouched in the weeds. A car was parked next to the house. As she passed, the reflective letters on the old metal mailbox at the end of the drive flashed the name Waite.

She drove well past the house, around a bend in the road, and continued on for about half a mile before pulling onto the shoulder and shutting off the lights. An overgrown ditch, really. The weeds helped to conceal her car. A perfect spot to approach the house from the back. However, if she did find Tonio, he might not be able to walk the distance back. She shook her head. If he was here, Satan himself wasn't going to stop her from getting him out.

Locking the car, she pocketed her keys, made certain her cell phone was on vibrate, shoved it deeper into the front pocket of her jeans, and started through the woods. The sky had begun to gray in the east. As thankful as she was for not having to stumble blind through undergrowth, the loss of total darkness meant she had to quickly find a good place to wait, out of sight. Though she hadn't seen evidence of any agents, they were close enough to come running if Chris gave the go-ahead. A comforting idea right about now.

The woods gradually thinned, and she found herself staring at the back of a dilapidated old barn squatting about thirty yards behind the house. The gray, weathered structure wasn't very large, more like an oversized storage shed that had never seen an animal and was probably crammed with an assortment of ancient junk.

No signs of life. Stealthily she crept from the trees and dashed at a half crouch to the back of the barn. Pressing herself against the rotted boards, she inched to the corner and peeked around the side—and nearly had a heart attack. Rab's car was visible from here. Which meant Tonio was probably on the premises. Nothing to do but wait.

*Please, let Rab leave.* Her heart knocked a tattoo against her ribs. What if he caught her? What if Harold awoke and alerted Chris before she completed her task? Shit, he might've woke up already!

*Breathe, focus.*

The grating rasp of an engine turning over nearly sent her into cardiac arrest. Hand on her chest, she peered around the corner again in time to see Rab's car back out of the driveway and pull away at a normal speed.

Gone! After waiting a few more moments, she decided none of Rab's men were there. She had to make her move. Where to start? Keeping close to the barn, she rounded the corner and crept down the side. Reaching the front, she walked to the wide door, which stood ajar, and looked inside. Junk, just as she'd thought. Tractor parts, rotted water hoses, weed killer that obviously hadn't seen combat duty, and a tiller. Inside the house was the most likely place, then.

She sprinted across the scruffy yard to the back of the house. A high window on her right seemed like a good place to start. Standing on her toes, she looked into a small kitchen, surprisingly clean and tidy. And floral, including the wallpaper and the curtains.

Wrinkling her nose, she methodically looked into each window. So much for staying out of sight, but no one came bursting through the trees to arrest her. All the blinds were tilted open enough to see that the tiny house was empty. Two bedrooms, one living area, one bath. All clean. She checked the base of the house and found it to be a solid concrete slab, unlike many homes in Tennessee. No basement.

Tonio wasn't here. Despair swamped her, grief filling her soul. She'd been wrong. Rab could've hidden Tonio anywhere. Chris was right. Three days was far too long.

Tonio was most likely dead.

She sagged against the back of the house, tears blurring her vision. Through the haze, the open barn door snagged her attention. A slight breeze kicked up, causing it to swing on rusty hinges. Beckoning.

But the building had yielded nothing.

*Take another look. Why not?*

Wiping her face, she walked to the structure, this time stepping inside. To her surprise, her boots made contact with wooden flooring instead of dirt. She glanced around the depressing space, unsure what she was looking for.

The sun had started to come up, and light filtered through the cracks in the walls, allowing her to see better. The outlines of various garden tools hanging on hooks took shape. Hedge trimmers, a rake, a hoe, and a shovel. Little else.

She moved farther inside. The boards squeaked under her shoes. Frowning, she stamped a foot. A hollow echo answered. Planting both feet, she bent her knees and bounced. The flooring gave.

"No ground underneath." Her pulse sped up, yet she stood still. Listening, letting her gaze touch every corner of the building.

And there, in the far left corner, was a cutout square in the flooring. A square with no hinge, but a metal handle affixed near one edge for lifting the entire piece off.

In an instant, she was squatting next to the square, yanking the handle with all her strength. At last, she was able to free the panel from the floor and drag it out of the way.

A set of rickety wooden steps descended into darkness. She didn't waste a second scrambling the ten feet or so to the bottom. She blinked, allowing her eyes to adjust.

And there, in the dim light filtering from the trapdoor above, was Tonio.

"Oh! Oh my God!"

The cry tore from her throat as she rushed to his side. He'd been bound to an old bed frame with thick ropes, naked and spread-eagle. His body was battered, a deep, infected wound in his shoulder, and he'd been badly abused.

She knelt, reached out, and smoothed his hair away from his face. Heat radiated off his skin. "Tonio? Can you hear me? Please, baby, wake up."

Long black lashes rested against his cheeks, dark with stubble but pale underneath. His lips were cracked, every harsh breath crackling like dry leaves in his chest. Her gaze swept downward, taking in the multicolored, festering wound on his right shoulder. Thin cuts marred his chest and torso. Nearly every inch of his skin was smeared with blood.

She rested a palm on his burning cheek. Merciful God, he was so sick. She couldn't have found the man she loved only to lose him!

The cell phone in her pocket vibrated a greeting. Snatching it out, she spied Chris's cell phone number on the display. Bracing herself, she answered, "Chris?"

"Where in the fuck are you?" he shouted. "Angel, I swear to God—"

"I found him! Tonio's here and—"

"What? Where?"

"Sharon Waite's grandparents' place! Chris, he's in bad shape. Hurry, please," she choked.

"Shit! Angel, listen. Get out of there—do you understand? Rab is on his way there. We got a tip he was seen driving that way. Get out now!"

The blood drained from her face. "No. I can't leave him. I have to try and get him to my car."

"Do it fast. We're already en route, just a few more minutes. I'll explain later. Hang tight, okay?"

"Just hurry." Angel ended the call, hooked the phone to her jeans, and patted Tonio's cheek. "Honey, please wake up."

"Nooo." He turned his head, moaning. "No more."

Her stomach pitched. No more what? No time to

think about what horrors he'd endured. Hands shaking, she went to work on the knots in the ropes binding his wrists, breaking three nails in the process. Five minutes and only one wrist freed. Too slow. Panic swelled and she squashed it with an effort. *Think!*

The hedge trimmers! Heedless of the unstable steps, she raced up to the main level and plucked the tool from the wall. These would make short work of the ropes.

Rushing back to his side, she leaned over his chest, capturing the rope binding his other wrist in the jaws of the trimmer. In seconds, the tool sliced through the thick bond. His freed arm dropped to the mattress and Tonio stirred, groaning.

"That's it, sweetie," she encouraged, setting to work on the bindings at his ankles. "Wake up so I can get you away from here."

Done. They'd worry about removing the rope tied around the one wrist and his ankles later. She tossed the hedge trimmers into a corner and scrambled back to his side. His dark eyes were half-open, dazed. Her heart leaped with hope.

She took his face in her hands. "Tonio? It's Angel. Look at me."

Tonio turned his head toward her voice. His glassy eyes found her face. Widened. "Angel?" he croaked.

She tried for a laugh, but it emerged as a sob. "Yes, baby. Listen to me. We have to get you out of here. Can you sit up?"

"I'm . . . dreaming." He smiled, started to close his eyes. "Good dream."

She patted his face, putting more sting behind it. "No, you don't, copper. Let me see those gorgeous eyes of yours."

He blinked, then stared in astonishment. "You're real. *Dios*, Angel." His voice broke. "You shouldn't have come. He'll hurt you, too."

Christ, what had that lunatic put him through? She swallowed back her own tears. "Shh, sweetie. I need for you to listen and try to follow, okay?"

"All right."

"First, I'm going to help you sit up. Try to scoot toward me so we can put your left arm around my shoulders."

He did, clenching his teeth against the pain the movement must be causing his right shoulder and arm, which were angry red and swollen with infection. She helped him sit up and drape his arm around her. Just that bit of exertion had him panting.

"You're doing fine. Now comes the hard part. You've got to get up those steps so I can help you to my car."

"I don't know . . . if I can walk. Sick. And the drugs."

Rage scored her soul. The crazy asshole had kept him drugged! "You don't have a choice, hotshot. Rab is on his way back, so we need to get your ass moving."

"I'm naked."

"Yeah, like you've ever had a problem with that around me before. Come on." She tried to lift him up, but he shook his head.

"Blanket's over there," he insisted, jerking his chin toward a dark corner.

An old, dirty thing from the looks of it. But it would do. "Okay. I'll get the blanket, but we'll get you up the stairs before I wrap you in it, so you don't trip."

She retrieved the blanket and tucked it under her left arm, then sat beside him. He put his good arm around her shoulders again and they pushed up together. He swayed and nearly fell, but managed to steady himself. She gave him a few seconds to get his bearings.

His forehead beaded with sweat, but he nodded, jaw clenched in the stubborn determination she knew so well. "Let's go."

They shuffled forward. At the bottom of the steps, Tonio motioned for her to go first. She hurried up, then knelt at the edge of the hole and held out a hand to encourage him. He more or less crawled upward, stopping only once to catch his breath. When his head emerged, she grabbed his uninjured arm and pulled.

At last he was out, on his hands and knees, trembling violently. He sat up, bracing his palms on his corded thighs. Lifting his head, he gazed at her through a fall of damp, spiky black hair. "I love you. So much."

She touched his cheek, afraid of the misery in his eyes. The pain running far deeper than the physical. "I love you, too."

He hesitated, looking torn. Hurt. "You might not feel the same when you know how weak I was. When I wanted to die."

"No." She placed her fingers over his lips. "Nothing will change my love for you. You're mine, for better or worse. Now, we'll talk about all the bad stuff later, for as long as you need. Let's focus on getting you to my car, as fast as possible."

The shadows on his face eased, but only some. The

abuse Rab had put him through was going to take a while to heal. And he'd need a lot of love.

She helped him struggle to his feet, then wrapped the blanket around his hips. Tucking the loose end in at his waist, she put an arm around him and urged him toward the door.

Tonio squinted against the morning sun, trying to wrap his mind around what had just happened. His beautiful woman was here, had rescued him. How?

Nothing made sense, but that was likely the lingering effect of the drug. All he really understood at this point was her haste to get him away from this living hell. A damn fine idea.

He leaned on her for balance, careful to keep the brunt of his weight off her frame. This strong, brave woman was actually carrying him like one soldier helping another wounded comrade off a battlefield, and it made his heart swell with love and pride.

Dried grass pricked at his bare feet as she guided him into the backyard. She stopped and looked up at him, her gorgeous face scrunched in concern. Her long dark hair was pulled back into a ponytail, making her look like a fresh-faced young girl of twenty.

"We've got to hurry. Chris is on his way with backup, but they're a few minutes out. My car is parked down the road, about half a mile past the house. Can you walk, or should I run and get the car?"

"I can make it."

"But he won't be going anywhere."

Beside him, Angel gasped, tightening her grip on him.

God, no. Not when they'd been so close.

The earth spun as Rab stepped into view from the corner of the house, holding a gun trained on them. The fringes of his vision grayed, and he willed himself not to pass out.

"Get behind me," he rasped, taking his arm from Angel's shoulder and moving in front of her. She laid a hand on his back, but stayed put, not uttering a sound.

Whatever had made Rab human at one time was gone. In his gaze, Tonio saw the hatred for both him and Angel.

"Where do you think you're going?" he hissed, leveling the gun at Tonio's heart. "Good thing I decided I couldn't stand to spend the day away from torturing you, or I wouldn't have caught my sister sneaking off with her worthless cop."

*Jesus.* "Rab, you don't really want to hurt me. You kept me in a dark hole with no food or water, sure. And I'm sick, but if you had wanted to kill me—"

"Really? I want to kill you so fucking bad I can taste your death in my mouth." His lip curled. "I want to hear you scream."

"It's not going to happen. This ends here and now, Rab. Why don't you stop blaming me and everyone else around you for your mistakes?"

"What would someone like you know about mistakes? You've probably been coddled since you were a baby." His lips twisted into a snarl and he thrust the muzzle of the gun at Tonio's chest for emphasis. "My daddy was a crook and my mother's a worthless bitch."

"Be a man, Rab. A man makes his own choices. You get to decide who you want to be." *Until they cart you off to prison again.* Best to leave out that part. Christ, his shoulder was on fire.

Rab gave a cold laugh, finger tightening on the trigger, and Tonio hurried on. "I know a lot about making mistakes. My fiancée left me at the altar and ran off with my best friend. I wished they'd rot in hell and they died in an accident shortly after that."

Nausea cramped his gut, and a wave of vertigo nearly sent him to his knees. *Hold out a little longer, keep the bastard talking.*

"That's not a mistake," Rab scoffed. "That's shitty timing. You're a liar and you betrayed me. You deserve to die for that."

"I'm a cop, and I want to help you," he said. "I understand the torment you've had to deal with all your life, or at least I'm trying. I'll get help for you. Counselors, whatever you need—"

"They don't give headshrinkers to people like me!" he cried. "All I ever wanted was to be important. Be somebody like my old man never was. Was that too much to ask?"

Yes. He'd murdered two women and who knew how many others? The nightmare had to end.

"Rab, put down the gun."

"Why couldn't you be the real deal?" he asked in confusion. "I thought this really cool guy, not those other losers, wanted to be my friend. I thought finally I'll be somebody. We'll do jobs together, and be tight, like brothers. I always wanted a brother." The gun wavered in his hand, lowered a bit.

"We can still be tight. I do care about you. I saved your life, didn't I? What does that tell you?"

Suddenly bodies detached themselves from the trees on both sides of the standoff. Chris had arrived with Shane and Shane's partner, Taylor. Tonio didn't dare allow his focus to stray from Rab, but out of his peripheral vision, he saw figures dart to either side of the barn. Chris and Agent Worth appeared at each corner of the house, behind Rab, quietly moving in with guns drawn. The agents had the gang leader neatly surrounded, but unless Tonio could talk the man down, this wasn't going to end well.

Behind Rab, Chris waved frantically. A movement caught Tonio's eye and he spared a quick glance to his right. The sight made his blood freeze. Angel was easing around him, slowly moving even with Rab's left side.

He licked his cracked lips, held Rab's gaze, and went for broke. "Put the gun down and we'll leave together, wherever you want to go. Like brothers. Please." He held out his hand, took a couple of steps closer.

Rab heard the deception in his voice. And he knew it was over. Everything, really over. His face crumpled and he let out a low moan of anguish, like a wounded animal. His eyes locked with Tonio's, and Tonio read his fate in their depths one split second before he jerked the gun high.

Pointed it at his head.

"Fucking liar!" Rab shrieked.

"No, I—"

Angel leaped just before Rab fired, but Tonio beat her to him. He charged straight into Rab, slamming him into the ground as the gun went off. The pain Tonio expected didn't happen, and he prayed the shot hadn't hit anyone else.

They struggled for control of the gun, and Chris rushed for them, getting Rab in a headlock. The thug was as strong as a bull, and wasn't surrendering the weapon. He and Tonio had the gun in a death grip, and if Tonio let go, he was dead.

Slowly the tide began to turn. Their muscles strained. Rab's grip weakened and finally Tonio was able to wrest the gun from him. Kneeling, he gathered the blanket around his hips, which wasn't doing too much good shielding him at this point, and stood. Chest heaving for breath, he kept the weapon trained on Rab. The other man stilled, palms up.

"You got me." He laughed a little, as though in disbelief.

"You have the right to remain silent." Chris was trying to get the man's hands behind him, got one cuff on a wrist and was trying to get the other when it all went to hell.

"But you forgot my backup."

"Anything you say can and will be used against you . . ." Chris snapped the second cuff in place—just as Rab's smirk, and the meaning behind his words, registered. A glint of sunlight reflected off a barrel in the trees, and he glimpsed Phil's face.

Tonio shouted, "Angel, everybody, down!"

Angel and the others dove. Tonio turned to face the threat and opened fire, distantly aware that he was standing right in the middle of the gun battle as gunshots were returned. He knew a moment's satisfaction when Phil tumbled from the brush facedown.

And then one more shot from the trees. Another. A punch to his chest, to his abdomen. Tonio fell, legs folding, fire igniting in his torso. He hit the ground hard, fighting to stay conscious, stay alive. He hurt, everywhere.

Cops and FBI shouting. A woman's stricken screams.

Angel?

"Officer down! Officer down! Get CareFlite in here!" Chris's voice, urging. "Breathe, buddy. Damn you, don't give up now."

"Tonio? Please don't leave me!" Angel begged.

*I won't,* he tried to say. But his lips wouldn't move.

*So hard to breathe, so hard . . . Don't want to die.*

No use. He couldn't stop the rising black tide, and the darkness engulfed him.

Over and over, the horror ran through Angel's head, unfolding in freeze-framed snapshots. Knowing she was about to watch Tonio die, and her helplessness to prevent it.

Rab, coming unhinged.

The dawning horror on Tonio's face when he knew Rab's men had ambushed them.

The gunshots. Screaming.

Tonio, crumpled on the ground, unmoving.

Touch-and-go. Three words spoken by kind, well-meaning doctors. Hated words that had filled her life—all of their lives—with renewed terror for the past four agonizing days.

She couldn't take much more, not without some sort of reassurance, any small sign, that Tonio was going to pull through.

But as she turned from the small window of his hospital room for the hundredth time and drank in the sight of him, so silent and pale, she knew that for a fat lie. She loved him so much her insides ached. As long as it took, whatever it took, she'd see him back on his feet.

Tonio turned his head, moaning low in his throat. Her heart thudded with hope, quickly tempered by a stinging reality check. He'd been moving a bit and making small sounds all day. Trying to come around, the doctors said, which he'd do when his body was ready.

"Nooo." He stirred again and flinched, jerking away from some unseen terror.

She sat beside him, reached out, and smoothed the soft black strands of hair off his face as she'd done so often in the last four days. Careful of his injuries, she stroked him wherever it was safe to touch, offering what comfort she could.

"Shh, baby. I'm here, and I'm not going anywhere. Try to wake up and open your eyes. Can you do that for me? Your family is here. You mom, Maria, Julian, and Grace. A whole crap load of cops, too. They're all waiting to see you."

Not yet. He stilled, and hours dragged by before he stirred again. But she sensed—prayed—he was making his way back. Finally.

A movement flickered behind his lids. At last, his long lashes swept upward. Dark eyes stared back at her in confusion from an angular face made sharper from weight loss. God, he was still the most beautiful man she'd ever seen.

"Welcome back." She smiled. *Do not cry.*

Awareness of his surroundings, of her, seeped into his expression. His gaze cleared and he gave her a lopsided grin.

"Hey, *bonita*," he whispered. "You haven't run for the hills yet?"

She bent over, kissed him gently on the lips. "Not a chance, cop. I paid my dues and now you're stuck with me."

"Good. You'd have a tough time . . . getting rid of me." Abruptly his happiness morphed into worry. "Austin?"

"He pulled through, sweetie," she reassured him.

Tonio blew out a breath, relieved. "That's great."

"A miracle. He woke up a few days ago. He's regaining his strength, but it's going to take time. If he behaves, the nurses are going to wheel him in tomorrow to visit you. I think they're tired of him pestering them to get out of bed."

"I can't wait to . . . see his ugly face again." His attempt at good humor faded and he stared at her, swallowing hard. "There at the end. I knew I was going to die."

"You were wrong." She cupped his cheek, waiting. He had more to say, a terrible weight to get off his chest.

"I wasn't afraid of death." His throat worked convulsively as he struggled for the right words. "I knew that in one second, the world would go on without me. You would go on and I'd never hold you again."

"Oh, Tonio," she choked. "Come here."

Taking great care not to bump his healing right shoulder, she cradled his head with her left arm. He leaned into her, nuzzling his face into her neck, brushing a sweet kiss at the hollow of her throat. His hair tickled her cheek and she held him for a long while, loving the feel of his solid body against hers. Alive and warm.

He drifted into sleep again, waking deep into the night.

Shaking off exhaustion, she kissed the top of his head. "Dumb question, but how do you feel?"

"Tired," he admitted. "I feel like I've been beaten with hammers."

"I'll have the nurse bring you something."

"Later. Talk to me."

She smiled at the little-boy tone in his voice. "About?"

"How long I've been out of it. What happened?"

Angel pulled away and helped him ease back into his pillow. Once she had him settled again, she took his hand.

"You've kept us out of our minds with worry for four days. Especially your family, who are all here, by the way. Well, not actually in the hospital at the moment. I coaxed them into leaving to get some rest, which wasn't easy, I'll tell you. Your mom and sister are staying at your place with me."

"Good." He smiled weakly.

She squeezed his fingers. "Anyway, you took a bullet to the chest and the abdomen. You've also had a severe concussion, which is part of the reason you've been unconscious so long. The real danger was how sick you'd become during captivity."

"My lungs feel heavy. Kinda wheezy."

"The infection from the knife wound in your shoulder and the other smaller cuts had spread. You'd developed pneumonia, too. You nearly died," she said quietly. "After all you'd been through, I almost lost you."

"But you didn't, *dulce*. You saved my life." His face tightened with emotion.

"When I saw you get shot, I thought I'd cost you your life." There. Her secret, all-consuming guilt, spoken aloud. "If only I'd waited for Chris, you would've been fine."

"No. I was a dead man, Angel. He was returning to kill me and who knows if they would've made their move in time to stop him? They wouldn't have known for sure where I was." His gaze sparked onyx fire. "But don't ever do anything like that again. You could've been killed."

The burden of his shooting lifted some. She had done what she felt was the right thing. In spite of his fussing, she'd do it again.

"What about Rab?"

"He's in jail without bond until his trial for at least two counts of murder and the attempted murders of a cop and a federal agent. Chris is saying he'll never see the light of day again, and believe me, I'm fine with that." She touched his beloved face. "Now you should rest. You're talking too much."

The corner of his mouth hitched up. "I've been resting for four days, and missing you for longer than that."

"I missed you, too, sexy cop."

"How did you find me?"

"An article I found online about Sharon Waite's murder. There was a small mention that she used to spend time at her grandparents' place." She scowled. "But that was only one of a bunch of locations they were scouting and the information was taking too damn long to come in. By the third day after you'd gone missing, I was in full-blown panic. Chris and his team were moving in to search the property, but Rab was ahead of them. He'd turned around to come back to the place after I thought he was gone and I was in the clear for a while. I'd already found you. Otherwise he might have—"

She shuddered, unwilling to think about how the entire episode might have turned out if Rab had arrived faster.

"My hero," he teased, already tired.

"Rest, please."

Tonio was quiet for several moments, a troubled frown knitting his brow. "Angel, even after all the horrible crimes he committed, I feel sad that he wasted what could've been a good life. I mean, look at you. You're a success, so why couldn't he be? He murdered two women and almost killed both of us, yet I also feel bad because he could've been different. Is it wrong to feel that way?"

"No, sweetheart. That means you're the good, kind man I fell in love with. A man who can feel empathy for a tormented individual and the families he devastated. I feel sad, too."

"I honestly hope they can all find a measure of peace now, even Rab."

"Me, too."

One touchy subject remained unspoken between them. One that couldn't remain taboo if he was going to heal completely.

Curling her fingers against his cheek, she encouraged very softly, "I want you to talk to me about those days after Rab took you. Tell me what he did to you."

He sucked in a sharp breath, soul-deep agony burning in his eyes. "I won't lie to you. He pumped me full of drugs. Tortured me physically and mentally," he said, nearly strangling on the confession. "For a while, I thought it would be better to let go." He shifted his gaze, couldn't meet her eyes.

"No, look at me, Tonio." She waited until he did, and wanted to weep for the terrible trauma he'd had to survive. "You have nothing to be ashamed of, do you hear? Nothing. You did the best you were able to do in a horrible situation. Whatever you were thinking and feeling was and is totally normal and doesn't change how much I love you."

"God, I love you, too," he whispered.

Her heart squeezed. There wasn't going to be a quick fix for this part of his ordeal. "I see only my brave hero, the man I love and respect. We're going to get through this, together. You have my promise, and my heart."

He brought her hand to his lips, kissed each finger. "You have mine, too. Thank you for loving me."

"I want to spend the rest of my life doing just that. If you can tolerate sharing your home with me," she breathed.

A teasing smile played about his lips, the shadows banished for the time being. "Hmm, I don't know. Depends."

"On what?" *Oh, please!*

"On whether you're my wife." His smile widened, love shining in his eyes along with more tears. Happy ones. "Miss Silva, will you marry me?"

"Oh yes!" she squealed. "Yes, yes, yes!"

His laugh ended in an oomph as she gave him a tight hug. She tried to sit up. "Your shoulder! I'm sorry—"

"Never mind," he rumbled, arms tightening around her. "Let me hold you."

She relaxed against him, reveling in the feeling of his hard chest. The steady thump of his heartbeat in her ear. The strength of his muscular arms encircling her.

"We have a lot to discuss," he murmured after a while. His voice had grown quiet, sleepy. "Selling your house, wedding plans. Lots of stuff. Your mom and mine will want to help."

"We'll talk about all that. Sleep, baby."

He did. In moments, he'd fallen sound asleep again. Even exhausted, he clung to her tightly, reluctant to let go. After some maneuvering, she managed to wiggle out of his arms so she could sit and admire him. So precious to her, this wonderful man she would spend the rest of her life with.

The days ahead wouldn't all be easy, but she'd be by his side to help him heal. They'd come through the worst already.

And she'd be right by his side, every step of the way.

The smells from the grill were fantastic. Tonio relaxed in his lounger on the back deck and sipped his beer—one of his first since being able to ditch the pain medication. He savored the taste, along with the sight of his friends gathered all around him having a great time.

In particular, he was enjoying watching Angel laughing and talking with them. His lady had blossomed before his eyes in the past few weeks like a thirsty flower finally getting a good rain, and her confidence was beautiful to see.

Had he really thought she was so different from Grace and the other women? Well, she was, and yet she was comfortable, too. Held her own among them, and he was so proud of her.

"That's some woman you have there," Julian said, taking a lounger beside him, beer in hand.

"Isn't she?" He couldn't help the smile that spread across his face. It was a permanent fixture now.

"Yeah. You're a lucky guy."

"So are you." Turning his attention to his brother, he narrowed his eyes. "You gonna tell me what's been eating you about the accident?"

Julian glanced around, but there was nobody nearby at the moment. The others were either manning the grill, in the yard goofing off, or on the other side of the deck making merry.

"I can talk about it now, but it's still hard." He paused, looking miserable. "I made Clay drive the ambulance that day."

Tonio's heart froze. "What do you mean, made him?"

"Just what I said. It was my turn to drive, but I talked him into taking the wheel." Julian's eyes were sad. "Now he'll pay for the rest of his life."

"Listen to me, bro. You didn't *make* him drive. He did it as a favor, and neither of you could've predicted what happened. It was a senseless accident, and the driver of the truck caused the wreck. It wasn't your fault," he emphasized.

"I know that, and I'm working on it."

"Keeping up with the counseling?"

"Every week."

"Good."

Julian had gone back to work, but he was having a tough time. Clay's recovery was progressing, but slowly. They still didn't know if he'd ever be the same. Tonio's heart went out to them both.

"I'm here," he said to Julian. "Whatever you need."

"I know. Thanks." He attempted a smile. "But hey, this is a celebration of my big bro getting well and going back to work. I think today should be all about fun."

"I couldn't agree more," Angel said, walking up to them. "Can I steal my man for a bit?"

"Go right ahead. I'll make myself scarce."

"No need." She held out a hand to Tonio. "Take a short walk with me?"

"You bet."

Taking her hand, he rose and let her lead him out of the yard, away from the chaos. She seemed content to take him for a stroll down the sidewalk, and it became apparent there was something on her mind.

"Is your brother okay?" she asked.

"Yeah, but it's taking time. He told me he talked Clay into driving the day of the accident. It's been killing him."

"Oh no." Concern marred her expression.

"He's actually doing better, I think, since he started counseling. I told him I'd be there for him no matter what."

"That goes for me, too. Him and Grace. They're wonderful people."

"Yes, they are." They walked a bit farther, and he studied her face. Her expression had smoothed out into contentment. Happiness. "Something on your mind?"

Halting, she pulled him to face her, lips curving up into a smile. “There is, my sexy cop. We have something to discuss.”

“We do?” He stared at her, puzzled. “What is it?”

Angel took his hand and very deliberately placed his palm on her lower abdomen with his fingers spread. “Yes, we do. And I don’t know what it is yet.”

“Wh-what?” he stammered. “You mean you’re—we’re—”

“Yes, we are.”

He couldn’t breathe. “How?”

Her laughter warmed him from the inside out. “If you need to know that, we have a real problem.”

“I mean, when?”

“I think it was the morning after we got to the lake cabin. You didn’t use protection.” She shrugged. “But who knows?”

“Oh my God.” He blinked at his beautiful woman. “I’m going to be a dad.”

“Yes. Are you upset?” She chewed her lip, worry creasing her brow.

“No! God, no.” A huge grin spread across his face. “You’ve made me the happiest man in the world. And my family is going to go over the moon, especially Mama.”

“Good,” she said softly, eyes shining. “I’m glad you’re happy. I am, too.”

“The day I met you was the luckiest day of my life. I think now you’re going to have to make an honest man out of me.”

“I already accepted your proposal!”

"I know, but we haven't set a date. How about next month?"

"How can I refuse?"

"You can't. And I'll spend the rest of my life making sure you never regret it."

Taking her in his arms, he held her tight against his heart.

Right where he planned to keep her, forever.

## *About the Author*

National bestselling author **Jo Davis** is best known for the popular Firefighters of Station Five, Sugarland Blue, and Torn Between Two Lovers series. As J. D. Tyler, she's the national bestselling author of the dark, sexy paranormal series Alpha Pack. *Primal Law*, the first book in her Alpha Pack series, is the winner of the 2011 National Reader's Choice Award in Paranormal. She has also been a multiple finalist in the Colorado Romance Writers Award of Excellence and a finalist for the Booksellers' Best Award, has captured the HOLT Medallion Award of Merit, and she has been a two-time nominee for the Australian Romance Readers Award in romantic suspense. She's had one book optioned for a major motion picture.

Connect Online

jodavis.net